YOU ARE SO
UNDEAD
TO ME

YOU ARE SO UNDEAD
TO ME

Stacey Jay

razor
bill

You Are So Undead to Me

RAZORBILL

Published by the Penguin Group
Penguin Young Readers Group
345 Hudson Street, New York, New York 10014, U.S.A.
Penguin Group (USA) Inc., 375 Hudson Street, New York, New York 10014, U.S.A.
Penguin Group (Canada), 90 Eglinton Avenue East, Suite 700, Toronto, Ontario,
Canada M4P 2Y3 (a division of Pearson Penguin Canada Inc.)
Penguin Books Ltd, 80 Strand, London WC2R 0RL, England
Penguin Ireland, 25 St Stephen's Green, Dublin 2, Ireland (a division of Penguin
Books Ltd)
Penguin Group (Australia), 250 Camberwell Road, Camberwell, Victoria 3124, Aus-
tralia (a division of Pearson Australia Group Pty Ltd)
Penguin Books India Pvt Ltd, 11 Community Centre, Panchsheel Park, New Delhi
– 110 017, India
Penguin Group (NZ), 67 Apollo Drive, Mairangi Bay, Auckland 1311, New Zealand
(a division of Pearson New Zealand Ltd)
Penguin Books (South Africa) (Pty) Ltd, 24 Sturdee Avenue, Rosebank, Johannesburg
2196, South Africa

Penguin Books Ltd, Registered Offices: 80 Strand, London WC2R 0RL, England

10 9 8 7 6 5 4 3 2 1

Library of Congress Cataloging-in-Publication Data

Jay, Stacey.
You are so undead to me / by Stacey Jay.
p. cm.
Summary: Megan Berry, a Carol, Arkansas high school student who can communi-
cate with the Undead, must team up with her childhood friend Ethan to save home-
coming from an army of flesh-hungry zombies.
ISBN 978-1-59514-225-2
[1. Zombies--Fiction. 2. Dead--Fiction. 3. Supernatural--Fiction. 4. High schools--
Fiction. 5. Schools--Fiction. 6. Interpersonal relations--Fiction. 7. Arkansas--Fiction.]
I. Title.
PZ7.J344Yo 2009
[Fic]--dc22
2008021056
Printed in the United States of America

For Laura Mae-daughter, friend, and fellow smartass.

PROLOGUE

The cold wind swept across the hill, whistling through the headstones that poked from the ground like dozens of crooked baby teeth. In the sky, a sickly yellow moon transformed the graveyard's bare trees into guardians made of old, white bone, and somewhere in the distance, an animal screamed.

Call me crazy, but I figured whatever was going to happen next *wasn't* going to be fun. Creepy graveyards aren't your typical location for good times of the cute-fluffy-bunny-and-rainbows variety.

My lips parted and I tried to cry out, but no sound came, nothing but a pathetic gurgling as the ground beneath me buckled.

Gnarled tree roots burst from the hard earth, wrapping around my arms and legs, lifting me into the air. More silent screams ripped from my throat as the roots flung me down the steep slope, toward the oldest part of the graveyard.

I threw my arms out to the side, trying to stop, but I'd already built too much momentum. Faster and faster I rolled, skin tearing, rocks bruising my bones. By the time I reached the bottom of the slope there was blood on my hands, on my face, smearing across the dead leaves at the edge of three open graves.

And there, from holes in the earth, three sets of glowing red eyes stared into mine, three pairs of gnarled hands reached for my flesh. I knew what they were at once. Zombies.

Rotted flesh hung loosely on their faces, chunks falling away as they groaned in anticipation of their meal. The smell of decay hit me like a physical blow, making me gag. I fought the urge to yack as I gasped for breath, still unable to make a sound.

"Help!" I finally managed to scream as soft, rotted hands latched around my ankles.

There was someone nearby, someone who could help me. I was sure of it. But before I could call out again, the third zombie was on top of me. Ancient teeth tore through my clothes, shredding fabric to get to skin.

I screamed, so loud it seemed someone else was screaming along with me. Frantically, I shoved at the zombie now digging into my shoulder so deep I could hear teeth scraping bone, kicking at the others near my feet and praying someone would hear me before it was too late.

"Nice outfit, Megan." It was Monica Parsons, fellow zombie Settler and general mistress of evil. She stood above me, watching the zombies feed.

"Help me!"

"Sorry, not into rescuing fashion victims."

I glanced down, gasping in horror as I saw the god-awful circa-1980s prom dress that had somehow found its way onto my body. The monstrosity was bright fuchsia except in the places where blood stained it black and probably the most wretched garment ever to see the light of day.

Or the light of the full moon, in this case.

"Does Josh know you're wearing *that* to homecoming? I really think he should be clued in to what a freak you are." She whipped out her cell, ready to document my shame with her camera feature.

"No!" I wailed, torn between fighting the zombies on top of me and trying to cover my face to conceal my identity.

"*Desino! Absisto!*" Another voice sounded from the darkness and suddenly the zombie on top of me froze mid-chomp. Seconds later a blurred shape slammed into it, knocking it to the ground, where the pair rolled over and over, all the way to the side of the old church.

I screamed as a chunk of skin disappeared with the zombie but didn't waste time getting to my feet. My lips were buzzing and blood flowed down my arm to drip from my fingers, but I pushed myself to move faster.

I had to save the person who had helped me, keep him from being eaten. But he was so far away, I'd never reach him time. But I *could* reach—

"Give me your hand!" I screamed to Monica, stumbling across the rocks on my bare feet. Now I was wearing nothing but a torn sleep shirt. I had no idea where my shoes and the '80s eyesore had gone and I didn't care. I just needed to get to Monica, get her hand in mine and our power combined before—

"Megan, Monica, run! Get the others, get—" The boy's voice became a strangled sound and I knew the zombie he'd knocked off of me was back in motion.

I risked a brief look over my shoulder to see the other two zombies lumbering forward, arms outstretched. Something yellow that looked like pus dripped from their mouths, making it clear they were hungry for a taste of the red trail I was leaving behind. But they weren't that close, not close enough to stop me before I reached Monica.

I grabbed her hand, clinging to it even when she tried to pull away.

"Let me go, freak, we've got to—ouch!" Digging my fingers into Monica's palm, I released every barrier to my power, every wall I'd first learned to erect to keep zombies from following me to the playground when I was five.

"This is it. You are never going to make the pom squad!" But I barely heard Monica now. All I could hear was the roar of blood rushing through my ears and the quieter hiss of more power than I'd ever felt sizzling along my nerve endings, all the way down to my fingertips.

"*Reverto!*" I screamed the word, flinging the power at the approaching zombies with a wave of my free hand. For a moment, the two coming for me hesitated, faltering in their steps.

But then they were on the move again, howling this time, their red eyes glowing with hate and hunger. I screamed, tightening my grip on Monica, unable to make my legs move now that the zombies were so close.

"Say it again! *With me* this time, you stupid—" Monica yelled.

"Okay! Okay," I sobbed.

"Now!"

"*Reverto!*" We screamed the word together. This time, the zombies spun around, turning toward the woods with another horrible groan. My eyes flew to the tree line, where a figure in a black cloak was disappearing into the forest.

We were safe. At least, Monica and I were. I still hadn't seen—

"Hello? Are you? . . ." I spun toward the boy who had saved my life, but the world spun as well. My head felt so light I was sure it would float off my neck any minute.

"Wow, Megan. Desperate for attention much?" Monica asked, her words transforming into wicked laughter—laughter in which was soon joined by the hundreds of people attending the Carol High homecoming dance.

"No!" I wailed, trying to cover myself with my arms.

But it was too late. Everyone had already seen me buck naked in the hot spotlights illuminating the platform where the homecoming queen should have been standing to receive her crown. My shame was complete, my life utterly and completely ruined. I would *never* be able to show my face in Carol again and—

"Ohmygod!" I bolted upright, drenched in sweat despite the fact that I'd deliberately cranked up the air-conditioning before heading to bed. It was a dream, just a dream . . . at least, most of it.

Everything except the attack. The scar on my shoulder wouldn't let me forget how real that had been.

The puckered flesh ached a bit as I huddled back under the covers, determined to get back to sleep and *not* to dream. Not to remember. It had been years since I'd been able to recall so many details about that night, and I certainly didn't want to dredge up any more. My mind had buried those memories for a reason, and they should *stay* buried.

Just like corpses should stay in the ground.

CHAPTER 1

My cell rang at ten till six. Jess was talking before I could even say hello.

"So what are you wearing, the dress or the butt jeans?" she asked, sounding nearly as breathless as I felt.

This was it: the first night of the rest of my life, the beginning of my social ascension at Carol High School. Pom squad tryouts were a couple of weeks away, but it looked like I was going to be accepted into the ranks of the trendy and gorgeous even before I was issued my official Cougar Pride dance team uniform.

I'd scored a date with the hottest guy in school over a Bunsen burner in junior chem. I was a year ahead and Mr. Hottie a year behind, but it was clearly fate—and not smarts or a lack thereof—that had made us lab partners.

"The dress," I said, taking one final spin in front of my mirror. "The one with the yellow and brown flowers."

"Yellow and brown? I thought they were red."

"Nope. Remember, it's the one we got at—"

"Take a picture and send it to my e-mail," she said. "The stepmonster is still borrowing my phone until hers is fixed, but I'm online and—"

The doorbell rang and I did my best to stifle a squeal of excitement. "He's here!" Josh Pickle—lame last name, but trust me, he's studly enough to pull it off—was really here to pick *me*, Megan Berry, only marginally cool sophomore, up for a date!

"Okay, go! But IM as soon as you get home. I want to hear everything!"

"Will do. Bye," I said, already halfway to the front door. I had to get there before my parents. Dad was wearing his weird "who flung poo?" monkey pajama pants and could not be allowed to interact with *anyone*. Therefore, I could not afford to play it cool and make my senior sex god wait at least a few seconds so it didn't seem like I'd raced to the door like a total loser.

But whatever—Josh had to know I was into him. It wasn't like I was very good at hiding my feelings where he was concerned, and he'd still asked me out.

"Right. Deep breath," I whispered, my biggest smile on my face before I'd even opened the door. "Hey, give me just a sec and—"

Oh. My. God. There was a dead person on my porch.

Again.

My flesh crawled and my stomach threatened a second showing of the seven-layer salad we'd had for dinner.

"Mom!" I screamed, barely able to force out the word through the massive, softball-size lump in my throat. I slammed the door in the guy's face and fumbled with the lock, doing my best not to hyperventilate.

This could not be happening! Josh was supposed to be ringing my doorbell, not some dead guy.

It *was* a guy, right?

I opened the door just a crack. Yep. Definitely a dude. The shoulder-length hair had thrown me for a second. The fact that his face was half covered in grave dirt—eww!—didn't help things either. At least he hadn't decomposed . . . much. He must have been a fairly recent member of the Unsettled.

"What is it, Megan? Dad and I were right in the middle of— oh my God!" Mom spied the dead guy and jumped about a foot in the air, then turned and raced back into the kitchen. She emerged seconds later with a bunch of newspapers and began spreading them on the floor near the front door.

Déjà vu hit like a ton of bricks. It was suddenly as if the past five years hadn't happened, as if I hadn't been zombie free and normal long enough to be lulled into thinking that my freedom was permanent. Even with the creepy dreams I'd been having lately, I'd never thought my powers were coming back. After the attack, my entire family had assumed I was done with Settling the Dead.

But the guy on the porch, the newspaper on the floor to catch the dirt . . . God, it was so horribly familiar I expected to look down and find myself wearing the Hello Kitty pajamas I so loved when I was ten.

"Invite him in, Megan. I'll go get the record book. I'm sure I stuck it somewhere in the walk-in." My mom brushed her long brown hair out of her eyes and shot me an excited smile. She was *excited* about this! *Excited* that I was once again one of the freakiest kids in the South.

"No way, Mom. Josh could be here any second. I'm not going to do this tonight!" Or any night if I had my say about it, but there was no need to go there just yet. I knew my mom considered our family's legacy as Settlers of the Dead something wonderful, a vital paranormal service to those recently troubled in death and blah, blah, blah.

"Megan Amanda Berry. You invite that boy in. Now. That is a person out there, a person in need of your help, and—"

"I know it's a person, Mom, but it's a dead person. His life is already over. Mine doesn't have to be."

"Megan—"

"Seriously, my life *will* be over if Josh shows up for our first date and sees a corpse in the entryway." I used my most reasonable tone and willed her with wide brown eyes to take pity on me in my moment of desperation. I mean, couldn't she understand the position I was in? Everyone felt sorry for the kid in *The Sixth Sense*, and he was the only one who could see the dead people. Creepy, yes, but at least he didn't have to worry about a zombie tailing him to softball practice and scaring half the population of Carol, Arkansas.

"Well, then, you'd better hurry and take his statement before Josh gets here." She disappeared into the kitchen, no doubt on her way to her and Dad's room to look for the Book of Unsettled Records. I'd thought I was done with that thing after what happened, after that night—

Even with the humid air streaming into the house, I shivered. I didn't want to think about that night. Not now. Not ever. The dreams were bad enough—I didn't have to torture myself while I was awake.

I turned back to the zombie, eying him up and down. He seemed normal enough—for a zombie. He didn't drool or lunge at my throat. He just stood there, looking a little spaced out, the way most Unsettled did until you gave them the cue to start spilling their guts.

I motioned him inside with a resigned sigh, being careful not to let him touch me as I shuffled around to close the door. It wouldn't matter how hot I looked if I smelled like a decomposing corpse.

The musty, slightly rotted smell of the Unsettled was hell to get out of clothing, and there was no way I was ruining the outfit that had taken me two hours to pick out. The white strappy sundress with brown and yellow flowers was retro without being too prissy. It picked up the goldish swirls in my brown eyes and looked great with my end-of-summer tan.

Over the summer I had finally outgrown the last of my awkward stage and looked good in clothes, even though I still had barely enough up top to fill out the built-in bra of my dress. My mother's fault. We look scarily alike, and she's always been super thin, with a not-quite-B cup.

"Hey, Meggy, heard you had a visitor." Dad popped his head out from the doorway to the kitchen but didn't come any closer. He still wasn't completely cool with the zombie stuff, even though he'd been married to Mom for twenty-three years, the first eight of which she'd been on active Settling duty. Her zombie-summoning power had started to fade when her offspring—that would be me—started showing signs of power.

Dead people started showing up on my porch when I turned five. Dead kids, to be specific. Settlers usually attract people of around the same age, something to do with the quality of our Settler vibes that I never really understood.

"Yeah. What a great surprise, right?" I smiled at Dad, trying to act like this wasn't freaking me out as much as it was. The dead guy grunted and shuffled on the papers, but his eyes remained fixed somewhere in the distance. I guess he could tell I wasn't talking to him yet. Normal zombies are fairly perceptive that way and far more mannerly than your average *Walking Dead* movie would have you believe.

"Your mom said this might happen, you know, as you got older and started to . . . develop." Dad looked like he'd just swallowed expired milk. I didn't know what was bothering him more, the zombie or discussing my hormones. Mom had warned me almost a year ago when I'd started my period that hormonal fluctuations sometimes enhanced Settler skills.

As if T-zone breakouts and cramps from hell weren't enough.

"Right. Did she find the book yet?" I asked, ready for a subject change.

"Not yet, but you know how things are in the Closet," Dad said.

The way we say *closet* in our house makes it clear the *c* is capitalized. The Closet is great and fearsome and full of more crap than any three-person family should own, let alone try to squeeze into a four-by-six-foot space. I nearly killed myself trying to sneak a peek at my Christmas presents when I was twelve and hadn't been in there since.

"Crap." I checked my watch. Less than ten minutes to arrival if Josh was on time. "Dad, could you just grab me that notepad Mom uses for the grocery lists? I'll write the stuff down there and transfer the info later."

"Is that SOP?"

Dad's retired air force and believes there's an SOP—standard operating procedure—for everything.

11

"No, but neither is letting someone outside the family see an out-of-grave phenomenon."

He nodded at the wisdom of that statement. "I'll grab you something to write with and then help your mom look. Be back in two minutes." He practically ran from the room, obviously not wanting Josh to see the zombie in our foyer any more than I did. Before I was born, a neighbor caught on to what was happening at the Berry house. My mom and dad had been forced to move halfway across the country from sunny California to Sticksville, Arkansas.

That *would* happen before I was born, so I couldn't even have the cool factor of saying I was born in Cali despite the fact both of my parents grew up there. Luckily my dad had been able to transfer to an air base in Arkansas last time, but I could tell he worried where we might be sent if we were discovered again. Settlers' Affairs doesn't mess around when it comes to being discovered. If you break cover, they decide how fast you run and how far.

Apparently Dad didn't want to find out if we'd be relocating to Outer Mongolia if my movie date met up with my zombie date. He was back in a flash with pen and paper. "I'll go check on your mother. If you hurry, you can have this guy out the back before I dig her out of the Closet."

"But she gets pissed if I let them walk through the house," I said, though something other than violating Mom's house rules was bothering me. I hadn't done this in so long. What if I forgot something?

"I'll vacuum after you leave for your date." Dad smiled and disappeared, and I couldn't help but smile back. For a man who had been adamantly opposed to letting his not-quite-sixteen-year-old go out with a senior, he was being incredibly cool.

Right! Screw doing things the Settler way. I had to get this guy out of here and get on with my real life.

Taking a deep breath, I turned back to the dearly departed. Hopefully, I still remembered how this was supposed to go.

"Welcome to your after-death session. My name is Megan. May I have your name, last name first?" The words rolled off my tongue with the same practiced ease they had years ago. And here I'd thought I suppressed all that zombie stuff.

"Anderson, William." His eyes focused in on me and I could see they had once been quite a nice shade of blue. Nearly as nice as the grin he flashed as the human part of him came online. Even with the dirt in his teeth, you could tell that smile had broken a few hearts when he was alive. "Hey, nice to meet you."

"Nice to meet you, too." I felt that familiar flash of sadness that always came with dealing with kids my own age who had already met their end. Settlers were a fairly spiritual group, and I'd been raised to believe these troubled souls would be going to a better place after they got their earthly business off their chests . . . but still, it was sad, especially with people so young.

"Can you give me your address before death, William?"

My pen flew across the paper as he rattled off an address not too terribly far away. Then I asked him for a phone number and a list of surviving immediate family. You had to get all the basic details out of an Unsettled before you let them tell you whatever was bothering them so much they actually had to crawl out of their grave and go looking for supernatural intervention. If you didn't, chances were you'd never get the 411.

Once they spill their guts, zombies can't get back to their graves fast enough, and it's never a good idea to try to slow down a determined zombie. They are freakishly strong. The movies have that right, but the whole eating-brains thing—completely bogus. Only Reanimated Corpses crave flesh, and they don't care about your brains. They'll eat whatever they can get their teeth into.

I shivered again, wishing I'd worn the matching brown shawl that came with my dress. The scar on my shoulder had faded and hardly anyone noticed it anymore, but I suddenly wanted it covered up.

Clearing my throat, I did my best to concentrate. Josh could be here any second, no time to angst out. "Now, William, tell me what it is you don't like about your death." Okay, so that wasn't standard lingo. I'd just watched too many *Nip/Tuck* reruns over the summer.

"I just wanted to tell my girlfriend, Sherry, that I never went out with that skank at the mall. I mean, I took her to the corn dog shack once, but I'm planning on . . . I mean I *was* planning . . ."

His voice wasn't sad as much as confused, but I still wanted to give him a hug and probably would have if it hadn't been for the smell. It had to suck coming to terms with your own death. But he kept stinking worse and worse the longer he was indoors, killing my urge to hand out friendly snuggles. That windy night must have been helping air him out while he was still in the doorway.

"But you were planning to . . ." I prodded gently. I felt way bad for the guy, but the clock was ticking. Two minutes if Josh was on time!

"I was planning to tell my girlfriend that I still loved her. And to tell Monica to go back to the Gap and leave me alone, you know?"

Well, well, if it wasn't old home night at the Berry residence. There was only one skank named Monica who worked at the Gap— my fellow Settler, Monica "I put the psycho in psycho hose beast" Parsons.

How ironic would it have been if he'd ended up on *her* doorstep instead of mine? Maybe that was why the powers had summoned me back into service for the night, to spare William the agony of seeing Monica after death. And now everything would go back to normal and I would be spared Settler service until another of the Monicster's victims needed to come get some post-burial business off his chest.

Riigghht . . . and Josh is going to show up with flowers and kneel down on one knee before he asks you to homecoming.

As if summoned by my slavishly devoted thoughts, the doorbell rang.

He was here! One minute early!

"Wha?" William jumped, clearly startled by the noise. He stumbled forward, knocking into me hard enough that I bounced off the computer hutch and then back into his undead arms. We fell to the ground in a heap, and by the time I untangled myself, Josh was ringing the doorbell again and my dress was covered in grave dirt.

Argh! Now I was going to reek!

"Hey, Josh!" I yelled through the door, hoping he couldn't hear William groaning as he stood up. "I'll be right back! I . . . forgot my purse!" Frantic, I ran for my room, mind racing as I tried to figure out what I could throw on that was clean and would be even remotely as cute as the word's most perfect sundress.

I skidded to a stop among the piles of clothes on the floor and started to strip. I was *not* going to let my first date with an older, cooler, drop-dead-gorgeous guy—okay, I'll admit it, my first real date *ever*, since I hadn't been allowed to get in cars with boys last year—be ruined by a zombie blast from the past. If Mom was right, if my powers had somehow been reactivated after lying dormant for so many years, then I would deal with it. But I would deal with it *later*.

I'd struggled into a tightish pair of Seven jeans and was flinging tank tops in ten different directions, searching for something that wasn't too schoolish looking for date wear, when I heard the crash.

"Crap!" I ran back to the front door, pulling on the shirt I'd had in my hand as I went. A quick look down at my chest revealed I'd had the misfortune to choose the LOOKING FOR A SUGAR DADDY shirt I usually only wore to dance class.

Great, real classy choice. But there was no time to change now. William was careening around the living room like a college freshman at his first kegger, banging into things, knocking Mom's Lladró porcelain collection to the ground. I was *so* dead. William was even now crushing beneath his feet the collectible mommy figurine Dad had given Mom when she was pregnant with me.

Of course, if I skipped out now, hoping Josh wouldn't notice the weird undead person roaming around in my living room when I opened the door, I would be in even deeper monkey-flinging poo than collectible destruction could ever cause. I would *never* be forgiven for leaving my zombie unattended.

And probably never allowed out of the house either.

Groaning inwardly, I raced back to the door. This was so horribly unfair! I was going to have to tell Josh I couldn't go out and deal with William. Grr! Couldn't this déjà zombie action have waited until our second date? Or at least until Josh had already asked me to homecoming like I'd dreamed he would do tonight over a greasy bucket of popcorn?

"Josh?" I shouted at the door, wincing as another Lladró crashed to the ground behind me.

"Um, yeah. Are you . . . coming out, Megan?" he asked, his voice so perfectly sexy I was fairly certain I was going to pass out from disappointment.

"I can't. I . . . I've got . . . My family has guests and I can't leave."

"But I thought you said you forgot your purse?"

"Um, no! I said I forgot the . . . worst . . . the worst thing I had to tell you. Which was that I couldn't go out with you tonight." William was moaning now. I had to make this quick with Josh no matter how stupid I sounded. If I didn't finish up with William, he was going to go Rogue and then I would be dead.

Because my mother would *kill me* if I let a zombie of mine go all rabid and start terrorizing the populace because I'd forgotten to send him back to his grave. Rogue zombies weren't like Reanimated Corpses. They weren't hungry for blood, but they could cause a hell of a mess and scare the average population to death if they got loose.

"So anyway, I'm so, *so* sorry. I'll call you later, okay?"

"Can't you at least open the door? Come out for a few minutes?" he asked, sounding—justifiably—like he thought I was nuts.

Crash. Groan. And then William was headed toward the back door. Ahh! "Nope, can't come out talktoyoulaterbye!"

I dashed to the back door, scrambling after William as he fell down the porch steps, one of his arms falling off along the way. Leaping over the appendage, refusing to waste time puking, I lunged for him, managing to get a hand on his other arm.

"Thank you, William. I'll take care of telling Sherry you still love her and thought Monica was a skank—now go rest in peace!" I shouted. Immediately he calmed down, his groans transforming to one long, satisfied sigh.

Then he was gone like a flash, moving with the preternatural speed of any naturally Unsettled. Which would have been fabulous . . . if he'd remembered to take his arm with him.

Great. This was going to be a *lot* of fun. Before I recorded his info in the book Mom was hopefully finding, I was going to have to take his arm back to his grave—which I had no idea how to find. Even staying home and calling Jess for a sulk session over missing my date would be more fun than this. Of course, having my gums resurfaced would probably be more fun than this.

Hurrying inside, I grabbed a garbage bag to hide William's arm in, not bothering to tell the parents buried in the closet where I was going because I knew Mom would *freak*. Then I headed out to my bike, praying Josh was far away and wouldn't see me trolling around Carol on my bicycle. If my weirdo behavior at the door hadn't turned him off, thinking I'd lied about not being able to leave the house certainly would.

Then not only would tonight *not* be my entrée into the realm of popularity, it would be the nail in the coffin of my terminal uncoolness.

CHAPTER 2

Judging from the path he'd taken out of my backyard, I figured there was only one cemetery William could have gone to. And *of course* it was the one farthest from my house.

I was dripping with sweat by the time I reached Mount Hope—which is not on a mountain, so I don't know what the people who named it were smoking. Mount Hope is a pleasant little patch of green not too far from the river that, thankfully, has almost no trees, so I could see well enough to read the names on the headstones in the fading light.

It was going to be dark soon, however, so I wasted no time. I hadn't been out after dark by myself in five years, and I wasn't ready to start now.

Flinging my bike to the ground, I dashed through the cemetery, searching for fresh graves. There were only two, and the second headstone I checked belonged to William Peyton Anderson—Beloved Son and Grandson, Taken Too Soon. My heart did a little flip as I read the inscription, but I refused to cry. Now that he had his earthly business off his chest, that beloved son would be going to a better place. And all I had to do was get his arm back to him and *I* would be too: home, with my secret chocolate stash.

19

After quickly scanning the cemetery to make sure I wasn't being watched, I pulled William's arm from the bag, trying not gag at the combo of stiff skin and smushy stuff underneath. I wasn't going to think about smushy stuff or the slight wriggling I could feel coming from the decomposing flesh. Maggots happen. It's a fact of life.

I set the arm on top of the dirt, then sat back on my heels. I rubbed my shaking hands on my jeans, even though I knew the smell wouldn't come off until I'd had a nice long shower. Man, I wished I'd thought to bring hand sanitizer! The whole Settler gig was so gross. No wonder I'd done my best to forget all the repulsive details.

Okay, okay, now I just had to relax and think. What was the command that would make the arm sink through the dirt to rejoin the rest of William? I closed my eyes and dug back through my mental files, searching for any spark of inspiration, but all I got was brain static. Brain static and a few images from the night of my attack—the red eyes, the graying teeth tearing through my pajamas, the feel of those strong hands gouging into—

"Errr!" I groaned through my tight jaw, eyes flying open.

Why couldn't I remember anything but those freaking Reanimated monsters? I was sure I'd known the second-stage dissolution spell at one point, even though I wasn't supposed to have been studying those things until I was at least thirteen. What had happened to all those memories, to the mental files of the girl I'd been before the attack? In my dreams I always remembered the commands I should use to work the different spells, but by the time I woke up in the morning, they were gone.

Of course, it wasn't like I'd been trying to stay current with the

Settler lingo. The very opposite, in fact. And now I was going to pay for being in Denial with a capital *D*.

I could still remember bits and pieces of my former life and knew the basic stage-one Settler stuff my mom had made me stay fresh on for the last five years. But for the most part, I drew a big freaking mental blank where Settler lore was concerned. Which meant the only way I was getting rid of this dead person's arm was the old-fashioned way.

I was going to have to dig. With my hands, because I. Didn't. Bring. A. Shovel.

"Shit!" I cursed, grabbing a handful of grave dirt and flinging it at the arm.

"Nice language."

I spun around, heart pounding, doing my best to hide the arm with my body as I checked out the guy who'd snuck up behind me. He was tall, but not Josh tall, and was dressed a little like one of the emo skaters who hung out near the Dairy Queen, his lean frame made even leaner by his fitted black jeans and striped sweater. His dark blond hair hung down over one eye, obscuring his face, but not so much I couldn't tell he was totally hot.

Like, Abercrombie model hot. Hot enough that I probably would have had issues thinking up something to say to him even if I hadn't been scared to death he would see William's arm and turn me in to the police for grave robbing or worse.

"Um, I was just—"

"Just trying to dispose of some unwanted body parts?" he asked in his deep, manly voice, taking two steps forward before he squatted

21

down in front of me. He was close enough I could tell that his eyes were a gorgeous shade of green and that he was *not* a happy camper. In fact, he looked *pissed*, and I could only assume he was pissed at me.

"Um . . ."

"I'm going to need something more than 'um.'" His voice got even deeper and would have been terrifying if it weren't weirdly familiar.

"Listen, I know this looks bad, but—"

"It doesn't just look bad. It *is* bad." His eyes narrowed, and my heart raced in response. I was suddenly aware of how very large he was, at least compared to my five-four and a hundred and change. He could kill me with his bare hands and have me buried in the fresh dirt behind me without breaking a sweat. "You really messed up, Megan."

And he knew my name! He was probably a psycho stalker serial killer of teen girls who had been waiting to add me to his list of victims . . . or something equally scary. Crap! Didn't I know by now that I should *never* leave the house without parental permission? I'd only snuck out two times in six years, and both times I'd found mortal danger.

". . . only get worse. Do you understand me?" he asked. He'd evidently been talking for a while, but I'd been too freaked to hear.

"Shit," I whispered, my voice shaky.

"Last time I checked, that wasn't an official command," he said with a sigh. "And aren't you a little young to have a mouth like that?"

His eyes drifted to my mouth and for a split second I thought he was checking out my lips. Even weirder, for a split second, I really kind of *hoped* that he was checking out my lips and that he might consider an even closer inspection.

I was having make-out fantasies about a serial killer. The realization was enough to snap me out of my inspection of the dude's own lips.

Grip! Must get grip! "I'm sorry, I didn't hear what you said. You're kind of freaking me out," I confessed.

"Elder Pruitt saw your Unsettled run across the football field without a halo," he said, as if the halo thing should make any sense to me.

So he was a Settler. He must have been if he was in touch with the Elders from Settlers' Affairs, the ruling body that kept the rest of the town Settlers in line. This was good news, mostly. At least he wasn't going to report me for grave robbing. But what he'd said *did* make me wonder why an Elder from Settlers' Affairs would be hanging around the Carol High football field. I would have asked for the 411 if I wasn't still more than a little worried.

I mean, I knew he wasn't going to kill me, but I could still be in deep trouble if I'd somehow broken the SA rules. "Um, listen, I'm not sure exactly what you're talking about. I had an accident when I was still a first-stage Settler and I—"

"Yeah . . . I know," he said, looking at me with a mixture of confusion and frustration. Didn't this guy have any expression that wasn't colored by massive amounts of negative emotion? He really needed to work on his happy face.

"So I don't remember what I'm supposed to do. I mean, I never really *learned* what I was supposed to do as a second stager, so when this guy showed up on my doorstep, I was a little unprepared for—"

"You shouldn't have been unprepared. Jennifer should have made

23

sure you weren't." Whoa! Now this guy was dissing me *and* my mom? Where did he get off? "Just because you weren't manifesting for a few years didn't mean you wouldn't start. You needed to know how to handle second-stage Settling without screwing it up."

"That's Mrs. Berry to you," I said, getting angry. "She's way older than you are, so I think the first-name thing is out. We do live in the South, and manners are expected, in case you hadn't noticed."

"Manners aren't going to do you much good if you get reprimanded by SA or your family gets relocated because you got caught running around town with random body parts."

"Fine, then I'll talk to Mom about catching up or something," I said, even though that was the last thing I wanted to do. I didn't want to catch up—I wanted out. Forever. "But it might not even matter; this might have been a fluke. I might go back to normal and never see a zombie—"

"Unsettled, have some respect," he said, obviously even angrier. "And you *have* gone back to normal. Being a Settler *is* normal for you."

"How would you know?" If he wanted to escalate this little confrontation, that was fine with me. "Who are you, anyway?"

"Ethan." He gave me a hard look, as if his name should mean something to me, then continued with a sigh. "I'm with Settlers' Affairs, Protocol Division, the people SA calls when screwups need an attitude adjustment."

I stared into his undeniably gorgeous green eyes, mind racing as I tried to remember where I might have met him before. The name did niggle something in the back of my mind, but I couldn't concentrate on the niggle when the rest of my brain was thinking about the whole

"Protocol" revelation. This guy was the equivalent of a Settler cop, and I was truly in deep trouble if he'd been called in. Some backpedaling was clearly in order.

"Okay, I'm sorry. My attitude is ready to be adjusted, I swear."

He just stared at me for several seconds.

"I'm Megan Berry," I said finally, when the tense silence had lasted too long. I might as well introduce myself properly, even though this dude obviously already knew who I was.

I held out my hand and he took it after a moment. A tiny buzz of Settler power jumped between us as his much larger hand engulfed mine, along with a zing of something much more human.

Wow, this guy had some intense personal energy. If I weren't totally into Josh and this guy weren't a Settler cop, I had a feeling I would be able to get a pretty intense crush going on Ethan in a very short time.

"Yeah, I know, but I was hoping you'd let me call you Schmeg."

"Schme—" The nickname made the niggle in my mind turn into a tidal wave that broke through some wall deep inside my head. I was suddenly overwhelmed with memories—Ethan and me playing in my backyard, eating tofu bake over at his house, watching scary movies in his rec room, me sneaking along to the graveyard the night of his second-stage ceremony because I didn't want to be left behind. He was three and a half years older and getting ready to—

"Seal your first grave," I mumbled, my lips numb. Ohmygod, *that* was why I'd been out alone on the night of my attack. And Ethan was the boy at the graveyard, the one who'd saved my life. I remembered his face now, the way he'd looked when he was thirteen.

Other details spilled into my brain, filling in an abundance of the holes in my personal history and Settler education. Now I knew why I was in trouble with Protocol. I was supposed to have marked William before I let him go. I should have touched his forehead, which would cause that halo thing and let any fellow Settlers who saw him know someone was following him back to his grave. Then I was supposed to go to his resting place and seal his grave after he returned to it, to make certain no one could resurrect him through black magic.

To make sure no one could turn him into a Reanimated Corpse, like the ones that had attacked me five years ago.

"You remember," Ethan said softly, and I could tell he was talking about so much more than me recalling what my new duties should have been.

"I'm sorry, Ethan." Oh God, this was really Ethan. *My* Ethan. Well, not my Ethan now, but back then . . . well, not even really back then, but . . . wow, this was so weird. "I mean, I . . . You know, after that night . . ." I sucked in a frustrated breath.

I was so confused, shaken by how much of my old life I had locked away in my head. How could I have forgotten him? Especially considering that my memories of Monica had come back within a few months? I mean, true, he went to a private Catholic school in Little Rock, where his dad taught, so it wasn't like I saw him every day or anything, but I should have remembered him eventually. What kind of sick cranium did I have that I would choose to remember my history with the witchiest girl I'd ever met—Settler or otherwise—but not my old best friend?

"Partial amnesia." He shrugged. "I know. Don't worry about it. I saw you at the bowling alley a year after the attack. I asked you what time it was even though SA told me to leave you alone until your memory came back. I was sure you'd recognize me if you saw me, but . . . you had no clue." He stood, then stuffed his hands in his pockets.

"That must have been weird," I said, standing up too. Of course, it was even weirder that I still remembered that day. I'd wondered why a totally cute older boy was talking to a lowly eleven-year-old.

I suddenly felt like two different people trapped in the same body and wasn't sure if my skin was big enough to fit both of us inside.

"Sorry about the Jennifer thing. It's just . . . a lot of people at Settlers' Affairs have had issues with the way she's handled this. They think she should have tried to help you recover your power sooner." He crossed his arms. "And then to have you botch your first job because she didn't have her act together—"

"Listen, Ethan, I took William's information and sent him on his way by myself. Then his arm fell off and I knew Mom would be pissed so I snuck out without saying anything. Don't blame her. I'm sure she would have shown me how to do the job if I'd stuck around."

"It was your first job out of retirement. Don't you think you should have asked for help before running out with a dead kid's arm?" he asked, sounding like a full-fledged grown-up, not the prank-pulling troublemaker I used to know. Was this really the same guy who had hidden a remote-control fart machine in my backpack?

"Give me a break. I was doing the best I could."

"No, you weren't. I know how smart you are, and this isn't even close to your best. I mean, bicycling through town with an arm in a garbage bag is pretty dumb, Schmeg."

"Don't call me that. I know what that means now, okay? And I really don't enjoy having a nickname derived from a slang word for dirty boy parts," I said, blushing because I'd said something dorky like "dirty boy parts" in front of the totally hot guy Ethan had become. God, this was so weird, to compare what he used to be to me to what he was now.

Which was . . . nothing. He was nothing but a zombie Settler cop, not my friend. The sooner I got that through my thick head the better.

"Fine," he said, eyes growing colder again, like he remembered that we were strangers now too. "Just make sure you get your training up to par before your next Unsettled."

"*If* I have a next one," I said, hurrying on before he could argue with me. "I will. I'll talk to Mom as soon as I get home."

"Good, because I have bigger things to worry about than cleaning up your messes. *Reverto terra.*" As he spoke the last two words he twisted his hand toward the grave behind me. I turned just in time to see William's arm sinking into the earth.

Reverto terra, return to earth. Crap, why couldn't I remember that before?

"I already sealed the grave before you got here—I was just waiting on the arm." Ethan pulled a set of keys from his back pocket and disarmed the security system on a very smooth BMW Mini Cooper parked a little farther down the street from where I'd thrown my bike. I guessed the Protocol job must pay rather nicely since Ethan and his family had been a little strapped for cash back in the day.

"I've got to go. I can give you a ride as far as the high school football field if you want," he said, triggering my curiosity again.

Why was he going to my school's football field? He was three and a half years older and he'd never even gone to CHS, so there was no way he'd be visiting for nostalgic reasons. Was there some sort of supernatural Settler weirdness going down at Carol High?

The thought made my heart race. Returning Settler powers ruining my first date with Josh was bad enough, but what if some kind of zombie crap was going down at my school? There were only two weeks until homecoming, and the football field was a *highly* necessary part of the festivities.

My mind was suddenly awash with high anxiety. What if I never got to see Josh play his senior homecoming game? What if the homecoming court never got to parade down the freshly mown grass? What if, heaven forbid, they canceled the dance because the football field was all messed up from grass-eating zombies or something and with no game the powers that be figured there shouldn't be a dance and I would never get to slow dance with Josh wearing my new nearly-too-sexy-for-Mom-to-let-me-buy-it dress?

Gah! One heart shouldn't have to bear this much stress in one night! "Ethan, wait," I said, running after him. He didn't turn back, but he did slow down enough for me to catch up. "What's going on at the football field? Is it Settler stuff?"

"It's none-of-your-business stuff," he said, speeding up a bit. "Nice shirt, by the way. Does your mom know her fourteen-year-old is looking for a sugar daddy?"

"I'm fifteen, nearly sixteen," I said, refusing to cross my arms. "And it's a joke, obviously. Like a play on the Sugar Daddy candy so obviously shown below the words?" He laughed, a smug little sound I knew meant I was being laughed *at*, not *with*. "Anyway, that's not the point. If my powers are returning, then it *is* my business if something's going on at CHS. It's my school. I have the right to—"

"The only thing you have the right to do is head home and get to work making up for lost time." We were at his car by then, and he had the nerve to turn around and pat me on the head before he opened his door. Patting! On the head! Like I was a freaking dog or something.

I guess my opinion of the pat must have shown on my face because the jerk laughed, the smile on his face by far the most gorgeous smile I'd ever seen on anyone. "See you later, Schmeg," he said before sliding into his car.

"Don't call me Schmeg!" I yelled after him as he drove away, my heart beating as fast as it had been when I'd arrived at Mount Hope but for reasons much more mystifying than having a dead person's arm in a garbage bag.

CHAPTER 3

My entire day Sunday was spent cramming on first- and second-stage Settler material and helping Mom glue together the crushed bits and pieces of her Lladró collection. Not only was there no time to sneak away to the football field to investigate, I didn't even get a chance to call Jess until so late Sunday night that her wicked stepmother wouldn't let her come to the phone.

Actually, Jess's step isn't *that* wicked, but she gets pissy if I call after nine because she's afraid it might wake up James, Jess's terror of a three-year-old half brother.

Without the chance to calm my fevered brain with some quality phone time, I had a heck of a time getting to sleep. All night long, my mind raced, struggling to find a way to reverse my newly revamped powers. The only possibility I managed to come up with involved jumping headfirst off the balcony of the school lunchroom and praying for another bout of partial amnesia and power short-circuiting. Since jumping could also result in a broken neck, paralysis, or death—all of which would ruin my chances of going to homecoming with Josh—I didn't consider it really much of a possibility.

I had nada and was starting to feel my inescapable future pressing in all around me.

The only thing I felt at all in control of was ensuring that I reconnected with Josh and made certain he continued to see me as a homecoming-date-worthy chick. Therefore, I was up at five Monday morning, straightening my hair and applying light makeup and just a hint of brown eyeliner around my dark eyes. I donned the sundress Josh hadn't seen Saturday night—with the shawl, this time—and was off to school by six forty-five.

By five to seven, I had locked my bike at the racks and was booking it to the football field, determined to find out what Settler weirdness was brewing. I walked the length of the dew-damp grass, explored the area beneath both the visitors' and home team bleachers, and even went so far as to peek into the boys' locker room but came up with nothing. Everything seemed business as usual.

"The track!" I whispered aloud, thunking myself on the forehead with my palm.

I hadn't checked the track that ran around the field, which was completely stupid on my part. Circles hold great power for Settlers. We walk circles around graves to seal them, and several of the most advanced, third-stage magic commands involved tracing interlocking circles in the air while chanting.

A quick glance at my cell revealed I had plenty of time to investigate, so I hurried out of the field house and back into the cool morning air. I was three-fourths of the way around the hard-packed dirt track when I felt the vibrations of some seriously bad mojo rippling up through the earth. The stinging energy crept along the bare skin of my legs like an electric shock, making me yip and jump in the air. Lucky for me, I landed on the side of my sandal and was down on the ground seconds later, coated in thick, black mud.

"Ergh!" Why was I such a freaking klutz? I'd been in ballet practically since birth!

For the second time in three days I was coated in grave dirt or, in this case, grave *mud*—mud that had the distinct feel of black magic lingering in its gloppy depths. It was obvious SA had already been here to clean up most of the mess, but the faint flicker of dark power remaining in the mud was still clear enough for me to read. Apparently my ability to pick up dark vibes had returned along with my Settler mojo.

Whatever was going down, it wasn't Settler stuff. It was black-arts stuff, the kind of thing that led to nothing but seriously bad news for average humans and Settlers alike. And it was happening right here, inches away from the football field where dozens of innocent teens practiced every day—or mostly innocent teens: I'd heard a few stories about some of Josh's teammates that were fairly scandalous.

I was going to have to talk to Mom about this and force her to find out the 411. If my friends were in danger, I deserved to know about it, no matter what Ethan or the old Elder farts at SA thought.

But first, I had to get cleaned up. I wasn't sure if grave dirt smelled as awful to average people as it did to Settlers, but it didn't matter. I couldn't stand the stink of myself all day. There wasn't time to go home, so I was going to be forced to wear the gym clothes in my backpack for the entire day. *Not* the best way to remind Josh how hot I was but better than smelling like dead people.

I hurried back to the field house and snuck down the darkened hall leading to the girls' locker room. It was eerily quiet and strangely cold, considering it was already nearly seventy degrees outside. I felt goose bumps break out all over my bare arms and a sinking feeling in my stomach. Hopefully that wasn't a sign maintenance had remembered to lock this door.

"Yes!" I sighed with relief as the rusty door swung inward with a little shove. It was dark inside, but enough light filtered through the tiny windows at the top of the concrete wall that I could find my way to the showers. I flipped one on. Score: We had water. I wouldn't have a towel, but there was still soap, so at least I'd no longer smell of decaying flesh.

I dumped my backpack, whipped off my dress and underwear, and laid them on one of the wooden benches near the shower. Then, after twisting my hair into a knot on my head that I figured would hold long enough for a quick rinse, I stepped into the water.

"Sheeeeeesh!" I sucked in the word on a gasp. Holy crap! The water was cold—penguins-in-Antarctica-during-a-blizzard cold.

My fingers were numb and my goose bumps frozen into goose bump cubes by the time I'd soaped up. As I hurriedly rinsed off, my teeth chattered loudly enough to echo through the deserted room.

I was making so much noise, I barely heard the door opening behind me.

"Gunh?" The groan was barely out of the zombie's mouth before I was spinning around, screaming bloody murder.

The zombie stared at me while I kept screaming, clenching my arms across my chest as I scrambled across the wet tile toward my clothes. The only thing that kept me from snatching my dirty dress and running naked from the locker room was that the zombie just stood there, rigid and unmoving. Finally, I pulled it together and stood shivering in the buzzing silence, staring at my second zombie in three days.

"Welcome to your after-death session. I'm Megan," I said, my teeth chattering. "May I have your name, last name first?"

"Franklin, Terrence," he said, a lecherous look on his face as the human part of him came online.

His teeth were oddly white and clean looking against his dark, earth-covered skin, but he was just an average Unsettled, nothing more. He was a little older looking than William—maybe seventeen or eighteen—but not too old for a second-stager to deal with. And apparently not too old to be intensely interested in seeing me naked. Eww!

As I hurriedly pulled my gym clothes from my backpack and put them on—the fabric sticking to my cold, wet skin—I was inwardly freaking out. Why did the *first* guy to see me in the buff have to be *dead*? It was so unfair and potentially emotionally scarring.

"Dang, girl, no need to cover up so fast," Terrence said, making me move even faster.

"No need to be a perv," I snapped back at him, but the dead guy only laughed. What a skeeze. I didn't feel nearly as bad about this dude being one of the dearly departed.

Once dressed, I fished a notebook and pen from my backpack and tried to keep from trembling as I wrote down his name, address, and cemetery plot and number. But even as my skin warmed up I couldn't stop shaking. This had *never* happened to me before! Never! Unsettled didn't come to me during the day.

I'd learned to shield to keep that from happening when I was like six years old. Every Settler knows how to keep zombies away until nightfall, when our powers are strongest and we can't help emitting the subtle, paranormal signals that tell our deceased clients where to find us. Shielding is the first thing you learn how to do when your power starts to manifest, as simple as learning to sing the ABCs.

"Um, so what don't you like about your death?" I asked Terrence.

"Not a dang thing," he said, smiling so wide his teeth took up half of his face.

"Then why are you out of your grave?"

"Danielle and I were finally going to do it, but I died the day before." He looked sad for a moment, which almost made my heart soften toward the guy until he spoke again. "So I never got to see a chick naked. Pissed me off, man. I knew I should have done it with Ladonna even though Ray said she had some nasty body odor prob—"

"So you crawled out of your grave because you wanted to see a girl naked?" My tone was not pleasant, but I couldn't help myself. This guy was topping my list of skankiest zombies ever.

"Yeah, baby. And now I have." He licked his dirt-covered lips in a way that would have been gross even if he were alive. "Now I have."

"Okay, that is totally freaking gross and—"

"And not something you would have had to deal with if you were shielding properly." I gasped as I turned toward the door, knowing I should be relieved to see another Settler. But considering it was Monica standing there, in all her cruel and beautiful senior glory, it was hard to summon up the slightest bit of relief, let alone gratitude. "Really, Megan, summoning an Unsettled during the day. That's like . . . toddler stuff, you know that, right?"

"Listen, Monica, I just—"

"Just came back into your power. Yeah, I heard." And she was entirely unimpressed, as usual. But when wasn't Monica totally unimpressed with anyone other than herself? "Have you Marked him yet?"

"Not yet, but I—"

"Seriously, Megan, you really need to get it together."

"Hey," Terrence said, eyes narrowing. "You're that chick from the mall, aren't—"

"Nice to see you again too." Monica cut Terrence off with a sigh, putting one hand to his forehead while she fished her cell from the front pocket of her jeans with the other. "Return to your grave and rest in peace."

Terrence was already streaking away as Monica lifted the phone to her ear. "Hey, Sue. I'm here with Megan Berry. She summoned an Unsettled this morning and will need to have the grave sealed so she doesn't have to cut school." She snatched the paper from my hand and repeated the cemetery and plot number to the woman on the phone. "Thanks, Sue. Yeah, I'll definitely tell her."

"Tell me what?" I asked. Monica snapped the phone shut and shot me a look of completely false pity from her bright blue eyes.

With her dark brown, nearly black hair, those eyes always looked out of place to me but in an exotic, gorgeous kind of way. Everything about Monica was perfect and gorgeous, from the shiny straight hair hanging down to her butt to her size-two body. I supposed that was why she was part of the social elite, despite the fact that she was in training to be the devil's handmaiden.

"Sue said you should really go home and stay with your mommy if you can't even remember how to shield."

"I remember how to shield just fine," I snapped, mentally firming up said shields as I spoke. Maybe I hadn't been shielding strongly enough before, but I certainly was now.

"Right, that's why you're summoning pervert zombies." Monica looked me up and down, her upper lip curling with distaste. "But then again, maybe you *enjoy* dead people seeing you naked. Is that the only way you can get a boy's attention, Meg?"

"Give me a break, Monica," I said, wishing I could say something nastier, but knowing I had to at least fake civility.

Not only was Monica queen bee at CHS and capable of making sure Josh never spoke to me again, she was also cocaptain of the pom squad. Her vote would help determine whether I made the team next week. I couldn't afford to piss her off no matter how much I'd like to tell her to go eat about a pound of dog poo and die.

"Sorry, Megan, no breaks for Settlers who mess up." She flipped her hair over her shoulder. "I'll be telling my SA liaison about the zombie I saw streaking in here this morning and anything else funky you get up to."

"Please, Monica, I swear I—"

"Ethan told me he took it easy on you the other night, but I'm not willing to risk being discovered because you can't handle yourself," she said, picking her monster purse up off the floor.

She'd talked to Ethan? About me? He'd called the Monicster and told her about meeting me in the graveyard? In the old days he'd hated her as much as I had. Well, maybe not quite as much, since she'd never shown him her witchiest side. He was cute and flirtworthy, and she had always been in need of his advice and comfort and . . . Hmm . . .

There was something prodding at my memory, something about

Ethan and Monica, but . . . I couldn't place it. I was on the verge of figuring it out when someone called my name from outside the locker room.

"Megan? Are you in here? I—" Jess poked her fuzzy blond head in, smiling at me before she saw Monica and her eyes widened in fear. Poor Jess, she was far too sweet to handle the Monicster. "Um, hi, Monica."

"Hey, Jessica," Monica said, turning a megawatt smile in her direction. "Saw your name on the tryout sheet last Friday. That is so awesome. I caught your solo at recital last year. Totally fresh."

Monica knew Jess's name? Who would have guessed?

"Oh, wow. Thanks, Monica," Jess said, her pale blue eyes lighting up with pleasure even though she shot me a look that clearly communicated she was thinking the same thing I was. "I'm totally psyched for tryouts. Megan and I have been working on—"

"Yeah, that's good," Monica said, her tone cooling a zillion degrees as she turned to shoot me one last look before heading for the door. "Megan's going to need a *lot* of work if she hopes to be anywhere on par with what we need."

I knew she was talking about more than dance team tryouts, but her words still stung. I'd been dancing since I was three and training for tryouts all summer. I was an excellent dancer and she knew it, but she was obviously going to make it as hard for me to make the team as possible. Great. As if I needed one more thing to worry about right now.

"Wow, she's such a jerk," Jess whispered after Monica disappeared. "Don't listen to her, Megan. You're totally ready for tryouts. She's just . . . witchy."

"Thanks," I said, unable to keep from smiling. The fact that she was willing to call Monica witchy on my behalf made me feel loads better. "Come on, we'd better go or we won't have time to get to our lockers before first."

"Okay, but . . . don't you want to change?"

"Already changed. I'm stuck in gym gear for the rest of the day." I filled Jess in on my fall in the mud—though I fudged on the reason I'd been walking around the track. Jess wasn't clued in to the whole Settler business.

We weren't allowed to tell non-Settlers anything about our world, not that it had been an issue—until now, anyway. Jess and I didn't start hanging out all the time until more than a year after the zombie attack, when we both ended up in all the same classes in seventh grade. Since then, we'd been inseparable, our love of dance cementing our friendship into a bond nothing could break, not even Pickle, our joint crush, asking me out instead of her.

"So you've got to tell me, how'd the date with the Delicious Dill go?" Jess asked, as if reading my mind. "I almost died when Clara said you'd called last night, but she didn't give me the phone. She's still holding my cell captive, so I couldn't even try to call you back."

Delicious Dill was our code name for Josh, derived from the Pickle last name. Kind of lame, but we'd thought it up in eighth grade so we couldn't be held responsible. "It didn't go at all. My parents had these old friends over and made me stay at home."

I felt a flash of conscience for telling Jess a lie but pushed it away. No matter how much I hated it, there would now be secrets between us.

Unless, of course, I figured out a way to check out of Settlerhood forever, a possibility that was looking even sweeter after this morning's events. Stay a Settler and deal with weird black-magic vibes, pervy zombies, and wicked coworkers like Monica. Or be a normal sophomore whose dates weren't interrupted by dead people and who wasn't forced to lie to her best friend. Normal won, hands down.

Now I just had to figure out some way to make my dream a reality.

CHAPTER 4

Please, Mom," I begged, fighting the urge to tear my hands away from hers and make a run for my room to retouch my makeup. "Do you not understand he will be here in like fifteen minutes and I haven't even—"

"And you won't be going anywhere until you convince me your shields are strong enough." Mom smiled and gripped my hands even tighter. "I shouldn't be letting you out of the house at all. I'm sure SA wouldn't approve, even if Monica *is* covering for you until you've practiced grave sealing."

That made me smile. Ha ha, Monica.

Her call to Sue had totally backfired. The Elders were now convinced I couldn't handle any Unsettled by myself without further training, so Monica had to cover for me. Her liaison had given her a power boost that would last at least a few days, meaning any undead in Carol between the ages of thirteen and eighteen that crawled out of its grave was going straight to her house.

Ha ha, hee hee, na na na na na, na na na na—

"So," Mom said, interrupting my admittedly immature mental celebration, "if you want me to call Elder Thomas and ask if it's—"

"No, okay, okay," I said, recrossing my legs on the purple yoga mat we were both sitting on and forcing myself to relax. I was not going to miss a second chance at a first date with Josh because I couldn't get my Zen on sufficiently to suit Mom.

Ah . . . Josh. Sweet, understanding, gorgeous Josh, who—first thing fourth period—had asked me to go with him and some other seniors to the haunted corn maze in Waverly, a tiny country town about ten minutes from Carol. The idea of hanging out with seniors was way scarier than any haunted maze, but I was willing to risk it. I had to convince Josh how perfect we were for each other and soon. Homecoming was only ten days, two hours, and a dozen or so minutes away and—

"Megan! I mean it. If you don't focus, I will tell that boy to go home."

"Okay! Sorry."

"Now concentrate. Close your eyes."

I closed them and almost immediately felt a surge of power flow from Mom's fingertips to mine. It was a much larger amount than she'd tried a few minutes before, but I had no trouble deflecting it. I'd been so freaked by my first daytime zombie that I'd been working on my shields all day. There was nothing getting through those suckers.

"Wow. Good job, honey." Mom's voice sounded funny, and when I opened my eyes, the look on her face made my stomach bottom out.

"What's wrong?"

"That was all the power I could muster and . . . it didn't even faze you." She dropped my hands, wiping her palms on her yoga pants. "I mean, I can't actively Settle anymore, but I should at least be able to break through the shields of a second-stager."

"But you couldn't. Is that bad?"

"No, it's just . . ." Mom reached out and smoothed a hair behind my ear. "Honey, you always had advanced power for your age when you were younger. But now, I really think you've come into something extraordinary. You're manifesting more than most third-stage Settlers, and you're not even sixteen. That's just—"

"Awful? Horrible?" I asked, standing up and moving into the kitchen to grab a mint. I'd suddenly lost my will to fix my makeup for the fifth time since I'd gotten home from school.

"No," Mom said, ignoring my bad attitude, "but it's probably why you summoned during the day. Your shields weren't up to handling the amount of power you were emitting."

"Great," I muttered. If what Mom said was true, there was no way I'd ever be free again. SA wouldn't let somebody with super-Settler mojo back out of the biz. Heck, they wouldn't let somebody with a tiny spark of power out. There weren't enough of us around to let anyone who was manifesting off the hook.

"It's a gift, one you should be proud of," Mom said, following me into the kitchen to check on whatever weird hippie thing she was cooking in the Crock-Pot. Thankfully, Josh and I were getting burgers on the way. "And one that could pay your way to the college of your choice."

"Right," I said. But not even the thought of mad cash could lift my spirits.

Earlier in the afternoon—after I'd finally found the address for William the zombie's girlfriend and dropped the note containing his message in the mail—Mom had shown me this secret savings account from before my accident. When I was younger, she hadn't wanted me to think our gift was only about monetary gain, but apparently I'd been getting paid for Settling all those years ago. With interest the money wasn't bad, and now that I was a second-stager, I'd be getting paid even more.

Our organization was one of the oldest in the world and had invested its assets wisely. Apparently, back in the old days, cities used to pay their local SA a tidy sum for keeping the Undead off the streets. They shelled out enough dough that, even now, in times when people had forgotten zombies were real, there was plenty of cash to go around.

Every Settler was paid well for the work they did, from the time they started manifesting as children to the time their ability to summon Unsettled faded when one of their kids took over. Afterward, they still got a stipend for using their remaining power to train their offspring, as Mom had trained me.

So the job was not totally without perks, even though Mom said SA didn't let kids touch their money until they graduated to third-stage Settling. Of course.

But still . . . I wasn't convinced the ups outweighed the downs.

Take Monica, for instance. She'd had to find another Settler to cover for her every time the pom squad was scheduled to dance at a night game. That couldn't have been easy. There were only so many Settlers our age in the surrounding areas. Which meant *I* was probably screwed as far as getting anyone to cover me during games—even if I wasn't blacklisted from the team because I had negatively impacted Monica's evil existence.

Argh! Why did life have to get so annoyingly complicated all of a sudden?

"Now, let's do a quick pop quiz," Mom said, reminding me that things could always get worse. "I give you a situation; you tell me what you would do."

"Mom, please. We studied all day yesterday. Can't we just—"

"And we'll study all night tonight and you won't go on your date unless—"

"Fine! Pop quiz me."

"Okay." She smiled and snagged a few pretzels from the bucket on the counter, obviously thrilled to be playing teacher again. Poor Mom, she had to get a life other than training me and counting seeds or whatever the hell she did for a living. "You've gotten all the information from your Unsettled. Now what do you do?"

"Mark the forehead to summon a halo, send it back to rest in peace, then head over to the graveyard to seal the grave with the standard ritual." Which, thankfully, Mom had agreed I could wait to learn until tomorrow night so my social life wouldn't be totally ruined.

"All right, suppose you wait too long and it starts to go Rogue."

"Do my best to lay hands on the Unsettled and send it back to its grave. If it doesn't respond, try to contain the Rogue and call SA. Not that I'll have to worry about that since I am such a responsible and dedicated Settler, of course."

"Of course." Mom sighed and crunched a pretzel, revealing that my good-little-Settler act wasn't fooling her for a second. She knew I was less than thrilled about my powers returning. "Describe the third type of out-of-grave phenomenon and tell me how they come to be."

"Talking with your mouth full is gross, Mom. Why don't we—"

"If you don't know, then you don't go," she said, still talking with her mouth full and even opening her mouth really wide so I could see all the gross smooshed pretzel inside. Very mature. And this was the woman I was supposed to respect as the Yoda to my Skywalker. She was way more Wookie.

"Reanimated Corpses. They're raised by black magic. The witch—"

"Not all witches practice black magic. The proper term is *black-magic practitioner*."

"Okay, the *black-magic practitioner* uses a totem—like a piece of clothing or a picture or a doll that represents the person they want the zombie to munch on—to focus their energy."

"Does the Reanimated Corpse need to see the totem?"

"No." I rolled my eyes, making it clear I was not a total idiot. "Zombies can't think. The totem is for the wi—black-magic practitioner. They need it for the spell and have to leave it on the grave after the corpse has risen."

"So how do they reanimate the corpse?"

"They spill blood on the grave and the totem and chant the summoning spell—"

"Which is?"

"Which is something I *don't* need to have memorized because I am never going to raise a corpse," I said, glancing at the clock on the stove. Jeez, Josh *would* be late this time, when I was dying for him to hurry up and get here and spare me any more quizzage.

"Fair enough," she said, crunching on another pretzel. "Though you'll have to have it memorized for the third-stage test in a few years."

"Okay, fine, but that's in a few years. So are we done?"

"Not yet. So why do Reanimated Corpses end up killing people other than the person they've been raised to kill?"

"They are drawn to blood," I said, my mouth going dry. "Any blood, so if they sense an open wound"—like the ones I'd had after I fell down the hill that night at the graveyard—"they . . . um . . ."

"They'll be deterred from their course and could potentially go into a feeding frenzy," she said, her voice gentle. I'd told her the memory of the attack had come back in all its grotesque scariness. Maybe now she'd feel sorry for me and give me a break with the quizzing.

"Now, let's say you encounter a Reanimated Corpse. What should you do?"

Or maybe not.

"Run like hell?" I asked, trying to ignore the way my stomach was turning inside out just thinking about running into one of the undead.

"Megan, I know this is hard, but—"

"I can freeze it with one of the freezing spells to buy some time, then work the spell to send it back to the one who raised it. Once it gets a taste of the same blood that summoned it from the ground in the first place, it will go snuggle back in its grave and chill for all eternity."

"Good. So the freezing spells. What are they and why—"

Thankfully, the doorbell rang just then, sparing me further torture and lifting my sagging spirits. After all, how could I stay in the depths of despair when the hottest guy in the entire school was waiting on my doorstep?

"I can go now and we'll finish this later?" I asked, giving Mom the puppy dog eyes.

"Fine. But home by ten, it's a school night," Mom called after me as I dashed to the door, apparently deciding to be cool and not force me to introduce her to Josh before we left. Thank God for small favors—it seemed like those were the only ones He was handing out lately.

· · ·

"You ready?" Josh asked, tightening his grip on my hand as we headed to the second entrance to the maze. We were supposed to be getting ready to race Josh's friend Andy and his date, but all I could think about was that Josh was holding my hand.

Holding. *My*. Hand. Ohmygod, I could hardly control my psychotic pleasure.

Josh was looking hotter than ever in a pair of dark-washed jeans and a vintage ringer T-shirt that made his arms look even more muscled. He had a little gel in his shaggy, nearly black hair and it looked like the brows above his ice blue eyes had just been plucked, so it was obvious he'd put in the effort to get studly for me. He'd told me he let his big sister pluck his eyebrows for special occasions.

Yes, he did! He bared that horribly intimate detail! He's totally into you and is going to ask you to homecoming tonight!

It was so nice when my inner voice got on a positive tangent for a change. "I'm ready. We're going to kick some maze ass," I said, with my best flirty smile.

"Hell, yeah, we are." He leaned down, giving me a sloppy kiss on the cheek. His breath was decidedly beerish and the dampness of the kiss not quite sexy, but who cared? He'd kissed me! Really *kissed* me! And Andy's girlfriend, London, was driving, so who cared if he'd had a few beers?

Mom would care and Dad would care and if they smell beer on you, you will be so dead and never allowed out of the house again. Ever. Not even for homecoming.

How quickly the inner-voice worm turns, returning to its negative-tangent ways.

I casually swiped my cheek while Josh wasn't looking, hoping my sweater wouldn't absorb any beer-scented saliva.

"Ready, set, go, losers!" Andy shouted from where he and London stood at the other maze entrance ten feet away. London squealed as they took off, and I found myself making an equally girlish noise as Josh pulled me into the dark rows of corn.

Everything was going perfectly. London, who was normally a Monica minion inclined toward evil, had been totally nice to me since they picked me up. She'd even acted like it was no big deal that Josh had invited me, even though she'd had to tell Monica there wasn't room for her in the car. Of course, *I* knew that Monica was stuck at home on Settler duty anyway but still took great satisfaction in knowing the Evil One had been ditched by her friends because of me.

Like I said, I am not as sweet as Jess and therefore can take pleasure in the pain of others. Well, in the pain of Monica at least. I actually felt sorry for Josh's ex, Beth, who'd looked kind of upset when I'd passed her in the hall earlier.

Josh had broken up with her over the summer after two years

together. But Beth hadn't given me the evil eye or apparently said anything to London to make it clear I wasn't welcome in the inner circle. So I supposed we were still cool. Thank God, since she was also cocaptain of the pom squad.

It was a late-September miracle and thrilling enough to make me forget all about Settler stuff for a while.

"Come on, this way," Josh said, dashing to the right, going the complete opposite of the direction he should be going to reach the center. I'd memorized the first few turns we should make by studying the miniature plaque at the entrance to the maze, so I knew we were on the wrong track. But who cared?

Getting lost in a dark, spooky maze where actors were hiding to scare us wasn't a bad thing. Ghouls jumping out of the darkness were the perfect excuse for me to be jumping into Josh's arms in need of comfort. From there, it was only a hop and a skip from comforting to kissing. And then from kissing to realizing how wonderful we were together and from realizing how wonderful we were together to realizing he simply *had* to ask me to be his date to the first major social event of the year because—

"Damn, wrong way!" Josh spun in a circle, not even noticing my squeal as a man dressed as a vampire dashed out of one corner of the dead end. "Come on, let's go back. Andy bet me beer money for a month. No way I'm losing."

We dashed back the way we'd come, Josh pulling so hard my arm felt like it might be wrenched from the socket. Once again he took the wrong fork in the maze, but when I tried to say something, he ignored me. Ten minutes later, we were still no closer to the center and Josh was still completely unwilling to comfort me no matter how freaked out I pretended to be by the various ghosts, chain saw–wielding freaks, and white-faced undead vampire brides.

I was approaching a state of extreme frustration when I noticed a sound, and a smell, that had nothing to do with pretend Halloween fun. The groans were coming from inside the rows of corn and getting closer every second. My heart started racing and a cold sweat broke out along my spine.

Whatever was coming sure wasn't an average Unsettled. They never sounded like that, so feral and evil and . . . hungry. What were the chances? It wasn't like black-magically raised zombies were a common occurrence in a small town like ours.

Memories of the attack flooded my mind, making me tremble as I pulled my hand from Josh's and spun back toward the dead end we'd just left. For a second my scar burned, as if the nerves were having a flashback. I winced in remembered pain but forced myself not to run for London's car, even though every cell in my body was screaming for me to get the hell out of the maze and I was fairly sure I was going to throw up.

I had to go get rid of them, *by myself.* I'd forgotten my cell at home and even if I'd had it there was no time to call for help. In addition to that big, scary insight, I realized I also couldn't let Josh see what was going down or my family would be relocated or worse. Thinking fast, I pulled one earring from my ear and stuffed it in my pocket before Josh noticed I wasn't following him and turned back.

"Come on," he said, clearly frustrated that I was wasting time. "I know which way to go for sure now."

"I . . . think I lost an earring back there," I said, already backing toward the sound of the approaching zombies, struggling to keep my expression normal looking despite the terror making my heart pound a hundred miles a minute. "I'll just go look for it and meet you in the center."

"Are you sure?" he asked, already on the move.

"Yeah totally. You've got to beat Andy, I'll see you in a little bit." I turned and ran to meet the zombies the second Josh was looking the other direction.

Even though I was dying to find some place to hide and bury my head in the dirt, I couldn't. If I didn't disable them, the Reanimated Corpses could start eating innocent people. No matter who they'd been called from their grave to kill, blood would drive them to feed wherever they found it. There were tons of kids running around going crazy in the maze—which meant scraped knees and bloody noses galore—and who knew how many other people were sporting shaving cuts that might draw the undead. One of them might even be my date for homecoming.

Holy crap. I wasn't ready for this, not by a long shot, but Mom had said my power was strong. Surely I'd be able to freeze them, then sic the coming monsters back on their Creator . . .

If I could only remember the freaking commands!

"Oh God, oh God!" I froze in place, shaking my hands at my sides as if that would somehow jar my memory. Now I was really going to throw up. Throw up and then pass out in my own vomit, thus giving the raving undead a hassle-free meal with extra bile sauce.

Crap! Why couldn't I remember the spell commands! Mom had made me study them yesterday, and I'd just heard Ethan say one of them the other night. Why hadn't I answered Mom's last pop quiz question when I had the chance! I'd known the answer in the kitchen, but now . . . it was like fear had given me the Jedi mind wipe or something.

"Come one Megan. Come on," I chanted. I was almost certain the sending-them-back-to-their-Creator command started with an *r* and ended with something about earth, but—

Two zombies chose that moment to burst through the corn, eyes glowing red, clawed hands stretched toward me. My mouth went absolutely dry, my throat closed up, and I saw my life flash in front of my eyes—complete with several scenes previously deleted by partial amnesia.

I remembered slipping the fart machine Ethan had put in my backpack into Monica's and embarrassing her at dance class. I recalled the excitement of building my first tree house with Ethan and his granddad, the time my aunt Sharon had visited from California and brought me an old Settler diary, and the smell of my mom's perfume when she'd rushed into the hospital after my attack.

Great. My memory was finally returning, seconds before death by Reanimated Corpses.

And they were definitely Reanimated—the yellow drool leaking from their hissing mouths banished any lingering doubt about that. And both formerly female, judging by the shredded remains of their dresses. I had time to realize that they hadn't been dead long and that one of them bore a slight resemblance to a deranged Pepsi-era Britney Spears before they were on me.

No, scratch that, running *past me*. They hadn't even stopped to eye my usually irresistible living flesh, which was a good thing, since I hadn't done much more than cower in fear like a complete loser.

That meant they were after someone in particular in the corn maze tonight. It wasn't me, but that didn't mean I was out of the woods. If anything, it meant I had to try harder to keep them from finding their target. Those two zombie chicks were like loaded guns I had to find some way to disarm, and only one surefire method came to mind. The undead were drawn to blood, any blood, which meant . . .

"Oh, crap!" I hissed as I shoved up the sleeve of my sweater and raked my nails down my forearm with as much force as I could muster.

It stung like nobody's business, and immediately the grooves left behind began to fill with blood. And here Mom was always saying my thirty-dollar manicures were a waste of my allowance.

The zombies were already on their way back to me, drawn by the mystical lure of fresh blood. A quick glance down the available pathways revealed a group of junior high kids coming from my right, so I dashed to my left, heading back toward the dead end.

Luckily, what with the haunted maze theme and all, no one should be too freaked out by seeing me being chased by the undead. But seeing me attempt to kick their asses and possibly get eaten when said ass kicking went awry was another thing altogether. Even if I didn't make it out of here alive, the very least I could do for my family was make sure they didn't have to uproot everything and move because I'd blown cover.

"You're not going to die, you're not going to die," I breathlessly chanted as I rounded the corner and emerged into the circular area where I'd first seen the zombies. I spun around, assuming my best imitation of a fight position—which was totally lame because I'd never studied martial arts or boxing or anything of the kind. I was a dancer, not a fighter!

But I was going to have to do my best to fight, at least until I remembered the freaking commands to send these ladies back to their Maker, and it seemed better to stage my last stand out in the open. If I kept running through the corn, I might escape them for longer, but they'd eventually catch up. Black-magically raised zombies just don't tire out the way live people do.

They're a lot slower than regular Unsettled, but they're completely relentless. They wouldn't stop until they got their super-strong hands on me. And when they did, I'd be exhausted as well as hemmed in on all sides by corn and unable to even try to throw a punch.

The girls trudged around the corner and lunged toward me, shrieking, mouths open wide, ready to clamp down around soft, living tissue.

I tensed, fists raised and weight evenly distributed between my feet. It was going to happen. Right here. Right now. Me versus two supernaturally strong zombies with a rabid hunger for my flesh.

If I were the gambling type, I *so* wouldn't have put any money on me. Not a thin freaking dime.

CHAPTER 5

Britney got to me first. I reacted on pure instinct, lashing out with my leg, grand jeté–ing right into her face. I'd worn my Timberlands due to the roughing-it factor of hiking around in a field, so the sound as foot and face connected was entirely satisfying. Her head snapped back and her forward momentum finished the job of getting Britney flat on her ass, but there was no time for celebration.

Miss Undead Arkansas number two was already lunging for my throat.

I faked right and then rolled to the left, putting space between me and both my opponents, frankly thrilled to still be bite free. I never would have thought I'd be a good fighter, but my instincts thus far were fairly Buffy-esque.

"Hi-yah!" I shouted as I swept one leg out in a circle, tripping zombie two, who fell into Britney, knocking her back on her ass. Call me crazy, but the cheesy karate sounds were making me feel so much tougher.

Too bad they weren't helping me remember the freaking words to the return-to-earth spell.

"Return to earth! *Terra* is earth," I mumbled as I backed away from the zombies on the ground, readying myself for another attack.

I had the second part of the spell! If only I could remember the Latin word for *return*. Dammit! Why did these spells have to be in Latin? Didn't anyone realize that we were living in the twenty-first century, for God's sake?

"Hi-yah," and Britney was down again, thanks to a grand jeté to the face. The chick was not learning from her mistakes. "Hi—"

I screamed as zombie two sidestepped the kick meant for her and tackled me to the ground.

We rolled over once, twice, and somehow I ended up on top. There wasn't time to congratulate myself or scramble off zombie two, however, before Britney was on me from behind. Without stopping to second-guess myself I bent forward, then slammed my head back, straight into Britney's face. Dull pain throbbed through my skull, but Britney was barely fazed. Of course—zombies didn't feel pain, which was just one of the many reasons it was entirely stupid to waste time fighting them. And why I should have been using my energy to work spells instead of exhausting myself with my super-lame ninja action.

Somehow I managed to dig Britney's fingers from my shoulders and dodge the zombie beneath me as she lunged for my throat, but I knew I didn't have much time left. This was going to end soon, one way or another. Either these ladies were going to eat me or I was going to remember the freaking words to the freaking *reverto* spell.

"*Reverto terra!*" I screamed, a relieved smile on my face as I twisted my palms to face both the Reanimated Corpses. Before they could utter a final groan, both Britney and her partner in crime were sinking into the earth.

Thank you, mind! Way to come through at the last minute! I would have appreciated the words *before* my jeans were covered in dirt and before the shoulder of my sweater was ripped so that my bra strap was hanging out, but hey, I'd take alive any way I could get it.

"Megan, get up!" shouted a strangely familiar voice from a few feet away. I spun to see Ethan running toward me.

What the hell was he doing here? More important question—why couldn't he have gotten here a few minutes sooner, *before* I had to fight for my life all by myself?

"It's fine, I already—" I screamed and kept screaming as first one hand and then another burst from the earth, closing around my feet then clawing up my calves. I tried to run but fell on my face, giving the emerging Britney a convenient handhold on my arm. "No!" I cried, squeezing my eyes closed as her mouth burst through the dirt, her teeth headed straight for my nose. I smelled her rancid, undead breath and knew it was a only matter of seconds before a key part of my face was a thing of the past.

"*Reverto!*" Ethan's command vibrated through the air, making me shiver with the force of his power buzzing across my skin.

Or maybe it was relief. Whatever it was, I was shaking like it was twenty degrees outside instead of sixty by the time the zombies fled into the cornfield, bound for whoever had raised them in the first place. If I'd left the *terra* out of the command, I would have been fine. They were returning to their Maker, after all, not the freaking earth.

I was so, so stupid. And would have been so, so dead if Ethan hadn't shown up.

"Are you okay?" Ethan asked, crouching down in front of me, cupping my face in his hands, his eyes wide and freaked out as he searched for bite marks.

"Just *reverto*, not *reverto terra*," I muttered, trying not to cry. I'd already screwed up royally—no need to add to my humiliation by bawling like a baby.

"Megan, you scared me half to death," he said, transferring his hands to my shoulders, his fingers digging into my skin in a way that made me certain he was having to work hard not to shake me senseless. "You could have been seriously hurt or worse. What the hell are you doing out here?"

"I'm on a date," I said, lifting my chin, striving for a small degree of dignity.

"Yeah, I heard." His tone would have made his disdain clear even if he hadn't already rolled his eyes. "Your mom told me where to find you." He grabbed my hand and pulled me to my feet.

I dug my heels in as he tried to drag me away, doing my best to ignore the electricity sweeping over my entire body. Holding hands with Ethan was so different from holding hands with Josh. Josh's hand had just felt like . . . a hand. But Ethan's felt way more intimate, as if he were touching something far more scandalous than my palm and fingers.

Before I realized it, I was coming down with a case of the tingles unlike anything I'd ever experienced. Having my fingers wrapped up in Ethan's much larger, warmer hand felt soooo amazing. All I wanted to do was cling to him and let him lead me wherever he wanted to lead me, but that was *not* what needed to be happening right now.

"Let me go," I said, struggling harder to free myself. "Where are you taking me?"

"Home, eventually," he said, tightening his grip until I winced.

"Ouch, that hurts." He relaxed for a second, and I took the

opportunity to wrench my hand free. Thank God, now I could think a little more clearly without the whole tingle thing distracting me. "I can't go home with you! I'm on a date. Josh will think I ditched him."

Ethan made another grab for my hand, but I jumped back in time. He sighed like I was the most annoying little brat in the universe. "I already left a note on London's car saying you got sick and called someone to pick you up. Now come on."

"How do you know London?" I asked, narrowing my eyes, wondering why I was suddenly so jealous.

"She hangs out with me and Monica sometimes. Come on, sickie, let's get out of here."

"I am not sick, and I am *not* leaving!" I shouted, crossing my arms when he tried to grab my hand again. So he hung out with London and Monica, did he? Enough that he knew what London's car looked like. Wasn't that cozy . . . and strangely infuriating. "Now if you'll excuse me, I'm going—"

"You're going with me. Now." Before I could think of a clever retort to that threat, Ethan darted forward.

"Put me down! You jerk!" I yelled as he flung me over his shoulder and set off toward the entrance to the maze. "I mean it. Put me down or I'll scream."

"Fine, scream. It's a haunted corn maze, people are supposed to be screaming," he said, his tone annoyingly smug. "Good thing for you, or somebody would have noticed you and the RCs."

Reanimated Corpses. "Aren't you cute with abbreviations," I said to his butt. From my flung-over-the-shoulder position, I was getting a very up close and personal look at the body part. And dang, but the boy could fill out a pair of jeans.

I blushed as the tingles started again and closed my eyes. I was not going to think about Ethan or his butt. The RCs might have started the ruination of my date, but Ethan was finishing it. He was an ass who was basically kidnapping me and probably making sure Josh would *never* ask me to homecoming.

Furious! I should have been furious . . . but for some reason, I wasn't. Some sick little part of me was very happy to be bouncing along on Ethan's shoulder, headed wherever he decided to take me. My inner feminist tried to put the smackdown on that sick little part, but soon she too was distracted by the lusciousness of Ethan. Weakness, thy name is Megan's hormones.

I was so deep in tingle Happyville, I didn't even notice the chick leaning on London's car until we were nearly to Ethan's Mini Cooper. And even then, it took me a few seconds to recognize the identity of the scrawny size-two wench who should *not* have been anywhere near here.

Monica. Not only was she not home on zombie duty, she was out getting ready to crash *my* date with *my* Josh. I would have screamed for Ethan to stop long enough for me to ask her what the hell she was doing if I'd thought he would listen. Or if a part of me weren't a little freaked out to see her standing there, looking so strangely satisfied with herself.

Someone had to have raised those corpses, and a Settler would know how to get the job done. Could Monica? . . .

Nah. Not even her horridness was that horrid, and she certainly didn't look like she'd just been bitten by two RCs. A little pale and out of breath and shivering in her oversize sweater, sure, but . . . hmmm . . .

No. I wasn't going to go there. Yet.

She was a bitch, not a witch or a black-magic practitioner or whatever. But I decided right then it might be smart to keep an eye on the Monicster. You know what they say—keep your friends close, but keep your enemies closer.

• • •

An hour later, I'd decided I would be grateful for a lot less closeness with a certain ex-friend. Ethan had firmly vanquished every last shred of happy within me with the most boring lecture in the world on the various Unsettled commands and an in-depth briefing on grave sealing. It wouldn't have been so bad, but Ethan insisted on delivering his "lesson" in some nasty-smelling graveyard near a paper plant where he had sent one of his Unsettled earlier in the evening.

"Now, you ready? You're going to seal the grave."

"Me?" I asked, shuffling away.

"Yes, you." He grabbed my hand and pulled me back.

"But I— ow!" I jumped as Ethan jabbed me with the needle. It was a tiny little needle, the kind diabetics used to check their blood sugar, but I've never been a fan of getting stuck with sharp things. This was apparently part of the grave-sealing process, however, so I guessed I had to get used to the idea of stabbing myself on a regular basis.

The Settler gig just kept getting better and better.

"If you'd had one of these on you earlier, you wouldn't have had to scratch your arm to get those RCs' attention," Ethan said, though he didn't sound annoyed. I could tell he thought I was pretty brave for luring the Reanimated Corpses back to me instead of letting them find their target. Unfortunately, he wasn't sufficiently impressed to give me the rest of the night off Settler duty. Even when I'd sworn I'd known all four second-stage commands before I was scared half to death.

He'd been appointed my tutor by the powers that be and was taking the job very seriously. I figured Mom would be pissed to find out SA thought she wasn't suitable mentor material anymore, but when I'd talked to her on Ethan's cell, she'd sounded positively thrilled. She said she just wanted to keep being my mother and it was probably better for me to learn second-stage Settling from someone who had more recent experience and blah, blah, blah, . . .

So, no help was coming from that corner. Hell, she'd even extended my curfew by an hour.

"Now, walk the perimeter of the grave, holding that hand over the center." Ethan steered me to the edge of the grave with his hands on my shoulders while I did my best to ignore how undeniably nice his touch felt. "Stay close to the edge. If any blood falls, it has to hit the grave," he said, standing back to watch my progress with a critical eye.

"Does blood *have* to fall?" I asked, feeling a little queasy simply saying the word. The blood earlier hadn't bothered me since I was in the heat of battle and all, but now my aversion to the red stuff was coming back with a vengeance.

"No, it doesn't. Settlers used to think blood had to be spilled in a circle around the grave, but somebody eventually figured out just breaking the skin was enough."

"All around the grave? Didn't they pass out?"

"Not their blood, animal blood."

"Animal blood?"

"Yeah, chickens or sometimes goats. They'd slit the animal's throat and drag it around the edge of the grave," he said, as casually as if he were discussing the directions to the nearest gas station.

"Oh." I suddenly felt even colder. Yuck. My stomach clenched and I stumbled the last few steps around the grave.

"Hey, are you all right?" he asked, catching my shoulders again, but this time we were facing each other and his touch was a lot softer.

"Yeah . . . it's just been a long night."

"Well, it's almost over. That's all you need to do to seal the grave. Easy, right?"

"Right." I sucked in a deep breath, inhaling the wonderful smell of him—soap and something spicy that was all Ethan. Wow, he smelled so very good. It was almost impossible to resist the urge to lean into his chest. I wanted to press my face against his gray sweatshirt, wrap my arms around him, and hold on for dear life.

"Rough night too, huh?" he asked, continuing on without waiting for an answer. "Well, it could have been a lot rougher. You could have died. Give me the two commands to freeze an RC."

Okay, well, *that* pretty much killed the snuggle urge.

"*Desino* and *absisto*. And thanks for reminding me about the dying part." I tried to step away, but he wrapped his arms around me, pulling me in for I guess what you could call a hug.

Though it was unlike *any* hug I'd ever experienced before. As soon as his fingers interlocked at the small of my back, I couldn't remember how to breathe. The tingles proceeded to skyrocket off the charts, and I was fairly certain I was going to pass out before I got up the guts to look him in the eye.

"I don't want you to be scared, but you've got to get serious about catching up. Especially with someone out there reanimating corpses."

"I know." I dared a look up into his face, illuminated by the light of the moon, and tried not to get freaked out by the fact that our lips were four inches apart. "And don't forget about the black magic at the football field."

"What do you know about that?" he asked, though he didn't sound mad, and his lips got a tiny bit closer to mine. Close enough I could smell the cinnamon on his breath.

Okay. Hold the freaking phone . . . was there some chance Ethan was feeling the same way I was feeling? Did he actually maybe want to kiss me as much as I was *dying* to kiss him? Was that even in the realm of possibility? I mean, he had already graduated from high school and thought I was a complete dork-brat-idiot. Right?

"I asked you a question," he said, still in that soft, sexy voice.

Hmmm . . . what was the question again? So hard to concentrate when so very near to the sex god Ethan had become. Who would have guessed he'd grow into that huge nose he had when he was thirteen? Or that he would get even taller? He had to be six feet if he was an inch, and—

"About the field, Schmeg?" he asked, a hint of laughter in his voice.

Oh yeah, the football field. "I, um . . . did some investigating," I said, doing my best not to sound as breathless as I felt. No need to give the jerk anything else to laugh about. "And don't call me Schmeg."

"Some investigating, huh?"

"Yeah, I found that place on the track. Someone was working a black ritual, not ten feet from the CHS football field."

"Maybe, maybe not." His arms tightened around me and I was suddenly paying more attention to how solid he felt under his sweatshirt than to questioning him about the football field.

I wondered if Ethan realized that his hands were straying below my waist, down very close to butt territory? Or was this simply a friendly hug that I was totally misinterpreting?

What was wrong with me? My school could be in imminent peril and I was allowing myself to fall victim to raging hormones. Why couldn't I focus on truly important things instead of obsessing about whether or not Ethan wanted to jump my bones? It was just . . . I'd never felt this way about a guy before. Josh didn't make me tingle all over the way Ethan did, didn't make me want to see if he tasted as wonderful as he smelled.

Thinking about sampling Ethan like an ice cream cone made my eyes drift to his lips, his full, soft-looking lips that were totally moving closer to mine. Holy cow! He was going to kiss me! He was really going to kiss me and—

"Why didn't you tell me you were hurt? That looks like a pretty nasty scratch," he said, bringing his face even closer to my shoulder and sniffing. "And it smells like grave dirt. One of the RCs did this, didn't they?"

"Um, maybe . . . I didn't really notice before," I said, looking down at my shoulder to see a crusty place near my bra strap.

The zombie who'd ripped my sweater must have broken the skin. Great, now I was going to be on antibiotics for a freaking month, and they always gave me the most awful stomachache. *And* I'd nearly

67

embarrassed the bejeezus out of myself by trying to put the moves on Ethan. Could this night get any worse?

"Come on, let's go. We'll swing by SA headquarters and see the medic on duty before I take you home." He pulled away from me as if there had never been a single moment of tension. And there probably hadn't been. I had just imagined the whole thing because I was *such* a loser. Thank God Ethan hadn't seemed to notice me crushing on him.

"Fine, but you're telling me about whatever's going on at my school on the way," I said, making sure to use my crankiest voice as I followed him back to his car.

"Nope, don't think so."

"Yes, I *do* think so."

"Doesn't matter what you think. You are my lowly student and I the masterful teacher."

I laughed at that—I couldn't help myself. "This from a guy with a C average?"

"By the time I graduated, I had a B average." He opened the door for me and then ran around to jump in the driver's seat. "You missed a lot those five years."

"Yeah, I guess I did," I said, feeling a little sad. I had missed a lot. Maybe it would have been better if I'd never lost my powers, if I'd just kept being a Settler. Then Ethan and I would have stayed friends and maybe even . . . eventually . . .

No way. Ethan never was and never will be interested in you. You're like the annoying little sister he never had, and that's it.

Right. I had to stay focused on practical goals, like learning enough Settler stuff to keep from dying, making sure my school was safe from black magic, and convincing Josh to *finally* asked me to the dance. Ethan was just my tutor and maybe my friend when he was in a good mood, nothing more.

That shouldn't have made me even sadder, but it did.

CHAPTER 6

*T*he next day passed in a haze, probably because I'd been up until midnight and Mom refused to let me have coffee because she was afraid it would stunt my growth. I was obviously already done growing, but that line of reasoning only led to arguments about decreasing bone density, so I'd learned not to try to get my caffeine fix at home.

Sometimes Jess hooked me up with a latte from the 7-Eleven, but she was absent at a dentist's appointment all morning. I didn't see her until lunch, where the most caffeine we could get our hands on was a chocolate brownie. All the soda machines had been removed from the cafeteria last year to help combat childhood obesity or something lame like that. Hello, we were *teens*, not children, and Diet Coke had never made anyone obese.

By the time we got to dance practice, I was wiped, but there was no way I could miss. It was our second-to-last chance to work on our optional routine before tryouts started next week.

Of course, I would have been able to concentrate a heck of a lot better if it had been just me and Jess as planned, not me and Jess and my new tutor—who insisted on picking me up after school and driving us both to the studio so we wouldn't waste a second getting to the graveyard afterward.

"Megan, are you ready?" Jess asked, and I could tell from the slight concern in her voice that it wasn't the first time she'd asked. Focus! I had to focus. Settler crap had already ruined my second first date with Josh and put my homecoming date situation in peril. I couldn't let it compromise my chances of making the pom squad too.

"Yep, totally." I nodded to Kayla, who started the music.

"Five, six, seven, eight." Jess counted down the beat under her breath and we both launched into the hip-hop sequence at the start of the next eight count.

Four knees bent deep in unison; then we pushed into a roll across the ground that ended with a jump back to our feet, a scissor kick, a quick ball change, and some very sexy hip swivels. We were coated in fresh sweat and breathing hard by the time we tagged on the new sixteen count we'd just learned from Kayla.

"Awesome, girls!" She actually applauded when we finished, a rare event from our jazz/hip-hop guru.

Kayla had been second runner-up for Miss Missouri three years ago, and most said this achievement had been based on her mad dance skills alone. But mad skills or no, she certainly wouldn't have had a chance at a title this year. Not that she wasn't a cute college chick, but Kayla had become a bit too hard-core for the pageant circuit. With her jet-black hair and tendency to wear skull and crossbones–inspired clothing, she was committed to fashion choices that were not pageant-friendly.

"Let's take it back to the beginning and learn the twenty-four-count entry sequence. I think you two are ready to slip a triple in there before the pas de bourrée." Kayla took the center of the floor, and Jess and I fell in behind.

We set a crazy pace from then on, both of us determined to lock down this new routine before we started dance squad clinic next week. On Monday we'd be inundated with new moves and knew we wouldn't want to be worrying about the optional routine. Of course, we really didn't *have* to do a fourth dance, but we figured any chance to show off our strong points was a good call.

I couldn't wait for our extra class on Friday. If the rest of the week went anything like the past two days, I would be needing the stress relief by then, and dancing always made me forget everything that was bugging me. Well . . . almost everything . . .

Ethan sat out in the waiting room, and there was no way I could completely lose track of the fact that he was watching me. No matter how I'd tried, I couldn't stop replaying that moment in the graveyard, when he'd been holding me and I was so certain we were going to kiss.

Of course, kissing Ethan should have been the *last* thing on my mind. I had a mere week and a half to convince Josh to ask me to homecoming. Maybe less if he was really sick. He hadn't been in chemistry, and no one knew where he was.

"Good work, girls. I think you're ready. If you don't make the squad, your competition must be ready to dance backup for Rihanna." Kayla shut off the stereo and started packing up her dance bag.

"Thanks, Kayla," Jess said, pulling off her sweatshirt.

I stuffed my dance shoes in my bag as Jess turned to help Kayla gather her CDs. "Are you going to be here next Monday after ballet class, Kay? We'll know the first routine for tryouts by then, and I'd love to—"

"You might know more than the first routine," said a voice from behind us. Jess and I turned to see London standing at the studio entrance. She hadn't been at school today either, but I guess she was feeling up to dance class. "We're going to separate everyone into groups by ability. The advanced group might get in a routine and a half."

Advanced group! She'd implied that we would be in the advanced group, and she'd actually *smiled* afterward. Obviously she didn't hate me for skipping out on them last night. "Hey, Megan, you feeling better?"

I shrugged, trying to act as if it were normal for one of the coolest girls in school to be inquiring after my health, even though out of the corner of my eye I saw Jess's jaw drop. "Yeah, thanks. I felt better this morning. I think it must have been something I ate."

"Well, it's probably better you left. The boys were acting so retarded, daring each other to jump off the giant hay bales at the center of the maze. You heard Josh broke his leg, right?"

No! Not a broken leg! That would mean—

"He's out of football for the rest of the season," she said, as if that weren't a big deal. He was our quarterback, for God's sake! He was a vital part of our team. A broken leg was a catastrophe—one that could also mean he wouldn't want to attend the homecoming dance. What fun was a dance with a broken leg?

"I was at the emergency room with him and Andy until one in the morning. I'm so beat," London said, stretching her arms above her head until her tiny midriff showed.

Not that I would have noticed said midriff if Ethan hadn't taken that moment to enter the studio.

"Megan, let's go. I don't have all night," Ethan said, glaring pointedly at his watch.

"Hey, Eat!" London squealed, enveloping Ethan in a hug. Hello, didn't she remember she had a boyfriend? And what was with the "Eat" crap? What kind of nickname was that? "What are you doing here? Come to see Monica?"

"Not that I remember. Did we have a date, killer?" Monica suddenly appeared behind Ethan, hugging him from the other side. Oh my God, the boy was now the center of a hot senior girl sandwich. How dare they rub their half-naked bodies all over my Ethan?

Your *Ethan? Girl, you've got it bad.*

"Nope," Ethan said, seemingly unaffected by all the unnecessary fondling. "You stood me up for ice cream last time. I had to eat both cones myself."

"Oh, poor baby. That must have been so bad for your girlish figure." Monica slapped Ethan on the arm before stripping off her sweater, obviously looking for an excuse to show off her own tiny midriff in her cropped tank top.

This time I didn't notice whether Ethan's attention was lured to Monica's rock-hard abs, however, because my own gaze was pulled straight to the giant bandage on her arm. What the hell was that about? Not only was it hard to believe Monica would be generous enough to share her life essence with those in need, but her bandage was nearly three times the size of the tiny one Jess had gotten after she gave blood. Why would Monica need something that big to cover a tiny needle hole?

"Um, stare much, Megan? Don't you have somewhere to be?" She crossed her arms, wincing as her hand brushed against the bandage.

Looked like whatever was under there hurt way more than a tiny needle hole as well, like it ached the way a zombie bite (or two) would ache. The RCs last night definitely would have had to take a chomp of their Creator before they went back to their graves, and Monica had most certainly been near the scene of the crime.

"What happened to your arm? That looks pretty bad," I asked before I could think better of questioning the mistress of evil.

Her eyes got bigger, but she only paused a second before speaking. "I had an allergic reaction to that orange stuff they put on my arm at the blood drive. Just shows what you get for trying to help those in need."

"You only did it because Andy bet you five dollars that you wouldn't," London said, obviously amused by Monica's plight.

"Whatever," Monica said, giving me the signature what-kind-of-scum-are-you Monica glare. Like I was the one who had offended her instead of London. "This is the senior girls' class, Megan. So why don't you make like a milk-carton kid and get missing."

"Yeah, come on, Meg." Ethan bounded across the room and grabbed me around the waist, pulling me out of the room with Jess following close behind. "See you girls later."

I was so freaked out by the touchy-feely thing Ethan was pulling, gluing me to his side, that all thoughts of zombie bites fled my mind and I almost missed Monica and London looking at me like I was some total skank. Then I was so freaked out trying to figure out why they thought I was a skank that I didn't realize Ethan was pulling me toward his lips until said lips were pressed against my cheek.

For a split second, the entire world disappeared. Nothing existed except Ethan's strong arm around my waist and the feel of his lips pressing softly against my skin, only inches from my mouth. If I were to turn the slightest bit to the left, our lips would be touching—we'd really be kissing, just like we should have been last—

"You looked great in there, babe. I better step up my game before the homecoming dance," Ethan said, pulling me even closer before heading to the door.

Babe? Homecoming dance? I didn't have time to pick my jaw up off the floor before he was shooing me out to his car, Jess hot on our heels.

"What the—"

"You need a ride somewhere, Jess?" Ethan interrupted before turning back to my poor, stunned best friend.

"Um, no, just let me grab my sweater," she said, sticking her head in the backseat.

"Are you sure, Jess?" I asked.

"Yeah, I'm meeting Dad and Clara and James for pizza down the street." She slammed the door and started backing away. "But I'll talk to you guys later."

As Ethan turned back to me, Jess made a classic "ohmygod what haven't you been telling me" face and mouthed that I should call her and spill all as soon as possible. I smiled, trying to act like I knew what I was going to say to her.

"What the hell was that about?" I snapped at Ethan as soon as Jess turned.

"Your leotard crawl up your butt or something, Schmeg?" Ethan asked as he opened the door for me.

"I'm not wearing a leotard, doofus," I said, sinking into the passenger's seat, sensing he wouldn't give me a straight answer until we were alone.

"Doofus? Are we in third grade?" he asked once he was in the driver's seat.

"Fine, do you prefer assface?" I asked, turning to glare at him. "What was with the kissy-kissy?"

"I figured I would need a cover for hanging around you so much. Pretending to be your new boyfriend and date to homecoming solved that problem." He shrugged as if this were no big deal while I did my best to control my fury and embarrassment.

Fury because he'd decided this without even asking me. Embarrassment because I'd nearly taken the fake kiss and turned it into a real kiss, right there in front of everyone.

"But what about Monica? She's never going to buy—"

"She'll buy it. We've been friends forever. She knows I fall hard and fast if I fall at all."

Fall hard and fast? Did that mean Ethan had been in love before?

Better question, of course, was why did I care?

"What do you mean 'hanging around me so much'?" I asked, that part finally penetrating. "You're my tutor. How long can it take to learn whatever I need to—"

"That's not why I'll be babysitting you for the next week or two."

Babysitting? What was I, two years old? "Then why *will* you be—"

"Nope, can't tell you. Classified information." He dropped that bombshell and calmly continued to drive, as if the subject were closed.

"No way," I said, really getting angry. Angry enough to forget how cute he was and that he'd had me feeling all mixed up and crushy for the past day and a half. "If you're *babysitting* me, I deserve to know why. Just like I deserve to know what is happening at my school."

"No, you don't." Argh! "Haven't you heard ignorance is bliss?"

"So you're just going to boss me around and pretend to be my boyfriend and I have *nothing* to say about it?"

"Yeah, that's about it."

"Well, that sucks," I said, doing my best not to scream when he shrugged again. Fine—I would destroy his calm with logic. "What if I already have a date to the dance? Ever think about that?"

"You don't. Your mom told me last night."

God, Mom! When would she learn to keep her mouth shut? "So what? Josh was about to ask me. We're dating, and London and Monica . . ." Oh crap, the arctic looks they'd given me suddenly made sense. I groaned. "Now they think I was leading Josh on."

"They'll get over it."

"No, I don't think they will," I said, really starting to lose it. "And that means I might not make the pom squad."

"Then you'll get over it."

"Arrr!" I screamed, banging my hand against the glove compartment. "You are ruining my life!"

"No, I'm saving your life," Ethan yelled, so loud I jumped back against the door.

Jeez. Where had freak-out boy come from?

Neither of us said anything for a few moments while Ethan turned off on a side street and parked. He turned off the car and just sat there, staring straight ahead. I was getting ready to say something, just to break the totally weird and uncomfortable silence, when he started talking, really softly. "I carried you across the cemetery that night. You were so small and . . . you were bleeding so bad it was all over me by the time I reached the Elder who was supposed to be teaching all the new second-stagers how to seal their first grave."

I didn't know how to respond to the obvious pain in his voice, so I didn't say anything, just sat there trying to swallow past the lump in my throat. Wow, who knew he was still so upset about the night of my attack?

"I was pretty sure you were dead, and I was bawling like a baby." He took a deep breath and let it out really slowly. "Because I knew it was my fault. If I hadn't dared you to come, if I hadn't told you which cemetery we'd be at, you would have been at home in bed."

He turned to look at me, though I could tell it wasn't easy for him. "You would have been safe."

"Ethan, you didn't know there would be RCs in the graveyard. And you didn't really think I would take the dare. You were joking, I—"

"No, I wasn't. I knew you would come." He laughed, but it wasn't a happy sound. "I thought you were ready to move up. Sure, you were just a kid, but you were so powerful back then. You were way stronger than I was, and I knew how upset you were that Monica and I were going to second stage without you."

"So you didn't want me to be upset. How is that being—"

"It was being stupid. You were ten years old. You weren't ready, just like you're not ready to know Protocol secrets now. SA has assigned me to be your bodyguard for a few weeks, so just deal with it and don't ask questions you know I can't answer."

Oh. My. God. So that was it. Ethan felt guilty and thought he could protect me if he kept me in the dark. It was really sweet.

And really freaking stupid. Ignorance was not bliss. If I was in danger, I needed to know about it. Knowledge could mean the difference between knowing how to stay out of trouble and walking right into it.

This argument made sense to me, but I knew I would have to have something better to convince Ethan to talk. He'd been feeling responsible for my near death for five years. That was a long time for guilt to make him crazy.

Mind racing, I tried to figure out how I could have gone from a person in need of training to a person in need of protection in twenty-four hours. What had changed between last night and—

"The RCs. SA thinks they were after me," I said, with total assurance. That had to be it. "But why? They ran right past me."

"Megan, I mean it, I—"

"So . . . that means they were after someone else. Someone I know, probably," I said, thinking out loud. "Has to be, or I wouldn't be getting a babysitter. Did they find the RC graves and recover a totem? Something recognizable?"

I was so going to have to thank Mom for making me cram Settler stuff all day Sunday so that I was all up on my black-magic practitioner trivia.

"It would have to be something recognizable if they traced it back to me so quickly," I continued. "So what was it—a picture, a doll? Something that looked like one of my friends?"

"Stop, Megan. Please." The pleading looking in his eyes almost made me shut up.

"If one of my friends is in danger, shouldn't you be protecting them, not me?" I asked in my most reasonable voice. "I'm not trying to be difficult, I swear, but—"

"Good." Ethan started up the car and pulled out onto the street, clearly done with the conversation. "So, what do you Carol kids do for fun on a Thursday night? Let's go blow off some steam."

"I am not interested in going on a fake date with you."

"Who said it was fake?" he asked, shooting me a look I wanted to believe meant he thought of me as more than a kid he had to protect. Too bad I already knew the truth. Ethan had spilled his guts, and now I knew for sure he would always think of me as a little girl. A little girl he cared about, but not in the way I wanted him to care.

And I did want him to care. I really did. That made it all even worse.

"I want to go home. Now, please," I said, suddenly feeling very tired.

"Either come out with me and pretend to be half of a happy couple to help cement our cover—"

"Cement our cover? Really Ethan, we're not spies for—"

"Or come with me to the graveyard for another Settler lesson. Your choice."

I sighed. I'd had more than my share of graveyards the past few days. "Fine. Sonic. There should be lots of people there to observe our newly discovered love."

"I think we should have been going out for a while. Like, since the summer."

"That makes me look like a skank for going out with Josh. And remember Monica. Since you two 'hang' all the time and my powers only just came back?"

"True. Okay, so it was just fireworks at first sight that night at Mount Hope. I saw what a hottie you'd become and stole you from

Pickle." He smiled, obviously pleased with himself for his make-believe girlfriend stealing. "Who is a dink, by the way. His older brother is in my Psych 101 class."

"You're in college?" I asked, ignoring both the hottie and the dink remarks. Ethan didn't think I was hot. He was just building his little cover story and having way too much fun doing it, if you asked me. And Josh . . . well, maybe he *was* a little bit of a dink. But that didn't mean he wasn't gorgeous and a great football player and basically nice and completely boyfriendworthy.

"Yeah. I take classes up at Williams on Tuesdays and Thursdays," he said as he pulled into one of the empty spaces at the drive-in. "I'm going part-time until I decide my major."

We chatted about his classes and my classes and other neutral topics while we placed our order with the carhop and then ate our chicken sandwiches. Aside from feeding me a few of his fries, however, Ethan did nothing at all to act like we were a couple. Maybe he thought sitting in the car together was enough. We did get some curious looks from a couple of Josh's friends and his ex, Beth, flat-out stopped to stare.

She actually looked kind of pissed to see me with another guy, which was weird. Josh said he broke up with her, but maybe it was the other way around. That would sort of explain the anger, I guess. Maybe she didn't want him back on the market and potentially trying to hook up with her again.

Jeez . . . maybe Josh really *was* a total loser and I had been too blinded by his man beauty to see it. He *had* been fairly annoying last night with the arm pulling and the refusing to give me any attention once he was racing for beer money.

As far as Ethan and I went, however, I didn't know whether to be happy about the lack of fake PDA or not. I mean, how lame is it to enjoy having some guy pretend to like you? But then, it certainly was nice to be close to Ethan, like . . . the kind of close that seemed to occur only when I was about to pass out or he was playing my fake boyfriend.

I was so pathetic, especially considering I had much bigger things to worry about, like figuring out which of my friends was in danger. By the time we pulled up to my house, I was more mixed up than ever and very ready for a quiet evening at home.

Too bad the thing that came rushing around the side of my house had other ideas. It took me a second to realize it was a zombie gunning for Ethan's car, however, because the corpse was on fire. On fire . . . and wearing my homecoming dress!

CHAPTER 7

Ahh!" I screamed as the zombie lunged on top of Ethan's car, hitting the windshield with a loud thunk. The glass didn't shatter, but it was only a matter of time.

If the fists slamming into the windshield were any clue, this dude definitely wanted in and believed in taking the direct approach. Reanimated Corpses, not so good with the whole door concept, apparently.

And this thing had to be an RC, although the telltale red eyes weren't visible through the flames. I'd never seen an Unsettled act so aggressively, not even a burning Unsettled. Which I'd seen once before, believe it or not. It was the summer of first grade, and the Unsettled had run through the park, where they were setting off a fireworks display. I opened the door and saw a fireball standing on my porch. Thankfully, everyone else in our neighborhood was down at the park, so no one saw my dad putting the flaming zombie kid out with a fire extinguisher.

But we weren't going to need a fire extinguisher for this guy. I rather liked the idea of sending him back to his Maker still burning. The twisted chick deserved it for destroying the world's most perfect dress. And it *had* to be a chick. No boy mind was capable of concocting something so purely, femininely evil.

I lifted my hands, focusing my power before I cast in the way Ethan had taught me to do the night before. "*Rever*—"

"Not through the glass!" Ethan yelled, slapping a hand over my mouth before I could finish the command. "Glass screws with paranormal vibrations. The command won't work and it might end up reflecting back on us."

"But Unsettled commands don't work on live people, do th— ohmygod!" The zombie slammed his forehead into the windshield, finally succeeding in cracking the glass.

"No, they don't, but it would sting like nobody's—" Another slam of the zombie head and the crack grew longer. "This isn't the time for a lesson. Stay in the car."

"No, I want to help, I—"

"Stay in the freaking car, Megan! That's an order!" he yelled before jumping out of the driver's side. The zombie snarled and leapt at Ethan, no longer interested in getting inside the vehicle now that his prey was on the outside.

He was after Ethan, not me. But why? And why had someone stolen my homecoming dress from the cleaners and dressed a corpse in it before . . .

The truth hit me just as Ethan lifted his hands and cast. "*Exuro!*" The zombie burned brighter and brighter, and then suddenly the fire went out and the charred remains of the RC fluttered to the ground. Ethan did a quick scan of the area, then whipped his phone out of his pocket. He was probably calling Settlers' Affairs, a phone call I didn't want to miss a second of overhearing.

I grabbed my bag and rocketed out of the car, running around to Ethan even as he gestured wildly for me to get in the house. As if. He might be my tutor and bodyguard and fake boyfriend, but he was *not* my father. The sooner he got that through his head the better, especially considering I had vital information he would want to tell the people at SA right away.

"Yes, I can hold, but it's urgent," he said to someone on the other line before turning back to me. "Get inside, Megan."

"No."

"Yes. Now. Or I'll hang up this phone and go lock you in your room before—"

"You do and I'll call the police and report you. This is the twenty-first century: You can't get away with kidnapping women and locking them—"

"You're not a woman, you're a kid, and—"

"Wait! I know why someone's after me. I can help," I said, holding up my hands and backing away as Ethan took a menacing step toward me. So much for the women's lib argument. What a chauvinist jerk.

"Talk. Fast," he said while I did my best not to break into a victory dance. Those two words had just confirmed the fact that someone was after me. Some Settler cop he was, getting outsmarted by a fifteen-year-old.

"Someone doesn't want me to go to homecoming. They're trying to make sure I don't go to the dance," I said, waiting for Ethan to work through the same logic that had brought me to this conclusion and congratulate me on my brilliance.

Instead, he started to laugh. "Right. Okay, I'll be sure to share your theory. Now get—"

"It's not a theory, it's the truth," I said, getting angry. "That zombie was wearing my homecoming dress. Why would someone go to all the trouble to steal the dress from the cleaners and put it on a corpse unless they were trying to send me a message about homecoming?"

"Megan, please—"

"*And* that thing was after you, not me. It stopped trying to get into the car when you got out."

"So?"

"So," I said, my tone making it clear *he* was the one with very little brain, "you said you were taking me to homecoming. Whoever doesn't want me at the dance must have found out and decided to eliminate my date and my dress at the same time."

"But I just said I was taking you like an hour ago," he said, still looking incredulous but at least not flat-out denying my argument.

"Right in front of Monica and London, the biggest gossips in school. I'm sure they were on their cells sharing the news with half the senior class before we even got to Sonic." I bit my lip and turned to pace around the lawn, not quite ready to share my sneaking suspicion that Monica might have something to do with the RCs. I'd need concrete proof before I went there with Ethan since he and the Monicster had been friends forever. "Speaking of, anyone who saw us together at Sonic could be a suspect, assuming they can make a totem doll fairly quickly. Or if they had a picture of you or a possession of yours to use. Probably the doll since you don't know that many—"

"Megan, I can appreciate your logic, but isn't raising flesh-eating corpses to keep you from going to homecoming a little extreme?"

"It's not extreme. It's flat-out crazy, but that doesn't mean it isn't true," I said, watching his expression waver between patronizing and contemplative before whipping out my ace. "Especially considering the RCs last night were after Josh."

"How did you know that?" he asked, looking really angry. "Did your mom—"

"Mom didn't tell me anything—you just did," I said, doing my best to keep my satisfied smile from my face. "Half the school knew that Josh and I were going out last night and that he didn't have a date for the dance. Someone wanted to make sure he didn't get one, at least not if that date was going to be me."

Ethan chewed his bottom lip for a second, then slowly snapped the phone shut.

"What? Aren't you going to tell SA about—"

"I'm going to tell them, but I'd better do it in person. They're never going to believe this could all be about some high school dance." He sighed and ran a frustrated hand through his hair. "I'm still not sure I believe it, but I have to admit it makes sense. They found pieces of a football jersey on the two graves last night. When they searched the boys' locker room this morning, the number fifteen jersey was missing."

"That's Josh's jersey!" My stomach started churning big-time. Hearing the hard evidence that Josh had been the target made it all so much more real.

"But there are other things going on. Things I can't tell you about that make this more complicated. If it were just these two attacks, I would say you were completely right, but—"

"There have been more attacks? Is that what happened at the football field? Was someone attacked by—"

"Uh-uh, no way. You've already tricked me into saying more than

I wanted to." He took me by the shoulders and turned me toward my front door. "Go inside and get something to clean up these ashes. I'll take them with me to headquarters."

"Okay," I sighed, knowing I'd won as much information from Ethan as I was going to get. For now. Might as well satisfy my non-homecoming-plot-related curiosity. "I didn't know RCs could be destroyed by fire. I thought you had to send them back to their Maker. That only the blood of the one who raised them could make them go back to their grave."

"It's not destroyed," Ethan said, turning to point to the ground, where the ashes were starting to look more solid. "In an hour or two, it will regenerate enough to start attacking things again."

"No way." Whoa, that was twisted. Black magic was some seriously warped stuff.

"Yes way. I'll work the *reverto* spell on it when it reconstitutes. I just couldn't send it back to its grave on fire. People usually won't notice a zombie running back to its Maker, but they will notice a streaking fireball."

"Makes sense," I said, turning back to the house before spinning around again. "So, would you want to use the fire spell if there were a whole bunch of RCs raised at once? I know the *reverto* spell won't work if there are too many of them."

"I guess that could work in theory, but it would depend on how many you were talking about. The flame spell takes a lot of energy and usually a lot more time. I wouldn't have been able to take care of this one so quickly if it weren't already burning. So . . . I'd say you could burn maybe two or three RCs at a time, max, and that's if the Settler was pretty powerful."

"And by that time, the rest of them would be on you," I said, feeling my stomach sink.

"You don't have to worry," Ethan said, his voice softer. "You're not going to be attacked by a bunch of RCs, I promise you. Nothing like that has happened in the states since the thing up in Michigan in the early '80s."

A part of me wanted to believe Ethan, but my gut was telling me I should be ready for anything. Whoever didn't want me at the homecoming dance might decide to screw trying to get rid of my dates and go straight for the source. They'd been willing to kill Ethan and Josh, so why not me?

Someone had really tried to *kill* Ethan and Josh. It was like the truth was finally soaking in through my thick skull. My hands were shaking and my chicken sandwich threatening to crawl back up my throat by the time I darted in the house and came back with a garbage bag and dustpan. Thankfully, my parents had the news turned up so loud in the den they didn't hear me come in. I didn't want them to see how freaked I was.

"Ethan," I said, once I was back outside holding the bag as he scooped increasingly solid zombie remains into it with the pan. "Do you think maybe I could learn the flame spell anyway? Just in case?"

"The flame spell is third-stage Settler stuff."

"But what if someone tries to kill you again?" *Or me*, I thought, but didn't add out loud. Ethan was already way overprotective: no need to fuel that fire. "I want to be able to help. I should be—"

"Third-stage spells are for third-stagers, Megan. End of discussion. I'll teach you another second-stage method for taking care of RCs later," he said, turning back to his car. "Right now I need to get this cleaned up and get to SA headquarters. Are your parents going to be home soon or—"

"They're home already. They're watching the news. I swear Dad's going deaf, he always has the television turned up so loud. I guess that's why they didn't hear me screaming." I tried to laugh at the last part but couldn't. There was nothing funny about what was going on—not the part of it I knew about or the parts that Ethan and the Elders were keeping from me.

"Listen, don't worry. I'll be back later to check on you. Everything's going to be fine." Then he bent down and kissed me, really softly on the forehead, like a big brother would kiss a little sister who was scared of the dark.

I smiled and tried to look like I felt comforted as he drove away, even though I was feeling anything but. Ethan was wrong. I wasn't a kid who needed to be kept safe from whatever was going down in Carol. Whatever was happening, I was obviously a big part of it. I needed to know all the facts so I could help SA find the person responsible before this went any further. The homecoming dance was in danger, and people might end up getting hurt or worse. Suddenly, getting a date had become a secondary concern. What had seemed like the most important thing in the world was now a much smaller blip on my radar. If someone was willing to *kill* people to keep me away from the dance, there had to be some reason for it. A reason that was probably as flat-out evil as whoever was raising these Reanimated Corpses.

No matter how freaked I was, I had to keep my eyes and ears open and do my best to find the person behind the attacks before it was too late.

• • •

I was having a horrible dream, a mix of the night of my attack and the events of the past few days. This time the zombies who jumped on me were on fire, and when a corpse leaned over to bite me, the flames spread to my hair, my clothes. Soon I was engulfed, screaming in agony as my skin melted away from my bones. Yet somehow, I continued to live on. I was conscious as I burned, able to hear the laughter of the person who wanted me dead echoing in my—

"Megan Berry! For the last time, get your head off your desk."

"Wha?" I snapped into an upright position, swiping at a bit of drool on my cheek. The laughter in the room got a little louder.

Crap. Why did I have to fall asleep in English of all places? Mrs. Pierce was already riding my butt about letting my GPA fall to a mere 3.6 instead of a 3.8. Apparently, she held the secretary of the Honor Society to a higher standard than the average student. If I had known that going in, I so wouldn't have run for the position.

"Bring that diary to me," Mrs. Pierce said.

She *couldn't* take my journal! Not when I'd just been listing suspects before I'd evidently succumbed to exhaustion and fallen asleep. "Um, it's not a diary, Mrs. Pierce, it's just, um . . . some notes . . . and stuff."

"English is not the place for notes and stuff. Bring it up here. Immediately."

Laughter tittered through the room again, and I blushed a shade of red I knew wasn't cute. This was all Mom's fault for depriving me of caffeine. If she'd let me have a cup of coffee before school, this never would have happened!

I closed the journal and hurried to the front of the room, feeling like I was back in the third grade getting in trouble for reading *Princess Diaries* novels instead of my stupid assigned reading. Pierce glared at me the entire way, her tiny brown eyes narrowed in her pudgy face. She looked like an evil mole, and not even the cutesy sweatshirts she wore could lessen the resemblance. The pink ENGLISH TEACHERS ARE ALWAYS WRITE shirt she had on today only brought out the sallow color of her skin, intensifying the "I spend most of my time underground" vibe.

"You may retrieve this after school." She pressed her lips together as she snatched the book. "No more journaling or sleeping on my time, or you'll be on your way to the office."

"Sorry," I said, then turned and fled back to my desk, doing my best not to look at anyone but Jess, who I could tell was totally commiserating with me.

Too bad I couldn't say the same for the rest of my peers. Almost every girl in school had been a total witch to me today. They'd been jealous when I'd started getting attention from a hot senior, and jealousy had all too easily turned to loathing when I'd proved myself unworthy of that attention. It was shocking how fast the news of my new college "boyfriend" had spread, even to someone well aware of the workings of the CHS gossip machine.

Maybe once I told Ethan about my shunning today, he would be more willing to believe that the person raising the zombies had to be someone from my school.

Don't even go there. You know it's pointless.

I sighed and tried to look like I was riveted by Colin Danforth's reading of *Macbeth* while letting my mind wander back to the problem at hand. My inner voice was right. Ethan would never believe me. He

93

hadn't even wanted to hear my list of possible suspects when he'd dropped by last night after his trip to SA headquarters. He hadn't told me much, but from his bad attitude I guessed the Elders had laughed in his face when he suggested someone was raising the dead to keep me from going to homecoming.

Which meant there was a lot more I didn't know. Otherwise, even the Elders would see the logic of my argument. I was sure of it. They were old and out of touch, but most of them weren't stupid. So that meant I was missing something. Something big.

But since I had no way of discovering what that something was, I'd decided to concentrate on what I *did* know. And I *knew* someone was trying to keep me from homecoming. If I could just figure out who that someone was, then I'd be closer to figuring out the bigger mystery.

Now, maybe if I'd spent more time reading *Nancy Drew* as a kid instead of all the Princess Diaries books, I'd be prepared to get sleuthing.

As it was, I hadn't gotten much further than a list of possible suspects. Monica was the biggie and would have been the *only* if there had ever been a documented case of a Settler raising the dead with the black arts. Apparently we were all such goody-goodies, we didn't go there. I'd looked through every history book Mom had in the Closet and had found nothing, which was enough to make me branch out and look for other suspects.

London was on my list simply because she'd been at both the corn maze and the dance studio when Ethan dropped the homecoming bomb. I couldn't really think of any motive she would have for wanting me stuck at home, but there was a chance I wasn't seeing the big picture.

Beth, Josh's ex, was also on the list, despite the fact that she resembled a Barbie doll more than a voodoo practitioner and seemed to have the intelligence of a gnat. Black magic wasn't easy stuff, and I doubted someone in remedial math would have the discipline to focus her mind and energy in the way you'd have to in order to work a summoning spell. Still, at least she had a motive—to punish me for going out with her man. A little thin, but a motive nonetheless.

I'd also added Beth's little sister Annabelle to the list. She was in my grade and as different from Beth as Jack Skellington was from Island Princess Barbie. Annabelle was a super goth who had been arrested over the summer for putting sugar in the gas tanks of an entire lot of SUVs. She was a budding radical environmentalist and just all around . . . scary.

Of course, scary did not necessarily equal evil, and I couldn't think of any motive for her, except maybe wanting revenge for Josh dumping her sister.

If only I had something else to go on!

The bell rang, signaling the end of fourth period. Thank. God. At least now I could get to the cafeteria and try to scrounge for some caffeine. I stuffed my copy of *Macbeth* in my bag and hurried to where Jess sat three rows back. Evil Pierce made us sit in alphabetical order. If she hadn't, Jess would surely have found a way to prod me into wakefulness before I embarrassed myself.

"Hey, you need to stop by your locker before lunch?" I asked.

"Um, no . . . but I don't think I'm going to lunch," she said with a sigh. "I've got this killer test in biology, and I should probably hit the library."

"I could help you. I took that test last year," I said, not wanting to brave the cafeteria alone. So far I hadn't seen Claire or Del, our usual lunch pals, but I was afraid they might be giving me the cold shoulder too.

"No, it's okay. A few people are going to be there for a study group, so they'll help." Jess smiled and reached over to squeeze my hand as we followed everyone else out of the class. "Hey, don't worry. I saw Claire, and she couldn't believe everyone's being so mean to you. She'll help protect you during lunch."

"Am I that obvious? God, I'm such a coward." And I was. I'd only spent five minutes on the phone with Jess the night before because I couldn't handle the amount of lying involved with explaining the whole Ethan situation. I'd given her the bare bones and that was it.

"No, not at all. I just know you."

"What about Del, do you think she'll be cool?" I asked, walking with Jess toward the library. "You know, I don't think she's at school today. She called me last night, all freaked out about something, but she wouldn't tell me what it was." Jess lowered her voice as we blended in with the crowd in the halls.

"Really?"

"Yeah, she's been acting weird lately. I hope she and her dad aren't fighting again." Jess's usually cheery face drooped.

Acting weird lately, huh? And maybe she was upset last night because her second attempt to kill my homecoming date had failed? I hated to suspect Del since she was basically a friend, but . . .

"I just wish she could see what a great person she is," Jess said, making me feel even worse for adding Del to my list of suspects, "and not let it get to her so much when her dad freaks out."

"Me too." I put one arm around Jess's shoulder and gave her a squeeze, feeling older for a second. Jess has always been shorter, but after my final growth spurt over the summer I had at least four inches on her. Jess had topped out at barely five feet and was super-tiny but was cool with being short. We'd always joked it would mean she'd be in the front of all the dance formations once we made the pom squad.

Man, I wished that was all I had to worry about. Just making the squad and homecoming and nothing else.

"See you in gym," Jess said, heading down the steps to the library while I continued on to the cafeteria, trying to ignore the nasty looks I received from several girls I passed.

"What a difference a day makes," I whispered, pasting a smile on my face.

I wasn't going to let this get me down. I'd find out who was after me, dump my fake boyfriend, and everything could go back to normal. No matter how much a part of me would be thrilled to go to the dance with Ethan, I needed to live in reality. Ethan wasn't real boyfriend material. Josh was. And since he wasn't back at school yet, maybe I could convince him that the rumors about me and Ethan were all a big misunderstanding.

Positive thinking, that was what I needed. Too bad positive thinking was so very hard to pull off when you were fairly certain there was a killer on the loose—a killer who could be watching your every move, determined not to fail again.

CHAPTER 8

"Time for a review." These were the first words out of Ethan's mouth Sunday afternoon, making me fairly certain this Settler lesson would be as boring as Thursday, Friday, and Saturday's sessions. "Let's begin. To return."

"Ethan, I know all the basic commands. Trust me, I actually have a very good memory when I put my—"

"To return," he repeated, turning to walk deeper into the cemetery before I'd finished locking my bike to the metal gate.

Shepherd's Hill was only a five-minute ride from my house, so I'd said I wouldn't need Ethan to pick me up. I'd been allowed the brief respite from babysitting detail because the sun wouldn't set until five thirty, long after our lesson would *hopefully* be over. Please. God. Then there might actually be time to enjoy a tiny portion of my weekend.

Hanging with Ethan the past three days had been an exercise in boredom and frustration. He rarely spoke, except to grill me about second-stage material, and refused to teach me anything that might actually prove useful in defending myself or anyone else from Reanimated Corpses. Not that I was *quite* as worried about another attack since I'd made it known around school Friday afternoon I wasn't going to homecoming because the cleaner had ruined my dress.

This was a lie, of course, but I figured it was an excellent way to test my theory, which had been proven completely *right* so far!

Going to the dance = mad amounts of bloodthirsty zombies.

Not going to the dance = peace and tranquility.

At least for now. The longer I thought about it, the more certain I was that whoever tried to kill Josh and Ethan had something awful planned for homecoming this Friday night, something they didn't want a zombie Settler present to observe. I didn't have any real enemies—at least none who would want my date to homecoming dead—so it made sense that the attacks weren't directed at who I was but rather *what* I was.

But then, that would mean an average person had discovered I was a Settler, which seemed unlikely since I hadn't even been back on active Settling duty for that long.

More disturbingly, it meant whoever was raising these corpses knew I was a Settler because they were one too. Monica was looking more guilty with every passing second—not that it mattered, since everyone was intent on burying their heads in the sand and I still had no concrete evidence to share with Ethan.

"Hey, have you thought about what I said?" I asked, knowing I was flapping my lips in vain but heeding my conscience, which demanded I try to get through to him one more time. "That whatever's happening might be an inside job?"

"To return," he repeated, turning to face me once we reached the secluded clearing we'd been using for our classroom for the past few days. Thankfully, Indian summer was still going strong, so I hadn't been freezing my ass off as well as having my brain numbed by boredom. "Really, Megan, you should know this one by now. I can't believe you—"

"*Reverto,*" I snapped back at him, making no attempt to hide my crankiness. He was never going to break down and tell me anything about the ongoing Protocol investigation.

He was too stubborn, pigheaded, obnoxious, cocky and . . . whoa . . . incredibly hot.

I tried to play it cool as Ethan stripped off his sweatshirt, revealing a skintight black tee underneath. I'd suspected he was built, but seeing the proof in all its honed, manly glory was still pretty freaking distracting. Jeez, why did he have to be so gorgeous? It would have been much easier to deal with being treated like a bratty little sister if he'd looked a little less yummy.

"To return to earth."

"*Reverto terra,*" I said, trying to imagine the dude from *Napoleon Dynamite*'s head on Ethan's body to help calm my racing heart.

"To cease."

"*Desino.*"

"To desist."

"*Absisto,*" I said, rushing on before he could get to the next part of his little review. "*Absisto* and *desino* can be used separately or in conjunction for increased power. *Reverto* may only be used on Reanimated Corpses, while *reverto terra* can be used on Unsettled, random Unsettled body parts, and on Rogues once they've been immobilized, though I shouldn't try to immobilize a Rogue on my own. I should call Settlers' Affairs first."

"Okay, so—"

"And I already know how to seal a grave, how to conjure an aura around a grave to see if it's been tampered with, and how to give and receive power donations so I can cover for another Settler or have them cover for me. I'm basically set, unless you've got a different second-stage handbook than the one Mom gave me."

There. Now he'd have to teach me something new. Or, better yet, put an end to these tutoring sessions completely. If he wasn't going to help me learn anything useful, my time would be better spent trying to figure out who was raising zombies and what they wanted before they ruined homecoming. Call me crazy, but I was still dying to go to the dance, even with a fake date and half the girls at school giving me the cold shoulder.

Oh hell, why lie to myself. I was way more excited about my fake date with Ethan than I'd been about the real date I'd had with Josh. Even when Ethan was boring me to tears, a sick part of me was still thrilled just to be near him, to watch the way his green eyes got all sparkly when he was making fun of me, to see him laugh when I made fun of him, to feel his hand on mine as he corrected my placement when we were practicing spells, to—

". . . so what do you think?"

"Um, what?" I asked, trying my best to look bored. "I was zoning out again, sorry. After four days of the same thing over and over and over—"

"I asked you if you wanted to learn another way to disable RCs, but if you're bored, you can go home. I've got better things to do than—"

"No, I want to learn. I do," I said, trying not clap with excitement. Finally, something useful! "I swear I will not tell anyone that you taught me the flame spell. It will be our little secret."

"I'm not going to teach you the flame spell."

"But you said—"

"The flame spell is for third-stagers. Third-stage spells take a lot of energy and are dangerous to Settlers who can't control their power."

"I can control my power just—"

"It could kill you, Megan."

"So could a Reanimated Corpse, Ethan. Really, I swear I can handle—"

"We're going to learn the *pax frater corpus.*"

"Peace brother dead body?" I asked, sounding less than enthused. Not another freezing spell, not when I'd thought we were finally getting somewhere!

"Somebody's been practicing her Latin." He grinned and chucked me under the chin before pulling a tiny dagger out of his pocket.

"What's this for?" I asked, reluctantly taking the dagger when he held it out.

"You need something sharp and metallic for the next spell. This is something I picked up at headquarters, but anything that will pierce flesh would work—even a safety pin, if it comes to that."

"Cool. So what is it?"

"It's called the *pax frater corpus.* It immobilizes an RC permanently," he said, backing away a few steps. "Even without a taste of the blood that helped them rise, the corpse will remain inoperable until its grave can be found and the *reverto terra* performed."

"Wow, really? No bursting back up through the ground?"

"No bursting back up through the ground." He bent his knees and lifted his hands into the air, assuming what looked very much like a combat position.

"So what's the catch?" I asked, mirroring his pose. If Ethan wanted to rumble, I was *so* ready. Dad had been teaching me a few self-defense moves I was dying to try.

"Why do you think there's a catch?" He started circling and I countered, a smile on my face. Looked like today might be entertaining after all.

"There has to be a catch or we'd use the *pax*-whatever all the time," I said, tensed for him to lunge. "To avoid the risk of an RC being seen on its way back to its Maker, if nothing else."

"Deductive reasoning skills. So sexy in a woman."

"I'm not a woman, I'm a bratty kid. Remember?" I stuck my tongue out at him, doing my best to ignore the tingles threatening to take over a large portion of my body. He was just messing with me, trying to make me lose my focus.

"True." He smiled his big-brother smile, which helped kill the last of the tingles. When would my stupid body learn Ethan was not interested? "So the catch, brat, is that you have to pierce the Reanimated Corpse's body with something metal while chanting the words to the spell."

"Okay, stick the zombie while *pax frater corpus*–ing. Doesn't sound so hard."

"It might not be, if those three words were the entire spell." "So, what is the entire spell?" I asked, willing my mind to absorb the next words out of Ethan's mouth.

"*Pax frater corpus, potestatum spirituum inmundorum ut eicerent eos et curarent omnem languorem et omnem infirmitatem.*"

Oh. Smack. I was so never going to be able to say all that.

"Give or take a few words here and there." Ethan grinned, and his eyebrows arched with excitement. "Doesn't that sound fun?"

"It sounds like suicide. You'd be dead before you got half of that out."

"Yeah, so why don't we just try the first three words right now. I'll be the RC and you be Meggy the Zombie Slayer."

"Very cute."

He grinned. "And we'll see if you can take me."

Ethan circled a little faster.

"Okay, fine, let's go." I gripped the knife and tried to look menacing.

"First the wager. If you stick me and say *pax frater corpus* before I pin you, then I'll teach you the fire spell as long as you promise not to use it until you graduate second stage."

Breaking a promise was bad, but dying was definitely worse. So I rather quickly overcame the guilt I felt for knowing I'd use the flame spell if I needed it, still a second-stager or not.

"Sounds good." I forced myself to relax. Now I *had* to win, no matter that he was bigger and obviously stronger. I'd just have to stay out of reach until I got a good opening and then move and talk really fast.

Hmm . . . now might be a good—

"I'm not done," he said, holding up a hand as if he sensed I was getting ready to pounce. "But if I pin you first, you stop bugging me about the spell and the investigation, which is none of your business."

"It's my business if my school is in danger. And it most certainly is my—"

"Starting *now*!" He lunged forward and I barely had time to squeal and leap to the side.

"So unfair!"

Ethan groaned a very convincing Reanimated Zombie groan and made another grab for my arm. I sidestepped again, then made a break for the more wooded portion of the cemetery. He was faster in the open, but hopefully I had a dancer's superior coordination and—

"Ahh!" I tripped over something and went sprawling onto the grass.

A second later, Ethan's hands were on my wrists. I was flipped over and pinned beneath a hundred and sixty or so pounds of boy before I had time to realize I'd dropped the stupid knife. Now, even if I managed to get a hand free, it was over. Ethan had won, without even breaking a sweat.

Though he *was* breathing faster. But then, so was I . . . and not from our brief run across the graveyard.

Feeling Ethan's legs pinning mine to the grass and his hands encircling my wrists was giving my heart a workout far more intense than any cardio routine. My pulse pounded and blood rushed to my face, heating my cheeks as I realized his lips were only a few inches away from mine. Man, it was nearly impossible to pull my eyes away from those lips, but was I ever glad I did.

Because what was going on in his eyes was *waaayyy* more interesting.

Those gorgeous green eyes with the slight yellow swirls were glued to my lips and his breath was still coming fast. But when I flicked my tongue out along my lips—more because I was freaked that he was staring at them than anything else—he stopped breathing completely. Like . . . he couldn't even breathe because he wanted to kiss me so badly!

But surely not, surely I was just—

"I won," he whispered, finally meeting my eyes.

"Yeah, you did," I said, not even sure what I was saying my heart was beating so fast. "I'm a klutz."

"You always were, except when you were dancing." Something about the way he said those words made the sentence one of the sweetest things I'd ever heard. But I didn't have time to think up a response because, a second later, Ethan's face was moving closer to mine.

Closer. And closer, until I could feel the warmth of him against my lips and there was no doubt that he was going to kiss me. He really, really was! My eyes slid closed and every nerve in my body lit up with anticipation, every part of me knowing this was going to be the best kiss of my entire—

"Gunhhh . . ."

I screamed and my eyes flew back open, but Ethan was already on his feet, inserting himself between me and the zombie a few feet away.

I scrambled to a seated position, only slightly comforted by the fact that this was a normal Unsettled, no red eyes, no slobbering for human flesh. As far as I knew, a black-magic practitioner couldn't even raise a corpse during the day since night was an integral part of the spell. But then, I shouldn't be summoning another daytime Unsettled either. I'd been working on my shielding nonstop! I couldn't imagine how my power had somehow penetrated those shields . . . unless . . .

"It's here for you?" I asked, coming to stand beside Ethan. The zombie had a Williams College sweatshirt on and looked way too old to be in high school, but I still found it hard to believe Ethan had allowed his shields to drop.

"Yeah, sure is." Ethan looked embarrassed as he shoved his hand into his back pocket and pulled out his BlackBerry.

"Have you ever—"

"Never," he said, his tone sharp enough that I shut up while he got the Unsettled's basic info typed into the device. "Carter, what is it you don't like about your death?"

I grinned to myself, secretly pleased Ethan had stolen my *Nip/Tuck* line.

"I never told Kate I was crazy about her. We'd been friends forever and I was afraid to mess that up, but now . . . I just really wish I'd told her how I felt."

Ethan asked a few more questions about Kate to make sure he knew how to find her in order to relay Carter's message, but I hardly heard any of it. Part of me was busy mentally replaying those last moments before the Unsettled had arrived, when I *knew* Ethan had been about to kiss me. The other part was freaking out about Carter's request. Surely this wasn't a mere coincidence! This was a bona fide sign.

Maybe Ethan had secretly been feeling more than friendship for me too but had been afraid it might interfere with our tutoring relationship. But now, with the tutoring out of the way, he'd realized he could show me how he felt. And what better way to show me than with a kiss? Our first kiss. The first kiss of many, many kisses to—

"Hello? Megan?"

"Yeah? Sorry," I said, tuning back in to reality in time to see Carter dash away.

"Listen, I think I know what happened," Ethan said, shoving his BlackBerry back into his pocket. "When we were on the ground, I could feel a power current flowing between us, and it got stronger when I leaned closer. Kind of a buzzing feeling"

"Oh . . . really?" I'd thought the buzzing was purely hormone-related. I could practically hear my hopes shattering.

"Yeah. I think I absorbed a lot of your power but without even trying to link up the way we did the other day."

Ethan had forced me to practice linking my power to his to strengthen the *reverto* spell like ten million times on Thursday, even though I'd done the exact same thing with Monica when I was barely ten. That was how we'd banished the zombies who'd attacked me, so I obviously knew how to get the job done. But Ethan had still been obsessive about it.

For a guy who was trying to convince me there wouldn't be a large-scale attack, he was doing a fairly lousy job of it. Sure, when I was a kid I'd needed Monica's help to banish the RCs. But there was no reason for second-stagers to link power unless they were dealing with a hell of a lot of zombies.

"So does that mean I wasn't shielding firmly enough?" I asked, straining to sound normal.

"No, I don't think so. It felt like your shields were still strong." He finally finished messing with his back pocket. "I'll ask my liaison about it, but until then it's probably best we don't practice any of the combat stuff I was going to show you today. Too much physical contact doesn't seem like a good idea if it makes me draw Unsettled during the day."

"Yeah, totally. I'll just . . . ask my dad to show me some more self-defense stuff."

"Cool. I mean, you probably won't need it for zombies, but it's always a good idea for a girl to know how to protect herself," he said, running his hand through his hair before glancing at his watch. "Hey, I've gotta get going. I'm meeting some friends in an hour."

"Sure, cool. I'll just . . . bike home," I said, my voice not sounding nearly as perky and normal as I wanted it to.

I was just so disappointed and achy inside. It was stupid, really. I mean, Ethan was my friend and I was obviously attracted to him, but there was no reason to get so angsty. It wasn't like I was in love with him or anything.

Oh. No. I wasn't? Was I?

"No, let's put your bike in my trunk and I'll drive you." Ethan grabbed his sweatshirt from the ground and shrugged it on. "I want to make sure that you're home safe and that your parents know I won't be back for babysitting duty until Tuesday morning so they'll need to keep a closer eye on you."

"Where are you going to be until Tuesday?"

"I told you, plans with friends."

"Plans that last all the way until Tuesday?" I realized how stupid and weirdly possessive I sounded and tried to backtrack, but Ethan spoke first.

"Yes, Schmeg, when you're a big girl and go away to college, you'll learn all about—"

"Oh, please. Spare me. I know all about those kind of plans," I said, rolling my eyes and trying to affect a blasé attitude even though I was inwardly raging. "I'm almost sixteen, Ethan, and I was dating the hottest guy in school before you showed up and ruined it. Believe me, I know a thing or two about plans."

For a second, I would have sworn Ethan looked jealous, but then he smiled, making me think I'd imagined it. "Good for you, Megan. Aren't you a big girl?"

The patronizing tone was the last straw. "Screw you, Ethan. And screw your ride home!"

"Oh, come on, Schmeg. I'm sorry, I—"

"And don't call me Schmeg." I ran the rest of the way to my bike and unlocked it with shaking hands, doing my best not to give in to the ridiculous urge to cry. I didn't care if Ethan had plans with some girl until Tuesday morning. I didn't care that he didn't care if I had ever fooled around with Josh. And I certainly didn't care that he thought I was nothing but a little brat he enjoyed teasing.

I knew I wasn't the joke he acted like I was. I had a brain, and it was about time I started using it for something other than obsessing about him.

Starting tomorrow, I was getting serious about finding out what was going on at Carol High School. Ethan could spend the next day or two shacked up with some college girl drinking beer. I'd spend mine profitably and by Tuesday be well on my way to proving to everyone I wasn't a stupid child.

CHAPTER 9

"So what's up? You find out anything?" Jess asked, handing me my cup of white chocolate mousse frozen yogurt. She'd hit the TCBY while I'd hit the dry cleaner's.

Carapelli's was the only cleaner I'd trusted with the world's most perfect dress. In return, they'd allowed my dress to be stolen and used to cross-dress a zombie. Carapelli and all his umpteen-million relatives were *so* on my poo list.

I hadn't told Jess the real way the dress was destroyed, of course, just that it had disappeared from the cleaner's and they were refusing to reimburse me. Not that it would have mattered even if they had given me money to buy a new dress since there wasn't another size four at the store in Little Rock or any of their Arkansas locations. Even with all the other stuff going on in my life, this still inspired a brief period of mourning Monday afternoon.

"No," I said, digging into my extra-large cup, wondering if I could eat my way to a size six in less than a week. "But I think the guy is lying so he won't get in trouble for giving someone my dress without the claim slip."

"Well, since you still have the claim slip . . ."

I grimaced around a bite of white chocolate mousse. "I threw it out. I never keep them; I just give them our phone number."

"Hmm . . . okay, so whoever stole your dress must know your phone number too."

"You're right," I said, following Jess as she turned back toward school. We only had about ten minutes before the pom squad clinic, so we had to walk while we scarfed yogurt. "And we're unlisted, so that would narrow it down a lot. Man, why didn't I think of that before?"

I should totally have asked Jess for help earlier. She wasn't in the Honor Society or any of the advanced classes, but she was way more gifted than I was when it came to good old common sense.

"But wait, don't get too excited. Didn't you write your phone number on the sign-up sheet for pom tryouts last week?"

"Crap, I did." And those had been up on the gymnasium bulletin board, where anyone could see them. Back to square one.

Well, not exactly square one. Since Sunday, I'd added another suspect to my list. Oddly enough, Mrs. Pierce had made the cut when she still couldn't find my journal by Monday morning. Not only had she allegedly "lost" my list of suspects, she'd also proceeded to give me the third degree about homecoming.

Was I going? Was I sure I had a reliable ride? Did it seem smart to waste time at a dance when I was falling behind on my studies? It was just . . . weird, and enough to get her added to my new list—which I kept safely out of sight during English, of course.

Still, there was only one real suspect in my mind. And now I totally had a motive for her. I couldn't believe I hadn't figured out why Monica might want to ruin homecoming earlier. But then, it

wasn't until the homecoming court was announced at school on
Tuesday that the lightbulb illuminated.

For the first time in her entire high school career, the Monicster
was *not* one of the homecoming princesses.

Neither was Beth Phillips, Josh's ex. Instead, the senior class
princesses consisted of London, her friend Alana, and two of the
biggest nerds in the entire school. The football and the basketball
team had banded together to vote in the nerds, thinking it would be
a hysterical senior prank.

So far, however, no one was amused. Not the nerd girls and
definitely not Beth or Monica. Beth was actually crying in the girls'
locker room after school on Tuesday as we changed into our dance
clothes for the second day of pom tryouts, and Monica . . .

Well, Monica had looked ready to kill someone. Maybe several
someones.

If she'd somehow gotten a look at the voting results before the
announcement—which was entirely possible since she was on the
student council and they were the ones who counted the votes—then
she could totally have been responsible for the attacks on Josh, Ethan,
and my homecoming dress. She wasn't a princess and therefore
couldn't be voted homecoming queen, so she'd probably decided to
sic a few Reanimated Corpses on the gym and ruin the dance and
didn't want me there to sic the RCs back on her with the *reverto*
spell.

She was whacked enough to kill, I was sure of it. Anyone who
had ever been on the receiving end of one of her arctic glares could
see that, and she would consider Josh expendable now that he wasn't
dating one of her best friends. I could imagine her sending an RC his

way and not feeling an ounce of remorse, and God knew she had no love for me or my poor dress.

The attack on Ethan was a little harder to justify since they really were good friends, but Monica had been right there to hear him say he was taking me to the dance. She definitely wouldn't have wanted *two* Settlers at homecoming, and she knew Ethan could handle himself well enough to fend off one RC. Especially if it was already on fire and thus could be completely incinerated by a flame spell without much effort.

Basically, all things considered, I would have been ready to approach Ethan and the Elders with my suspicions but for two things: One, Monica had been at dance practice the entire time Ethan and I had been at Sonic, and therefore I couldn't figure out how she could have summoned the zombie wearing my homecoming dress from its grave, let alone stuffed it into my dress. And two, I knew the whole "not a single case in Settler history of a Settler using black magic" thing would make the Elders completely unwilling to see the situation with Monica clearly.

I could, however, totally see Monica being the first Settler to go bad. She *was* exceptionally evil.

"Wow, Megan. Do you know how many calories are in an extra large?" The first words to greet us as we entered the gym were enough to give me acid reflux. "I mean, it's fat free, not *sugar* free. Better watch it or you won't fit into any of the uniforms even if you do make the squad."

Think of the she-devil and she shall appear. "Thanks, Monica. I really appreciate your concern," I said, my tone so sweet it could have caused a diabetic to go into shock.

"Sure thing. Anytime." She smiled and I smiled back, wishing I had the guts to growl at her instead.

But I couldn't afford an attitude. Tryouts were Friday, only three days away, and I *had* to make the team. It was what Jess and I had been dreaming about for years, and I wasn't going to give the Monicster any excuse to blacklist me—or amp up her RC attacks. Mustn't forget about that. This wasn't only my future of pom-pom shaking that was at risk, but possibly my life as well.

"Someone should shoot that girl and put us all out of our misery," Jess whispered as soon as Monica was out of range.

I laughed as I threw away the last of my yogurt. Only Monica could make Jess's claws come out. "You ready to go in?"

"Yeah, just two more bites. I need calories if I'm going to dance for an hour and a half," Jess said, shoveling in another bite. "So, seriously, you have no idea who might have stolen your dress?"

"Not really. I mean, I sort of thought maybe Beth might hate me because of the whole Josh thing, but I mean, it's not like anything really happened between me and Josh," I said, hating that I couldn't tell Jess everything. "He's still cool in chemistry, but it's obvious he heard about the Ethan thing, so there's no more flirting."

"The Ethan thing?" Jess smiled. "Does your boyfriend know you call him a thing?"

"You know what I mean," I said, trying to laugh it off but failing. It just felt so wrong to be lying to Jess about anything but especially something as important as who I was dating.

Or *not* dating. Ethan was back on babysitting duty and had, in fact, probably been watching me and Jess as we walked to TCBY and back again, but nothing else was going on with us. Our tutoring sessions were apparently over, and he seemed to be doing his best not to spend any more time with me than absolutely necessary. That meant he drove me to school and home and stayed parked on the couch until Dad and Mom got home from work to take over the babysitting.

Since I was pissed at him, his lack of interest shouldn't have bothered me, but it did. A lot.

"You look sad." Jess, perceptive as always. "Is there something going on with you and Ethan? A fight or something?"

"No, it's fine. We're fine." I smiled, trying to look like one half of a happy couple.

"You don't look fine. You especially don't look like you're dating one of the hottest guys I've ever seen in real life."

I laughed for real. "He is hot, the jerk."

Jess smiled. "See there, I knew it. He's being a jerk. Well, tell him just because he looks like he walked out of an Abercrombie ad doesn't mean he gets to treat my best friend like crap."

"He's not treating me like crap. It's just . . . it's complicated." God, I wished I could tell Jess the truth: that Ethan was my fake boyfriend and probably not even that for very much longer. By Friday this would all be over, one way or another.

Not only was homecoming Friday night, it was also the night of the full moon. That alone made it a good night for bad magic since the full moon added power to all kinds of casting. But my Googling on Monday had also revealed there would be a lunar eclipse occurring at approximately nine fifty-eight that evening.

According to the third-stage book I'd filched from the Closet early Tuesday morning, lunar eclipses meant *major* energy mojo for black-magic practitioners. If whoever was raising the Reanimated Corpses was planning something big, Friday would be the night to do it, whether or not CHS homecoming was involved. Though I still *knew* it was, no matter that the powers that be thought my theory was ridiculous.

"So is Ethan upset about you guys not going to the dance?" Jess asked, eerily taking up where my thoughts had left off. How did she do that?

"Why would he be upset about that?" I turned to head into the gym and Jess followed.

"I mean, I know he's in college and all, but he seemed kind of excited to go last week. Are you sure you aren't thinking about going? I mean, couldn't you find another dress?"

I stopped dead in my tracks and turned to look at my best friend. Why was she so curious about whether or not I secretly planned to go to the dance with Ethan? I'd told her and everyone else I was staying home. What did Jess have to gain or lose if I didn't show up at homecoming? Could she possibly have a motive for—

"I mean," she began, her expression mildly tortured, "I didn't want to say anything because I didn't know if you and Ethan had other plans, but I was thinking maybe you and I could hang out. Just veg and eat junk food and watch old movies all night or something?"

Oh man. I was *such* a jerk. Here I'd been on my way to adding my best friend to my list of suspects. I sucked. Really, really hard.

Thankfully, I had a good idea of how to redeem myself.

"I love you," I said, hugging Jess impulsively. "You're the best best friend."

"Thanks. You too."

"But I know Kyle asked you to the dance today," I said. "I heard him talking about it in study hall. Didn't you tell him yes?"

"No, I haven't said yes or no yet. But I—" She broke off, and I could tell she was trying to think of some plausible reason she would refuse a date with a total cutie to hang out with her lame, no-dress-having girlfriend. "He's just so tall, and I'm so short. We'd look funny together, don't you think? I can tell him I have other plans."

"You do not have other plans! You're going with Kyle and . . ." Hell, I was tired of hiding from whatever freak was out to get me. Time to turn the tables! "And I'll find something to wear and we'll double."

"Really?" she asked, giving me a look. "Are you sure? It could be fun—"

"To stay home and miss the dance? No way. Doubling will be great. And I'm sure Ethan won't mind."

"Well . . . okay. I—"

"Um, if you two are done lesboing out, we're getting ready to start," Monica interrupted.

"I think we're done. Are you done, Jess?"

Jess paused, considering the question. "Um, yeah. For now." Beth Phillips and a few of the other girls laughed as we joined the lineup behind the seniors. I felt better than I had since this whole Josh-Ethan-homecoming thing started. I wasn't going to be the two-timer everyone hated for the rest of my life!

Now all I had to do was make sure everyone at the clinic today knew I was back on for homecoming and the news would spread from there. Sooner or later, it would reach the ears I was aiming for, and this time I'd be ready.

I was going to flush out the person responsible for the attacks before they had the chance to ruin homecoming or any of my friendships. I'd nearly started suspecting Jess, and that degree of paranoia was unforgivable.

There would be no more chickening out. I wasn't having any luck hunting for clues, so I'd make the clues come to me. Even if they came in the form of another RC, I could handle myself. I was Megan Berry, full-on second-stage Settler, with all the training I needed to send a Reanimated Corpse packing.

They could bring it. Because I wasn't afraid anymore.

Okay . . . so I was a little bit afraid, but a little fear was good. It would keep me on my toes.

I focused on the dance routines, and the rest of the hour and a half flew by. I was actually feeling pretty relaxed by the time we finished up and hit the locker room to change. So relaxed, in fact, that I was totally unprepared to be blindsided by an unholy trinity of angry senior girls.

"Megan, could you come here a second?" London was leaning against her locker, with Alana and Beth flanking her on either side. None of them looked happy.

"Sure, what's up?" I asked, shoving my gym clothes in my bag as I crossed the room.

"That's what I was going to ask you," London said. "What do you think you're doing, changing your mind about bringing Ethan to homecoming?" Wow, news really did spread fast. "I mean, aren't you embarrassed?"

"Um, about what?" I asked, playing dumb.

"About leading Josh on when you were already going out with

someone," Alana said, her tone making it clear I was a lower life form.

"Ethan and I weren't really going out. I mean, we were sort of dating, but not seriously," I said, wincing at how lame I sounded. I was such a bad liar! "So, you know, I thought it would be okay to—"

"Okay to what? Act like a skank?" Beth asked, her nose squinching as if she were offended by my scent. "Listen, Josh and I aren't together anymore, but I still care about him. I can't believe you're doing this."

"Yeah, it's really messed up," Alana agreed.

Jeez, what was with these girls? It was like they were stuck in the 1960s or something. Even if I had been dating Josh and Ethan at the same time, so what? If it wasn't serious with either one of them, I had the right to date both and *not* be treated like I'd committed a crime against girls everywhere.

But then again, this wasn't a crime against just any girls. It was a crime against the *popular* girls. They didn't like the idea of some sophomore nobody choosing another guy over one of their own. I had offended the social order of CHS, and now . . . I was obviously going to pay.

"So do you want to rethink this issue?" London asked, blue eyes wide.

"Listen, I really am sorry; I didn't mean to upset anyone," I said, thinking fast. "But Josh isn't even going to be at the dance, right? I mean, with his leg broken he can't—"

"Is that why you ditched him? Because he got hurt?" Beth asked, obviously angry. "What a shallow, selfish little—"

"Josh and I are going as friends, so he'll be there," Alana said, interrupting Beth, who looked ready to tear my hair out.

What the hell was up with her? She obviously wasn't over Josh, which bumped her higher on the list of my potential suspects. If she was this angry in public, what might she be doing in private? She *had* seen me at Sonic with Ethan and had had plenty of time and opportunity to get to a graveyard before we got home to my house. *And* she was a really good artist. She was always placing in the state competitions, so she was totally capable of making realistic representations of people to use as totems.

But if she was still in love with Josh, why would she send a zombie to kill him? It didn't make sense.

"So I really think it would be more pleasant for you if you didn't bring Ethan." London reached over and pressed soft fingers to my elbow, and I tried not to shiver. Her energy really creeped me out. It could have been just normal bitchy vibes, or it could have been that I was sensing some of her dark power. Maybe London was in on this too . . . for some reason I couldn't fathom.

God, I was really taking the crazy train to Paranoiaville. That was why I had to stick to my guns and my plan to draw the real culprit.

"I'm going to bring Ethan," I said, smoothly detaching from London's grasp. "But I'll call Josh to apologize and make sure it's okay with him first."

"That's the least you could do," Beth said, obviously not truly placated. "I still think you shouldn't go."

"But it's your choice," London said with a shrug. "We're just trying to make sure no one on our squad gets a bad rep. You're really talented, Megan, so it's pretty given you'll be one of us by Friday night."

"Yeah, and we haven't even seen your optional dance," Alana said. "Kayla said you and Jess have a routine that's hot enough to raise the dead."

My blood chilled several degrees and goose bumps broke out on my arms.

Raise the dead? Who would say that if they didn't happen to know I worked with zombies in my spare time? Did Alana know? Did they *all* know? I was going to lose my mind if I didn't get to the bottom of this!

"I hope so. We, um, worked really hard on it," I said, backing away from the seniors, really needing my space all of a sudden. "So I'll see you tomorrow."

"Right. See you," Beth said, her normally pretty face pinched and unhappy looking. London and Alana seemed a little more chill, but the vibes all three were giving out were not good.

No matter what they'd said about my dancing ability, I couldn't help but think I'd won myself three anti-Megan votes. And for what? So I could lure a psychopath into attacking me again? I so needed therapy or an intervention or something.

Hopefully I'd still be alive to get my head in a better place when all of this was over.

CHAPTER 10

$\mathcal{E}$than had mysteriously disappeared by the time I left the gym, and Mom was waiting for me in the parking lot. She usually had Wednesdays off from her job at the Arkansas Agriculture Commission, where she did . . . something with seeds. Sorting them or measuring them or . . . something.

I never really understood what Mom did the way I understood Dad's aircraft maintenance work but figured that was fine. I knew enough to know I didn't want to follow in her footsteps. Call me crazy, but sorting seeds sounded about as stimulating as organizing my sock drawer.

Still, Mom looovvved it.

She jabbered on and on about some hybrid seed they were working on while I did my best not to think about Ethan or give in to the temptation to ask where he'd gone. Probably to visit his *real* girlfriend or something really collegiate and important.

Whatever. I had things to do that I didn't want him to observe anyway.

I'd read enough in Mom's old third-stage Settler book over the past twenty-four hours to learn about the importance of full moons and eclipses in black magic, but I hadn't had the chance to practice any of the more advanced commands I'd read about because Ethan was always around. Since I'd just thrown out bait I firmly believed would bring on another attack, however, today seemed like an excellent time to get some real-life experience with the things I'd been reading about.

Especially the flame command. No matter what Ethan said about it taking up a lot of power and being so scary and dangerous, it still seemed like a pretty useful thing to have in your bag of tricks. The rest of the third-stage stuff wasn't as interesting as I'd hoped it would be—at least not as far as combating Reanimated Corpses was concerned—but it did make me more hopeful about the future.

According to the book, third-stagers had a lot more wiggle room when it came to how often they used their power. They could basically "shut off" for days at a time. As long as they spent one to two nights a week at home waiting for Unsettled, their power wouldn't get out of control. It made me feel way better about staying a Settler to know I'd have more freedom in a few years . . . or as soon as I advanced to the third stage.

Mom and Ethan had both said I was manifesting way more power than the average second-stager. Shouldn't that mean I could move up sooner? Getting to choose which nights I was "at the office" would really help me make sure I didn't miss night performances with the pom squad. And if I already knew most of the third-stage stuff before I started pestering Mom to talk to Settlers' Affairs for me . . .

Well, I didn't see how they could refuse, which made me even more rabid to get started.

Once we got home, however, I exercised great restraint and resisted whipping out the third-stage book until I'd finished dinner and read my English assignment. *Macbeth*. More like *Macblech*. So far I just wasn't into Shakespeare, which sort of made me rethink English as one of my possible majors in college.

Then I hopped on the computer to IM the news of *Macbeth*'s snooze factor to Jess, took a super-fast shower, and finally raced into the kitchen to snag a bag of Doritos because all the dancing had made me extremely snacky for junk food and Mom had cooked something gross as usual. So I was just getting around to memorizing the hand motions for the flame command when the phone rang.

I waited for Mom to answer it on the off chance someone was actually calling my house to speak to my parents—which had happened maybe once or twice in the past six months—while I hid the stage-three book under my mattress. Then, in an effort to appear innocent while I waited for Mom to yell for me to pick up, I turned on one of my TiVo'd episodes of *Engaged & Underage*, my favorite guilty pleasure.

It was like watching an angsty hormone-fueled train wreck and firmly cemented my resolve to be at least twenty-five before I considered getting hitched.

"Megan! Phone!"

The phone was already in hand, dearest Mother. "Hello?"

"Megan? Hey, it's Del."

"Hey, Del, what's up?" I asked, trying not to sound surprised. Del and I were friends, but she rarely called. We had more of an IM-every-once-in-a-while relationship.

"I was just wondering if you'd mind picking up my homework from the office tomorrow since you live closer than Jess or Claire. My brother was going to do it, but now he's got mono too."

"You've got mono? That sucks!" And meant she couldn't be my zombie raiser . . . unless this call was a deliberate attempt to throw me off her trail.

Her trail? What trail? You have no trail. You are the worst Nancy Drew ever.

The inner voice was back on a pessimistic streak. Why was I not surprised?

"I know, and right before homecoming! I'm so bummed." Del sighed. "But Zeke is the one who gave it to me, so I guess I wouldn't be going anyway."

Zeke, Del's man, *had* been absent all week too, so this was seeming pretty believable. Besides, Del and Zeke spent too much time making out to get around to raising zombies. It was only my paranoia that had made me suspect her. Well, paranoia and Jess's comments about Del's weird behavior lately and the odd phone call she'd gotten from Del the other day.

Maybe that was why she was calling me instead of Jess even though Jess lived nearly as close. Maybe she'd already weirded Jess out by being all freaky on the phone. Or maybe she was trying to lure me over to her house so she could tie me up in her basement to make sure I didn't get to the dance?

I made a mental note to make sure Ethan was with me when I went by Del's. It was better to be paranoid and safe than trusting and dead.

"No problem," I said. "I'll pick it up and bring it by after tryout clinic tomorrow."

"So how's that going?"

We talked about clinic and the gorgeous dress Del wasn't going to be wearing to homecoming for a few minutes; then I signed off with a promise to see her Thursday afternoon. I'd barely had time to get the stage-three book pulled out from under my mattress, however, when the phone rang again.

Hmmm. Caller unknown. How intriguing.

This time I didn't wait for Mom to answer because it was almost ten and I knew she'd get on me for late phone calls—probably while still *on the phone* with me and whoever had called.

"Hello?"

There was a brief, creepy pause before a scratchy voice came on the line. "I've got a present for you, Megan."

"Who is this?" I vaulted off my bed to pace around the room, for some reason feeling safer on the move.

This was it! This had to be my guy. Or my girl, rather. The person was obviously masking her voice, but it still sounded like a female.

"It doesn't matter who I am. It's who *you* are that's important." The weirdo laughed then, but the sound was inhuman, like a robot coughing up a hair ball. She was using something high-tech to conceal her voice, which made me even more afraid. A high tech voodoo freak didn't seem like a good combination. "I know you like to play with dead people, Megan."

"I don't know what you're talking about," I said, my voice shaking.

I wasn't going to give her confirmation if she didn't have it already, but in my heart I knew my cover had been blown. Someone knew I was a Settler. If this person *wasn't* Monica, that meant my family could be relocated, all of our lives ruined because some twisted freak liked to use Reanimated Corpses as her own personal murder weapons.

"Oh, I think you do. It's okay, I like to play with them too." The way she said "play" made my skin crawl. "Experimenting with new things can be such fun, don't you think?"

"Please, you're freaking me out. I don't understand—"

"No, you don't, but you will," she snapped, clearly near to losing what little sanity she had left. "I wish it could have been different. It's been fun playing with you from a distance, but I wanted to look you in the face when you finally died. Too bad it looks like that won't be happening. Still, at least I know you'll still be getting what you deserve."

The sharp click as she hung up the phone made me flinch. My mouth went dry and my lips opened and closed, with no words coming out. Someone wanted me dead. Someone *really* wanted me dead.

I frantically punched star-69 into the phone, but all I got was a recording telling me the number was blocked. Of course. Like a freak who went to the trouble to use voice-disguise technology was going to let a murder plot be foiled by *last call return*.

A murder plot. This wasn't about homecoming, after all. I felt the Doritos I'd eaten come racing back up my throat and barely made it to the toilet in time.

"Megan! Get to the door! Now!!" My mom's scream came just as I was flushing. I wiped a trembling hand across my mouth and dashed to the door, fearing the worst, but when I got to the foyer, it looked like Settler business as usual.

Well, not exactly as usual.

Just inside the door stood three zombies—all of them girls. And all of them with the same face and dirty shoulder-length blond hair. Triplets.

My mom stood next to the newspaper she'd laid out by the door, looking as struck by the sadness of this as I felt. Someone out there had lost three kids all at once. I felt so bad for their family. Combined with the terror inspired by the phone call, it was enough to make me tear up.

Mom must have seen how upset I was because she stuck close even after she'd handed me the official record book. Her hand on my shoulder helped me pull it together as I opened the book to the first empty page and clicked my pen. I just had to get through this, put these girls to rest. Then I could tell Mom everything.

I *had* to tell her, even though I hated to let her know our cover could have been compromised. No matter how many times I'd moaned about the lameness of living in Arkansas, I didn't really want to leave and start all over somewhere else. With a new school, no friends, no best friend, and no Ethan. I really wished Ethan hadn't disappeared right when I needed a friend—and a bodyguard—in the worst way.

"Hello, my name is Megan," I said, surprised my voice didn't sound shakier than it did. "Welcome to your after-death session. Could you please give me your names, last name first."

"Wellington, Shane," they all three said at once, creating a creepy kind of stereo effect as the human part of them came online.

"No, I'm Shane!" they said, again at the same time. They turned to look at each other, obviously confused. "Who are you? Stop copying me!"

"Okay, just relax. Let's try this one at a time." What was their problem? I'd never heard of an after-death identity crisis, but then, I'd never dealt with triplets before either. I motioned to the girl on the far left. "Let's start with you."

"No, we'll start with me, whatever your name is," said the one in the center in a snotty voice. I was starting to feel a little less sorry for her. "I'm the real Shane. I don't know who these other losers are."

The two girls on either side of her chose that moment to start groaning. Not a typical zombie groan—more like they'd been asked to take out the trash and were expressing their displeasure for the chore. Still, there was something . . . *off* about the whole situation. Especially coming so soon after the phone call.

I struggled to remember the exact words the crazy on the phone had used but kept drawing a blank. All I could hear was her creepy robot voice telling me she wanted to look me in the face while I died.

While I *died*. I couldn't *die*. My sixteenth birthday was only three weeks away!

"Shut up, freaks." Shane flipped her grave dirt–covered hair out of her gray eyes and glared first at me, then at my mom. "Would you people mind telling me what's going on here?"

"Maybe you could tell us why you've chosen to emerge from your rest?" Mom seemed fairly calm, so maybe this wasn't anything weird after all. She must have seen or heard about something like the three Shanes before.

Still, uneasiness niggled at my brain. There had been something about a present. The psycho had said she'd gotten me a present. Judging from the death threat, I could assume it wasn't going to be a gift I would enjoy, but I didn't see how this could be related. Shane and her sisters were normal Unsettled, no glowing red eyes or lunging for my throat.

Well, they weren't *completely* normal since the other two weren't really very talkative. But Shane certainly had normal Unsettled issues, which she revealed as she began spilling her guts.

"My cousin Melinda stole every last pair of shoes I owned while I was in a coma. She came in and told me about it while I was on life support. She thought I couldn't hear her, but I could." She sneered, her contempt for her shoe-stealing cousin clear in every line of her face, which was weird, considering the other two Shanes were looking less and less lifelike every second, their jaws growing slack and their eyes empty. "I want her to know that she can't have my shoes. I want them to go to like charity or something because there's no way that thief— will you shut up?"

The other two zombies were groaning again, louder and louder, making every hair on my body stand on end. They sounded like they were getting ready to go Rogue, which shouldn't be possible since they still hadn't told me what had made them rise from their grave along with their sister. This was so strange, so unlike anything I'd ever even heard of.

"Okay, so you want your shoes to go to charity. I've got it. Now what about the other two of you? Who wants to go first?" But the other two Shanes just moaned again, and their eyes began to glow a faint blue color. Okay, creepy. But at least not red. "Mom, what's going on? Have you ever seen—"

"No, but I've read about something similar," she said, and this time I could hear the fear in her voice. "Shane, are you sure the shoes are the only reason you came to talk with us tonight?" Mom edged slightly in front of me, as if to put herself in harm's way rather than her baby chick. "Go get the phone, Megan. I'll handle—"

"No, Mom, this is my responsibility. These girls are obviously here for me," I said, edging back in front of her.

"Megan Amanda—"

She didn't have time to get to my last name before the two sisters' blue eyes suddenly turned bright, Reanimated red. They lunged at me, claws raised as I stumbled backward into Mom. I had just enough time to notice that their French manicures were in awfully good shape for chicks who'd dug themselves out from under six feet of dirt before we were on the floor, rumbling like something from the WWWF.

CHAPTER 11

I heard Shane screaming and saw Mom trying to pull one of the sisters off of me, but they were too strong. Groaner number one shoved Mom away as if she weighed nothing and then turned her attention back to me with a swipe aimed at my eyes. I wiggled to the left just in time to catch the blow on the shoulder, not the face, but it still hurt like nobody's business.

"*Absis*—" Groaner two shoved her hand into my face, interrupting the freezing command even as groaner one made a lunge for my throat.

Mom grabbed a baseball bat from the closet and knocked the lunger's head hard enough to spin her face around to her back, then started whaling on the second zombie, but the thing barely seemed to notice. Argh! If only Mom could still command the dead!

But Mom hadn't been able to actively Settle since I was five years old and started manifesting. That meant she couldn't help me any more than the average terrified human parent. It also meant that, once these ladies had eaten me, she and Dad would have no way to get rid of them.

I had to get free. There was no other option.

I screamed and kicked and thrashed but barely managed to keep clear of one zombie's hands and the other zombie's mouth. The second one was getting way too freaking close to getting her teeth into me, a fact that made my heart beat triple time as I shoved at the hand still covering my mouth.

One part of me heard Mom yell for Dad, but the other part was back at the night of my first attack. I remembered the searing pain as the zombie tore into my shoulder, the feeling of flesh tearing away from flesh as I scuttled backward, screaming. I was suddenly ten years old again, helpless to do anything but lie there and pray for help.

No! You aren't that little kid anymore. Pull your head out of your ass and do something!

I forced the memory away as I reared back and head-butted the thing on top of me. Pain blossomed through my forehead, but luckily the zombie was dazed enough by the blow to be temporarily distracted from her bid to rip out my throat. Seconds later, Dad was there above me, kicking her away.

"Grab my arms, Megan!" I clung to my dad's forearms as he snatched me under the armpits and hauled me out from under the two feral versions of Shane.

I kicked the one with her face still in the right direction in the eye as my dad wrenched me free, giving us a few extra seconds to turn and haul ass. Mom was already holding open the door to my parents' bedroom, ready to slam it closed as soon as we were safely inside. Dad and I lurched through the opening, still awkwardly clinging to each other, but luckily we didn't fall down until we were near the bed.

"They're clones, I'm sure of it," Mom spoke into the phone at her ear as she closed the door and flipped the dead bolt. "Yes, I know that— listen, I— dammit, Carl, they were trying to eat my daughter.

We're locked in our bedroom, but I don't know how long the door will hold. We need backup. Now!"

As if on cue, something that sounded like a fist connected with the door, making it rattle. A second later, another blow hit and the wood groaned in a way that wasn't comforting. We had to get out of here before they found a way in.

"Mom, the window!" I was up and across the room in a second, throwing open the window next to my parents' bed. Our house is all one level, and the lot only sloped a little bit on that side. It was maybe a four-foot drop to the ground and from there only ten to twelve feet around to the side of the house where my dad's truck was parked in the driveway.

"We're going to try to get out to the—"

Mom was interrupted by a splintering sound as a white Mary Jane broke through the bottom of the door.

"Jennifer, come on!" My dad kicked out the screen and helped me through the window. I hit the ground and turned to see if Mom needed help getting through. I was reaching up to take her hand when she screamed.

"Behind you, Megan!"

On pure instinct, I ducked down. A second later, I felt the air stir as something zoomed over my head and hit the brick wall in front of me.

"Gunhhh!" Yet another version of Shane groaned as she struggled to stand, half of her head smashed in by contact with the bricks. Too bad zombies didn't need brains to function or I might have been able to eliminate her as a possible threat. But no, she was already up and at me—trudging forward, arms raised and hands ready to close around my neck and squeeze as soon as she got close enough.

I turned to run, only to find two other clones shuffling in from the front yard. I changed direction, rounding the house into the backyard.

If I'd been able to draw a big enough breath, I would have screamed.

The entire yard was filled with Shanes, at least two dozen of them. That evil freak on the phone had wanted to make sure I wouldn't survive this attack, so she'd made up for what black-magically raised zombies lacked in speed with pure numbers. My family was surrounded, and unless help showed soon, we weren't going to live to share the story of these clones with the rest of the Settler world.

"Reverto! Reverto!" I hurled everything I had at the clones, but it didn't do a bit of good. There were too many of them for the *reverto* spell to work. They wouldn't be going anywhere unless I miraculously gained more power or worked the *pax frater corpus*—which was impossible since I certainly hadn't memorized the entire thing.

I was out of options. Unless . . .

No, I couldn't try the flame command—not yet. I hadn't even had the chance to practice it once. I was likely to screw up the hand motions and end up shocking myself senseless and providing the corpses with an easy feast. Better to stick with what I knew I could handle.

"Desino! Absisto!" I focused my magic as best I could and hurled the power at the zombie closest to me. It froze in its tracks. The second-stage animation-arrest spells were fairly simple. Unfortunately, they only lasted for a few seconds, maybe a minute, tops. This was only buying me time, not really helping solve the—

I suddenly had an idea. The real Shane really *was* an average

Unsettled, though Mom hadn't seemed convinced she'd spilled the real reason she crawled from her grave. If I could get the 411 from Shane, Mark her, and send her back to her rest, maybe all these other Shanes would go with her. Surely they wouldn't be able to animate if the person they'd been cloned from was at rest?

Or so I hoped. Otherwise, heading back into the house was probably a very stupid idea.

"Absisto!" I used my hands to guide the spell toward the zombies on the porch steps, running past them as soon as they were momentarily out of commission.

"Megan!" I heard Mom scream, and could only hope Dad had pulled her to safety.

There was nothing I could do for her now except try to get rid of these zombies. Hand-to-hand combat was useless.

"Desino! Absisto! Desino!" I managed to freeze enough of the clones to get in through the back door. The living room was blessedly empty, but I could see the first two zombies that had attacked me making quick work of the door to my parents' bedroom. I had to work fast.

"Shane! Tell me what it is you don't like about your death!" I said, rushing toward the real Shane, who still stood by the front door, looking nearly as freaked out as I felt.

"My cousin . . . my shoes . . ." She trailed off, looking like she was going to cry. I'd never seen a zombie cry before, and it was completely unnerving.

"Desino!" I screamed at the zombie that was coming at me from the back porch.

I took Shane's hand and threw open the front door. There weren't

137

any zombies on the front lawn, thank God, so I pulled her through and slammed the door behind us.

"Okay, you want your shoes to go to charity. You're positive that's all."

"And . . . I want the police to know that it wasn't an accident." Her voice was small, childlike, and I felt a shiver run up my spine. I'd only had one murdered Unsettled as a kid, but I remembered it well. A six-year-old zombie had crawled from her grave to tell me about the foster father who had abused her into an early grave. I hadn't been able to sleep well for months after.

"Desino! Absisto!" I stopped the two zombies that were coming out the door, and then kicked them back inside while they were still frozen. The toppled over like big, corpsey bowling pins. Jeez! I wished I had a key so I could lock the door from the outside!

"What happened? Who was it?" I asked as I pulled her toward the mailbox

"My older sister. She ground up nuts and put them in the milk shake she made for me after I had my tonsils out."

"I'm sorry, I don't understand." The zombies were starting to come around the side of the house. *"Desino! Absisto!"* Crap! How much longer could this go on before one of our neighbors came out to see what was up? The houses were pretty far apart in our neighborhood but not *that* far. Even if we survived almost certain zombie death and managed to find the freak who'd called me before she spilled our secret, we *still* might have to flee the state.

"Hurry, Shane, explain to me! I want to help you, but you have to hurry!"

"I'm deathly allergic to nuts. My sister knew that when she put those walnuts in there. She wanted to get rid of me so that all of my grandmother's inheritance would go to her and she wouldn't have to share. She was going to inherit a million dollars already," Shane sobbed, swiping a hand across her nose. "I don't know why that wasn't enough."

"*Desino! Absisto!*" I hated to interrupt her, but there *were* zombies getting uncomfortably close.

"I think she might have been sorry after. She came and cried by my bed when I was in a coma . . . but it was too late." Shane was shivering and brought a hand up to her mouth and began chewing on her already ravaged nails. There was no doubt in my mind she was naturally Unsettled. She looked like she'd done the dirty work of getting out of her grave, and if a murderous sister wasn't enough to pull you from your eternal rest, I didn't know what was.

Still, the girl on the phone must have somehow gotten to Shane between her grave and our house and used Shane as her latest evil "experiment." That was what she'd said; I remembered it now—that she loved playing with the dead and that experimenting was so much fun. That. Witch. If I hadn't wanted her to pay before, I certainly did now. Messing with some poor, tortured soul who had been murdered was just . . . evil.

I wished I had the time or the heart to question Shane about what said evil girl looked like, but I didn't. The zombies had figured out where I'd run to and were closing in fast. There was no way I'd be able to hold them off for much longer. I didn't have a second to spare.

"*Desino!* Don't worry, Shane. I'll make sure your sister doesn't get away with this," I said, smoothing a piece of dirty blond hair out of her face.

She was younger than I'd thought at first, probably no more than thirteen. I was only three years older, but I felt almost motherly at that moment—I wanted to comfort her, and I also wanted to make sure her sister rotted in prison for the rest of her life.

"Thanks." She smiled and threw her arms around me for a hug. For once, I didn't mind the smell of death because the gratitude in her eyes was as real and alive as anything I'd ever seen.

"Just go get some rest." I touched her forehead lightly. "Rest in peace, Shane."

Seconds later, she dashed away, disappearing down the street with preternatural speed. I spun to check out the zombies, who were still approaching at *Night of the Living Dead* shuffle speed across the yard. With. No. Sign. Of. Stopping.

My guess had been wrong, and now I was going to die before I could keep my promise to Shane, before I could tell my parents I loved them one last time, before—

No! Hell, no. I wasn't going down yet, not before I at least gave my last resort a try. I traced the circular pattern for the flame spell in the air with as much confidence as I could, then forced my power out across the yard as I screamed the command. *"Exuro!"* I gasped as I was knocked off my feet by the force of the magic coursing through me, but I kept my hands directed at the approaching clones, praying this was going to work.

Seconds later, my prayer was answered . . . a little more thoroughly than I'd expected.

"Whoa!" I scrambled back into the street as the grass near my feet burst into flame, my head spinning dizzily from the amount of power

I'd used. Not only had the Shane clones gone up like a crack-house mattress, so had the grass, the oak tree in the front yard, and part of the wooden door to our garage.

Oh. Smack. This was bad. This was very bad.

"Megan!" My mom and dad came running around the side of the house, but my relief at seeing them alive was short-lived. Mom gaped at the fire and then at me, looking like she was going to bust an artery or something.

And that was before the Settlers' Affairs ambulances pulled up the street.

Several Settlers of the Elder variety jumped out, staring at the lawn in abject horror before whipping out cell phones. They were too busy running damage control to pay much attention to me, but I knew my respite from a major crackdown wouldn't last long. I saw the looks they were shooting my way. No matter that I'd saved my family and myself, I'd also broken a big, hairy Settler rule.

Executing commands above your station was a super-big no-no. Probably because it led to things like this.

• • •

"Mom, please, can't we just—"

"No, we can't. This is not debatable, Megan." Mom sighed as she pulled to the side of the smooth black pavement that wound through the Hidden Hills Cemetery, the swankiest cemetery in Little Rock. Midnight on a school night or not, I still had to seal Shane's grave, so here we were.

Shane hadn't lived in Carol but in a posh section of the capital. Still, for some reason, she'd booked it the forty miles up to my house instead of going to one of the Settler teens in her area. I assumed it was because the person who had cloned her had directed her my way, though neither Mom nor the Elders would tell me anything.

Well, Mom had spilled a little. She'd told me the person who sent Shane must have suspected she was murdered because only a soul with that kind of burden had the psychic energy needed to make a batch of clones. She'd also said that only someone very dangerous—translate, someone crazy deep into the black arts—would be able to pull off such an intricate spell. Unfortunately, after that, the Elders had pulled Mom aside and she'd refused to tell me anything else.

Except that I would be going to SA headquarters for an official review tomorrow after school, which was *so* not good news.

I'd never personally known anyone who'd gone up for review, but I'd heard stories. Sometimes all you got was a major chewing out, but sometimes reviewed Settlers just disappeared.

"Mom, please," I begged one last time. "At least tell me if using the flame command is the only thing I'm in trouble for. I'm your only child—don't you want me to be prepared to defend myself?" If even the classic only-child argument didn't work, I was screwed.

"No, Megan, I'm sorry. I can't."

I was screwed.

"Okay. Fine." But it wasn't fine—not fine at all.

"Honey, you're not going to have to defend yourself. You didn't do anything wrong, you—" She broke off, digging her fingers into her temples in a way that left no doubt this night had given her a migraine. "You *did* do something wrong, but I'm glad you did, even though you could have seriously hurt yourself if the Elders hadn't been there to help you deactivate the spell. Still, I'm glad you're alive and safe, and I'm going to do my best to keep you that way."

"Then why won't you—"

"I just can't tell you anything more about the review. If they use a lie-detector charm, I don't want you to fail because I said things I was told not to."

A lie-detector charm? Why would they work a lie-detector charm? Did they think I was lying about the phone call and the death threat? Or about how I learned the flame spell? Or maybe it was something totally unrelated to tonight. Maybe I—

Headlights suddenly cut through the darkness behind us. I tensed for a second, wondering if maybe the person who'd raised the zombies had decided to come after me personally when Mom's cell rang.

"Yes, that's us. Thanks for coming." She snapped the phone shut and turned to me. "I asked Ethan to meet us. I wanted to make sure you had a manifesting third-stager around for protection just in case."

"Oh, thanks," I mumbled, wondering where my bodyguard had been when I *really* needed him.

"Don't give him a hard time," Mom said as Ethan pulled up and parked behind us. "I can tell he feels horrible that he wasn't there tonight."

"Well, he *should* feel horrible. It was his job to guard me, right?"

"Yes, it was, but it's also his job to get an education so he'll have something to fall back on when his active Settling days are over. He has a huge test tomorrow and needed to study, so I told him I could handle watching you for the evening." Uh-oh, now Mom was pissed; she was getting her militant voice on. "If you want to blame someone, blame me. But I thought you of all people would understand that

Settlers have more going on with their lives than their responsibilities to the dead."

And now *I* was getting pissed. "Yeah, I do understand. I didn't even want to be a Settler again, let alone start learning third-stage stuff, but I didn't have a choice. It's not fair that I'm getting in trouble for trying to defend myself!"

"Well, no one said life was fair," Mom yelled.

"Thanks, Mom. You know, someone almost killed me tonight," I yelled back as I opened the door to the car. "But you're right, don't cut me any slack. I'll just go settle this grave and we can go home to the house I ruined because I'm sure you're pissed at me for that too!"

"Megan—"

"Whatever!" I slammed out of the car and stormed up and over the hill toward the older family plots without even checking to see if Ethan was following me. I didn't want to look at him or Mom or anyone else right now. Not when I was seconds away from bawling my eyes out.

How could the night have ended like this? I couldn't believe *I* was the one in trouble. I'd just received a death threat! It wasn't just unfair, it was cruel, and it made me feel more alone than I ever had in my life. Like I didn't have anyone on my side, no one I could trust.

Dammit! I *was* crying by the time I reached Shane's grave. I just couldn't hold it in.

"Don't cry, Schmeg." Ethan's voice was as soft as the hands he laid on my shoulders. Hands I shrugged off with a violent twist.

"Don't." I pawed through the pockets of my jeans, searching for the safety pin I'd shoved in there before leaving the house.

"Listen, I'm sorry. You don't know how sorry."

Argh! I couldn't find the freaking pin anywhere. "Do you have a needle I could use?"

"Yeah, and I'll give it to you as soon as you let me apologize," he said, his voice sounding weird.

I turned to look at him and knew immediately I wasn't really mad. I couldn't be, not when he looked so devastated. I could tell he was thinking he'd failed me, just like he'd failed that night five years ago.

Seeing him so sad and vulnerable looking made my heart flip over and my throat get tight. I suddenly realized I didn't want to yell at Ethan. What I really wanted, what I'd been dying for since I knew my family was safe from the clones, was a hug. And not just any hug—an Ethan hug.

I fell into him and started crying even harder, but he just wrapped his arms around me and held on tight. I buried my face in his chest and snotted all over his sweatshirt while he whispered things I couldn't really understand into the top of my hair. I don't know how long we stood there, but finally I calmed down enough to realize that—for the first time all night—I felt safe and . . . right.

In fact, nothing had ever felt as right. Nothing in my entire life.

"I promise I won't let anyone hurt you again," he said, his hand under my chin, tilting my face up to his. Before I could think what to say or wonder if I had snot dripping out of my nose, his lips were on mine and we were kissing.

Really kissing, not big brother–little sister kissing.

It was even more amazing than I'd thought it would be. Little explosions went off all the way down my spine and I got so dizzy I knew I would fall if he let me go. But I could tell he wasn't going to let me go, not anytime soon. The kiss to end all kisses was only getting more intense and showing no signs of stopping.

I found my arms around Ethan's neck without remembering putting them there. Then one of his hands was in my hair, pulling me closer and closer. Oh. God. French kissing had never been like this, never made me feel like I was becoming part of the other person, like somehow we'd become connected in a way far more intense than—

A scream suddenly interrupted both my thoughts and the kiss.

Ethan jumped away from me so fast I stumbled, but I didn't fall. Good thing too because whoever it was screamed again, louder and closer. Then Ethan and I were running across the cemetery, following a girl being chased by a Reanimated Corpse. A girl who looked a hell of a lot like Monica Parsons.

CHAPTER 12

The big buzz at school Thursday morning was all about football. Or, more specifically, how the hell the Cougars were going to win the homecoming game with *two* senior players out with major injuries. Word in the hall was that Mark Hastings had sustained a concussion when he ran his car off the road and into a tree on the way to pick up a burger last night—which just goes to show you should never give in to late night junk food cravings.

Especially if your brakes have been disabled by a psychopath.

Monica had only agreed to go to the dance with Mark three hours before his accident and seven hours before she was attacked by a Reanimated Corpse in the Hidden Hills Cemetery. It seemed I wasn't the only Settler whose cover was blown or the only Settler who *someone* didn't want at homecoming.

Now even Settlers' Affairs couldn't deny that the person raising these corpses looked like they had some tie to Carol High School, which meant stepped-up security measures on campus. There was one undercover Elder working in the cafeteria and another in the library. Mom had also volunteered to come hang out but had been told to stay home.

She wouldn't qualify to be an Elder even when she was older

because she'd had a kid and passed on her power. And apparently, the Elders were a cliquey bunch of wahoos who didn't want non-Elders or non-Protocol members getting involved in their investigation.

I'd never been so miserable about being right. There was no doubt about it: Someone roaming these very halls had it in for me—and Monica. Or so she would have people believe.

For me, last night was all it took to cement Monica as my prime suspect. There was no denying that her "attack" had been super-fishy. First of all, why had she really been at the Hidden Hills Cemetery? She'd said something about a phone call telling her to go check out a grave that had been tampered with, but hello, she wasn't stupid. Evil, yes—but not stupid. Why would she head out to Hidden Hills because of some weird anonymous phone call without telling SA or calling for backup of some kind?

And why—once she was there and saw the RC coming after her—didn't she banish it? She was nearly a third-stage Settler and surely had the mojo to work a *reverto* spell on a single corpse. So why had she run instead of working the command? She'd said she "just got so scared she forgot the spell," but I, for one, wasn't buying. She'd been studying second-stage stuff since she was twelve, for God's sake.

Besides, everyone knew Monica didn't *experience* fear; she instilled it.

But the weirdest part of the whole thing was: Why had the RC—who'd bitten her on the leg before Ethan made it up the hill—seemed to chill once it had Monica's blood in its mouth? I mean, Ethan had worked the *reverto* spell only a few seconds later, but I didn't think I'd imagined the way the zombie's face had already slackened, as if it was losing its black-magic charge.

Every Settler knew a Reanimated Corpse would go back to its grave once it had a taste of its Maker's blood. Could Monica have been that Maker and tried to kill her own homecoming date and staged the attack simply to cover her ass when she learned the Shane clones hadn't killed me?

Or was I just letting jealousy cloud my perception? There was no denying the way my stomach had dropped when Ethan pulled Monica into his arms after the zombies were gone. He'd looked just as upset as when he'd learned I'd been in danger and just as close to doing more than picking up the bawling Monica and carrying her down the hill to his car.

If I hadn't been following right behind them, would he have been playing tonsil hockey with Monica too? Maybe that was Ethan's response to seeing a girl cry. Maybe our kiss had meant nothing; maybe—

No. I wasn't going to go there. I did my best to banish all angst-ridden thoughts as I headed into the girls' restroom to see if I could do *something* with my hair before lunch.

I'd let it air dry this morning and it was now a mass of frizzy, 1980s-perm-gone-awry waves. Yikes. Maybe I should have skipped the extra sleep and opted for some blow-drying time instead, no matter how wiped I was after being up until two.

"Nice look, Megan." This evil pronouncement was accompanied by a snort that made it clear my look was anything but nice.

"Thanks, Monica," I said in my sweetest voice as I twisted my hair up into a bun and jabbed a couple of number two pencils through it to hold it in place.

Evidently the fact that we'd both been "attacked" last night didn't mean we were going to be new BFFs. Fine with me. Her getting bit by an RC didn't make me like her any more than I did yesterday.

In fact, I would have gone ahead and accused her of being the one behind all this . . . if a part of me wasn't scared to death of her. Not only was she the Monicster, she was a very powerful Settler, two years older than me and completely out of her gourd if she'd been raising zombies with black magic. I had to tread carefully and only play my hand when I had irrefutable proof—and hopefully several large, scary Protocol officers for backup.

"I was so beat I didn't have time to fix it. I'm so glad you still think it looks okay."

"Whatever." She rolled her eyes, making it clear how frustrating she found people who didn't get her sarcasm. Ha! Disarmed by my niceness. Now to see if I could get any information to solidify my case.

"Sorry to hear about Mark. Bad for the team and for you."

"It's not like we were going to beat Danderville anyway," she said, showing a decided lack of school spirit for someone who was cocaptain of the pom squad as she stalked across the bathroom, peeking under the doors of the stalls.

"You're probably right. Still, I—"

"What the hell are you trying to do? Make sure I get relocated too?" Monica turned back to me with a hiss. "There could have been someone in here."

"Sorry. I didn't say anything about the graveyard or—"

"Damn right you didn't, and you're not going to say anything now." She closed the distance between us, getting close enough I would have backed away if the sink weren't right behind me. "You might be fooling the Elders, but I'm not buying the innocent act, Megan."

"Innocent act?" I asked, totally dumbfounded. "What are you talking about?"

"Really, it's pathetic," she said, smiling as she backed away, giving me a slow, assessing up-and-down look, making clear just how pitiable I was. "I mean, are you that desperate for Ethan's attention? That you have to keep staging attacks on yourself?"

What?! "That's ridiculous, Monica, and you know it." *You're the attack stager,* I wanted to add, but didn't. She was close enough to claw my eyes out, and those nails looked very, *very* sharp.

"All I know is that you're going for a review this afternoon and I'm not."

"So what? That's because I used a third-stage command, not—"

"Right, sure you did. And you've been back on Settler duty for how long?" She laughed and stepped up to the mirror next to mine, checking her black-like-her-soul eyeliner. "You should just understand one thing. Whether you show up at school tomorrow or not, there's no way you'll have a chance to sic any of your little friends on me again."

I tried to laugh but couldn't. This just wasn't funny. "Strange you call them *my* friends, Monica. I was pretty sure that RC at the cemetery last night was something you cooked up."

I could at least accuse her of that, though I'd have loved to accuse her of a lot more.

"I don't need to do things like that to get attention." She whipped a lipstick from her purse and applied a smooth coat of gloss. "The Elders know it, and so does Ethan. He told me last night he'll be making sure I'm safe from now on."

"Of course he will. He's with Protocol and—"

"It's a little more . . . personal than that." Monica smiled and turned to face me, the triumph in her expression making me want to wring her neck. "You're going to need to find another date to the dance, assuming you're not in SA custody before then. Ethan will be taking me."

She wasn't lying—I could tell from the smug smile curling her evil lips. "Fine, so he'll be your fake boyfriend instead of mine. I couldn't care less." I shrugged, hoping I had done a decent job of concealing my surprise . . . not to mention my hurt.

How could Ethan have let me find this out from the Monicster? Didn't he think he should tell me he'd been reassigned himself?

"Fake boyfriend?" She laughed again. "There was nothing fake about what happened when he took me home last night. It was just like old times."

My mouth dropped open. I couldn't help myself, even though I regretted showing my shock the second Monica's eyes lit up in victory. That was what had been niggling at my brain in the locker room the other day. Five years ago, after Monica helped me banish the zombies, I'd tried to thank her. But she'd told me to thank her boyfriend. She said if they hadn't stayed behind to make out in the woods before the second-stage ceremony, they never would have heard me scream.

Her boyfriend's name? Ethan.

God! How could I have been so stupid?

Before I could think of a way to salvage what was left of my pride, she was heading toward the door, throwing her parting shot over her shoulder. "And remember—don't count your pompoms before those names go up on the gym wall Saturday morning."

Oh. My. God. She *didn't* just act like I wasn't a shoo-in for the team. Even distracted by murdering zombies, my crush on Ethan, and a dozen other things, I'd still learned the routines yesterday faster than anyone. *And* I'd danced them as well as, if not better than, the seniors running the clinic. So if Monica was insinuating I might not make the squad, she had to be planning something sneaky and underhanded.

Now I just had to find out if it was average senior-girl sneaky and underhanded or if she really was the one who'd tried to kill me. And if she'd have the guts to try again while a Protocol officer was tailing her every move.

My life was just getting more and more complicated, not to mention dangerous. And now it looked like I didn't even have a bodyguard anymore. If I hadn't been so upset, I would have tried to call Ethan during lunch to get his version of the story. But I didn't. I figured I'd find out the truth this afternoon.

If I went outside after pom clinic and he was still waiting to give me a ride to SA headquarters for my review, I'd know Monica was lying. If not . . . I'd deal with it. I *had* to deal with it and stay focused on exposing Monica or whoever else was raising murderous corpses. My life could depend on it.

· · ·

"Thank God you're finally here! Where were you?" Jess pulled me inside the house without even saying hi. Despite the fact that she hadn't even raised her voice, I knew she was pissed.

"I'm so sorry. I had to run by Del's to drop off her homework."

"You were at Del's all this time?" Jess asked, shooting me a strange look.

"No, I just stopped by really quickly." *Long enough to see that*

Del was clearly sick and not up for raising zombies, I mentally added. "Then I got stuck at my mom's work. She said she had to go get this one little thing, and that turned into two things, then three," I said as I bent over to take off my shoes, finding it easier to lie when I wasn't looking Jess in the face. "We just got home ten minutes ago, and I grabbed my stuff and came right over."

"Don't take off your shoes. We should practice in what we're going to wear for tryouts."

"But won't Clara have a meltdown?" I asked in a whisper, just in case her stepmom was nearby.

Clara was actually very cool about most things, but she was a total neat freak. She'd burst into tears one time when Jess and I spilled a bag of Doritos on the couch in the living room and hadn't stopped even after we'd picked them all up and vacuumed the area twice. Jess had said she was still crying an hour and a half later when her dad got home from work. I mean, I understand cleanliness is a virtue and all that, but Clara definitely had issues.

"No, I promised her I'd pay for the carpet cleaners to come do my room next month out of my allowance." Jess rolled her eyes and tugged me up the stairs, obviously not in the mood to talk about her stepmom.

Clara was the one person in the world who could get under Jess's skin. It was a shame she was forced to live with the woman until she was eighteen. Jess's bio mom had run off when she was still a little kid, a fact I knew had really messed her up for a while, even though she refused to talk about it. When we were in middle school, she'd cry every time we watched a movie that had anything to do with moms and daughters. Even *Dumbo* would make her totally lose it. And that wasn't even about people.

"So did you get a copy of the tryout CD they made?" Jess asked as soon as we were safely ensconced in her room, which was kind of like being inside our own giant loft apartment.

Jess's dad, Mr. Thompson, was a psychotically rich investor type and had specially designed this room for his Little Princess when she was ten and started getting really serious about dance. One corner of the massive space was totally devoted to her passion, with full-length mirrors on the wall and a dance bar and everything. Her sound system made the one we used at the Dance Zone seem positively ghetto.

"Yeah, I did, but when I put it in my mom's car, it was blank." I plopped down on the thick carpet to stretch. "Monica is totally trying to keep me off the squad."

And probably trying to kill me.

The list of things I couldn't tell my best friend was getting way too long for my personal comfort.

"That witch! I hate her," Jess said, and for once I really believed she hated someone. Of course, pom squad was the one thing that Jess was super-serious about and had been since we were tiny. It was natural that anything or anyone getting in the way of our dream would drive her crazy. It would have been driving me crazy too . . . if I didn't have so many other things on my mind.

The review hadn't gone as badly as I'd anticipated, but it hadn't gone really well either. The Elders hadn't reprimanded me for using a third-stage command. In fact, they'd been positively thrilled about how powerfully I was manifesting, certain I was going to be something really special in the Settler world.

I, of course, wasn't so thrilled. Especially when I heard about some of their plans for me, plans that involved special training camps in the summer that would put me on the fast track to an Enforcement career straight out of high school. Enforcement was so *not* my idea of the world's most perfect job. If Protocol were the police of the Settler world, Enforcement were the FBI. It was a scary, difficult, dangerous career, and I wasn't into any of those things.

Considering SA had shelled out the cash to resod our lawn and fix our garage door in the middle of the night so none of our neighbors would see the results of the fire, however, I wasn't in a position to argue with the Elders at the moment.

Even if I hadn't caused a major cover-up situation, they actually believed *I* was to blame for the clones. They thought my overabundance of power had negatively interacted with the energy of a murder victim or something lame like that. No matter how many times I told them about the threatening phone call, they seemed unimpressed.

They believed someone at my school had been raising corpses through black magic, but they were convinced the clone situation was unrelated because no teenager could complete such a complicated voodoo spell. Ethan had helped confirm this theory because he'd drawn an Unsettled during the day when we were training together. Even close contact with my power was enough to up his power, something SA had never heard of.

The Elders thought this was really cool . . . and really dangerous. Nothing had been decided yet, but there had been talk of security.

Like, big-time security, not a junior Protocol officer like Ethan.

My mom and I had been followed by one large, intimidating Enforcer guy all afternoon, and there was talk of adding two or three more to Megan detail. Like the one guy wasn't bad enough. Barker was freaky, and it gave me the creeps to even sit in the same car with him.

He was the one who had dropped me off a block from Jess's house and who would be waiting to escort me back home—where he would also be staying—after we were finished practicing for tryouts. Until SA decided what to do with me, tall, dark, and scary would be *living* with us.

The situation sucked. Especially because I couldn't stop thinking about what it would be like if it was Ethan in our guest room instead of the Enforcer thug.

"Hey, I got the music from London, so we're good to go. It's okay—don't look so sad," Jess said, laying a hand on my leg as she leaned deeper into her stretch.

"Thanks. Good thinking." I tried to smile, but it was so hard. All I could seem to think about was Ethan. How he'd testified about his daytime Unsettled without even looking at me. How he'd rushed from headquarters without saying hi and jumped into Monica's car, looking positively thrilled with his new assignment. I'd been upgraded to Enforcer thug bodyguard, so Monica had my Ethan as her bodyguard.

Not your *Ethan. He made that clear.*

Even if Monica was lying about whatever had happened on her porch, Ethan was obviously not into me. If he were, he would have called, text-messaged or . . . *something* to let me know that the thing with the Monicster was just an assignment and that the kiss last night had been more than a reaction to a stressful situation.

But he hadn't. And he wouldn't and I'd probably never kiss him ever again.

"Megan, are you crying?" Jess asked, grabbing my hand.

"No, no, I'm just . . . stressed." I sniffed, forcing myself to swallow past the lump in my throat. I would not let Ethan make me cry. I had to hold it together. "Mrs. Pierce was giving me a hard time today, and Monica's being a jerk, and . . . other stuff."

"What other stuff?" Jess waited a few seconds while I tried to figure out what I could tell her that wouldn't break Settler secrecy. "Come on, Meg, you know you can tell me anything, right?"

"I . . . " No, I couldn't tell her anything! I wished I could, but I couldn't. "I swear, it's nothing. I'm overreacting."

"Okay," Jess said, sounding like she didn't believe me. "Well, let's get started. I told Kyle I'd call him after we were done, so we've only got about an hour. Otherwise Clara will crack down with her phone curfew and I won't be able to call until tomorrow."

"She's so weird with the phone stuff. I mean, you're almost sixteen years old—you should be able to talk on the phone after nine o'clock. The way she checks the cell phone records to make sure you're not calling after phone curfew is just weird."

"I know! She's such a freak." Jess went off on a tirade, like I'd known she would, saving me from any further best-friend prodding about my fragile emotional state.

Still, I felt awful the entire time we were practicing. Jess had been a great friend to me for, like, forever. If I couldn't tell her about the Settler stuff, who could I tell? Maybe once all this craziness was over, I'd find a way to break the news—after swearing her to secrecy, of course. It would be so nice to have someone normal to talk to about all the weird undead drama.

"So what do you think? You ready for tomorrow?" Jess asked, still breathing hard after our third time through our final routine.

"As ready as I'll ever be. If we practice any more, I'll be dead." I collapsed on the floor with a sigh, the room spinning around me. All the late nights were catching up with me. I'd never felt so wiped at the end of a dance practice.

Jess laughed and flopped down next to me. "Make sure you get some rest tonight. Don't stay up until midnight talking to your man or whatever you've been doing that's making you fall asleep in English."

"Right. About that," I said, squeezing my eyes closed as I realized I had to break the news about my lack of homecoming date to Jess. I'd totally forgotten I'd said we'd double with her and Kyle! "It turns out I won't be going to the dance tomorrow night."

"What?" she asked, eyes round. "Why?"

"Ethan and I broke up." Crap. The words hurt so much it was like they were true.

"Oh no! God, Megan, I'm so sorry." She leaned over and enveloped me in a fierce hug, her obvious empathy only making me feel worse. "That's awful. What a jerk! The *day* before homecoming, too!"

"Yeah, pretty jerky." I sighed, knowing *I* was the real jerk.

"Listen, I'll cancel with Kyle and we'll stay home and veg as planned," she said, proving she was the best friend ever. But I couldn't let her make that sacrifice.

"No way. You've got to go—to report on Ethan for me if nothing else. He's going to take Monica to the dance instead of me."

"What!" Jess screeched, practically shattering something in my inner ear with her outrage. "Ethan dumped you for Monica? What the hell is wrong with him?"

"I guess he likes older, more popular girls."

"Older, more horrible girls is more like it." Jess slammed her hand down on the carpet. "This is awful. He can't take her! He just can't!"

"Apparently he can. And today I saw them out driving together in her car."

"No, this can't happen," Jess said, bouncing up to stalk around the dance space. She was as pissed as I'd ever seen her in our four years of friendship. "We've got to keep this from happening."

"No, it's okay, it's—"

"No, it's not okay. They're both awful," Jess said, turning flashing blue eyes to mine. "This is what you were so upset about before, wasn't it? What you weren't going to tell me about?"

"Yeah, I guess."

"Why weren't you going to tell me? I tell you everything, Megan." She paused, sucking in a big breath before dropping her gaze to the floor. "It really hurts my feelings that you weren't going to say anything."

"I'm sorry, Jess. Really, I—"

"Listen, I've got to call Kyle for real now, okay? I mean, if we're not doubling with you and Ethan, we're going to have to find another ride. He doesn't get his new car until graduation."

"Okay." I stood up and grabbed my dance bag, feeling like the lowest form of scum on the earth. "You aren't mad at me, are you?"

She crossed her arms, making me wait a horrible moment. "No, I'm just . . . sad, that's all. It'll be fine. Just talk to me next time, okay?"

"I totally will, I swear," I said, giving her a hug before heading to the door of her room.

I felt awful as I trudged to the dark car where Barker was waiting. If I wasn't careful, I was going to lose my best friend.

CHAPTER 13

I'd just made it back to my house and was sneaking a Dr. Pepper from the fridge—because I still had to study for a stupid *Macbeth* quiz and needed the caffeine—when the phone rang. I pounced on the kitchen cordless, answering before the ringing woke my parents. After our crazy time last night, they'd gone to bed at like seven thirty, right when I was leaving to go to Jess's house with Barker.

"Hello?" I whispered, highly conscious of said bodyguard.

As far as I knew, he was getting ready for bed, but I wouldn't have been surprised if he'd been given leave to monitor my phone time. My parents were all about giving other people control over my life—especially people who were supposed to keep me from setting anything else on fire.

"Megan, is that you?"

"Yeah, it's me. What's up?" It was Jess, which made me smile. She was probably risking an after-nine-o'clock phone call to tell me that she loved me and that we were still BFFs.

"Why are you whispering?"

"I'm in the kitchen and my parents are asleep. They had a rough time last night," I said, hoping Jess wouldn't ask me why they'd had a rough time, because I was so done with lies right now.

"Okay, well . . . jeez, I didn't think they'd be asleep already. Maybe I shouldn't have called."

"Why? What's wrong?"

"Well, I . . . I called Kyle after you left. Right?"

"Right."

"And I was telling him that Ethan was going to the dance with Monica."

"Yeah." There was nothing fake about how upset hearing Ethan's name made me.

He really *was* an ass. He'd had all day to call and at least leave a message on our home machine saying he was sorry for not telling me about his transfer personally, but he hadn't. It was now nine thirty, and he apparently hadn't been able to spare a single second in his busy, Monica-protecting schedule to pick up the phone. It hurt. Badly. I'd thought we were friends at the very least, if not on our way to being something more.

"Well, so I told him I couldn't believe Ethan had done that to you, and Kyle told me I *shouldn't* believe it because he was at the senior bonfire, and Ethan and Monica were there too, but . . ." She paused again, and it was all I could do not to freak out and beg her to talk faster.

"But what?"

"Well, he said they were fighting and not looking at all like a happy couple," Jess said, getting excited. "And that Monica stomped off into the woods after Ethan said something about you."

"What about me?" I asked, hope making me suck in a breath and hold it.

"I don't know. Kyle said he couldn't hear."

My breath whooshed out. "Oh. Well, I—"

"But he said Monica got in her car and left just a few minutes ago," Jess said, like this was the best news she'd heard all year. Maybe it was just my lack of sleep, but I didn't get what she was so jazzed about.

"So?"

"So! Ethan was still there, hanging out with London and some other people." Jess sighed, clearly frustrated by my lack of imagination. "If your parents were still awake, I was going to tell you to make them drive you out there and talk to him, see if you guys could make up so we can still go to the dance together. They're having the bonfire down the road from the old Carlisle farm and that's only like five minutes from your house."

A five-minute drive, but at least a fifteen-minute bike ride at top speed. Still, it was only nine thirty. My school-night curfew was usually ten, sometimes ten thirty or eleven on special occasions. I could be there by nine forty-five, talk to Ethan, and then be back by—

"No, I can't," I said, mentally shaking some sense into myself. "My parents are asleep and I would feel awful waking them to ask for a ride."

And my bodyguard would never let me out of the house to go make a visit to the small-town Protocol officer he'd replaced. I could tell already that Barker thought he was way too cool for Arkansas. He'd flown in from Missouri this morning to help the Elders deal with their problem child since Arkansas didn't have any full-time Enforcement people working in the state. Our population was too small to warrant such a presence—until my special situation. Wasn't I soooo lucky?

"Yeah, you're probably right. I mean, you can always talk to him tomorrow . . . though by then he and Monica might have made up," Jess said, sounding bummed. "But so what, right? I mean, he's a jerk for dumping you to go with her in the first place and—"

"Well, he didn't exactly dump me," I blurted out before I could talk myself out of it. I needed to tell Jess at least part of the truth or I was going to bust something. "Monica was the one who told me about the change of plans."

"What! Are you nuts, Megan? Why would you ever believe something that—"

"Ethan didn't call me to say it wasn't true! And I saw him earlier and he totally ignored me. So I figured Monica was being straight with me for once."

"No way—there must be some other explanation. You've got to go to him!" She sounded like a character from some sweeping epic set on the prairie.

"You've started reading romance novels again, haven't you?"

"I never stopped reading them—I just told you I did so you'd quit making fun of me." She laughed and I laughed with her, even as a rush of adrenaline dumped into my bloodstream.

I couldn't really sneak out of the house and crash the senior homecoming bonfire. Could I? But how could I *not* when my entire romantic future could be at stake? What if Monica had told Ethan some sort of lie too? Maybe that was why he hadn't talked to me all day. That had to be it!

"Okay, I'm going to go," I said, tiptoeing to the garage door before I could chicken out. A peek outside revealed the garage door was still open, so no one would hear me when I fetched my bike and hit the road. I threw on my jacket and searched my backpack for my phone. "But I'm taking my cell, so you have to promise to call Kyle and let him know I'm coming so he can call you if it looks like Ethan is going to leave before I get there. Then you can text me so—"

"No way—I'll call Kyle and make sure he keeps Ethan there for at least five more minutes."

"Fifteen more minutes. I'm not going to ask for a ride. I figure I can bike there almost as fast," I said, stepping out into the garage.

"Perfect!"

"Okay, so I'm going, in my dance clothes because I don't have time to change, but—"

"That's fine; you look hot in those black dance pants. Just be careful, okay?" Jess sounded a little worried now that she'd convinced me to go. "It's really dark on that road by the Carlisle farm, and you know the old man who lives there likes to shoot at people sometimes."

"I'll be prepared to duck bullets."

"And pull over if a car is coming so you don't get run over. I know a lot of the seniors are drinking tonight, so—"

"Don't worry," I said, getting a brainstorm. "I'll take Clint Street and then cut through Perkins Park to get to the other side of Carlisle's place. It'll be faster anyway."

"But what if there's some creepy homeless person—"

"We live in Carol, Arkansas, Jess. When was the last time you saw any homeless person, let alone a creepy one?" I laughed, and I could hear her giggle softly on her end of the line. "Okay, I've got to get off the phone now. Remember, call the cell if you need to give me an update."

"Will do. Go get your man, Megan Berry!"

"Right, okay, bye," I said, grinning like an idiot even though Ethan was hardly "my man."

At least, he wasn't yet.

* * *

God, but it was creepy riding my bike through the blackness at the end of Clint Street. The dense trees on either side of the road made it so dark I was forced to turn on my little bike headlight, which in turn made me certain I was going to get shot any second, even though the road was a good half mile behind the farmhouse where Nathaniel Carlisle lived.

Or where we all assumed he still lived. No one had seen or heard from the old man for years—except for the occasional shotgun blast— and the house was completely surrounded by rusted old cars from the '50s and '60s. Rumor had it that Carlisle didn't even have electricity, that he used candles for light and an old woodstove for heat because he hated other people so very, very much.

So very much he was willing to risk murdering them by *shooting* at them. My heart raced at the thought, and I pumped even faster.

A few minutes later, after riding so hard I felt like my lungs were going to burst out of my chest and then running my bike through the darkened park—which was kind of spooky even without the homeless people Jess was worried about—I realized the very large flaw in my and Jess's plan. Not only could Ethan have decided to leave before I got to the bonfire, Monica could have decided to *come back.*

"No. Way." I stopped dead at the edge of the crowd of seniors huddled close to the roaring flames, my heart crawling up into my throat and trying to puke itself out onto the leaves beneath my feet.

Monica was back and snuggled up very close to Ethan. *My* Ethan, who didn't look like he was upset with her. At. All. He didn't seem the least bit bothered by the fact that Monica's arm was moving around his waist, or that her hand was sliding up the inside of his sweater, or that her mouth was whispering something into his ear. In fact, he was so non-bothered by all of it that he turned to look down at her, giving her the perfect opportunity to move her mouth to his.

Unholy lip lock, Batman—and then they were kissing. Right in front of me. The night after Ethan had kissed me like my mouth contained the last breath of oxygen left in the world.

Monica finally pulled away and snuggled her cheek into Ethan's arm, a movement that turned her eyes straight toward me. Our eyes connected, but she didn't look the slightest bit shocked to see me. Instead, her victorious expression made it seem like she'd known I was there all along.

I turned around fast, gulping in air as I rolled my bike back toward the park, tears already blurring my vision. A few of the seniors I passed shot me strange looks—including London and Beth, who actually looked kind of sorry for me—but I didn't stop. I couldn't stop or talk to anyone or I was going to embarrass myself by sobbing over Ethan in public. I had to get away—far away.

I pushed my bike across the uneven ground a little faster and within a few minutes had left the glow of the bonfire behind. That was when I started to lose it so badly I actually had to quit walking.

I couldn't believe I'd been such a fool, to think Ethan would want to *talk* to me tonight, let alone tell me I was the one he really wanted. He was obviously very happy to be glued to Monica Parsons' skanky size-two body, and that was fine with me.

I hoped the two of them would be very freaking happy together.

The tears really started pouring now that I was out of hearing range. I didn't want Ethan to be with anyone else. I wanted him to be with me because I wasn't just crushing on him hard-core—I *really* liked him. More than liked him. *Way* more than liked him. Maybe even—

No. I was *not* going to think about that. I sucked in a breath and swiped at my nose, which was running again.

It always ran when I cried. Maybe that was why Ethan had decided he didn't like me. He'd gotten home and seen the snot on his sweatshirt from when I'd blubbered all over him last night and realized Monica was the better option. The prettier, tinier, less snotty option.

Hopefully Barker would be in bed by the time I got home so he wouldn't see what a mess I was. Or catch me sneaking back in. I was out of the house without permission, probably something that could get me in a lot of trouble if I were caught.

Which meant I should get moving.

"Gaaannnnnh." The sound came from the trees in front of me, but it was too dark to see anything clearly. All I got was the vague impression of something thicker and blacker than the rest of the night, with glowing red eyes, rushing at me before I was knocked to the ground.

I tried to scream but couldn't draw a breath. The thing on top of me was too heavy, easily the biggest zombie I'd ever seen. Or felt. I actually still couldn't *see* it, but I could feel its hands closing around my neck, smell the stink of its rotted flesh as it leaned toward my face, and hear the unmistakable groan of a Reanimated Corpse hungry for its first taste of the living.

"*Reverto!*" I forced the word out, spitting it into the face of the zombie who was doing a pretty excellent job of crushing my windpipe.

"Gunh," it groaned as it rolled off of me and crashed away through the park.

I flopped over in the leaves, gasping for breath, little pinpricks of light dancing across my vision. On my hands and knees, I crawled forward, feeling for my bike in the near complete blackness, my heart beating a million miles a minute. I had to get up, had to get back to the bonfire and tell Ethan and Monica what had—

Unless this was Monica's work.

"Gunh!"

"Gahhhnnn, gunh."

"Oh no," I whispered, jumping to my feet so fast the world spun. There were more of them, somewhere out there in the darkness.

Bike forgotten, I stumbled backward until my back hit a tree, then stood absolutely still, holding my breath and doing my best not to make a sound, straining to determine exactly where the groans were coming from. I knew I had to run, but it wouldn't do any good if I ran straight into the path of one of the RCs. No matter how much the terrified part of me wanted to haul ass, I had to be smarter than that. I'd barely squeezed out the *reverto* command last time and—

The *reverto* command! Would it work if I couldn't see where I was aiming the spell? It seemed logical to assume it would . . . except it obviously hadn't banished the rest of the corpses when I'd dispatched the first one.

Which had to mean there were a *lot* of them out there.

Oh. God. There *were* a lot of them. A dozen at least. How had Monica raised so many so fast? She couldn't raise this many corpses all by herself, could she?

Worry about Monica later—get out of here now!

Shuffles and groans came from the darkness ahead of me and from either side. Slowly, as my eyes adjusted to the dark, I began to notice spots of red floating in the blackness. It was their eyes, the glowing red eyes of at least twenty Reanimated Corpses, and those were only the ones I could see. There were probably more behind me, closing in on my location, ready to tear my body apart as they fought for the chance to feed upon my—

Stop it! You've got to think, not scare yourself to death.

Okay, okay. I had to think. Think!

All right, so the *reverto* command was out. It shouldn't have even worked the first time, considering the number of corpses I was dealing with. I could try the flame command, even though I'd already gotten in trouble for that once because, hello, I'd rather be in trouble than dead—but there was a chance that wouldn't work either.

The Elders seemed to think the *exuro* command had only worked so well last night because the zombies were clones and therefore easier to overwhelm with one command. Kind of like burning a bunch of paper dolls that were all connected. It would take more power to burn twenty separate corpses.

But I didn't have much of a choice. I still didn't have the entire *pax frater* spell memorized, even though I'd been working on it during study hall. Besides, I wasn't the type to carry a little dagger around in my wallet like Ethan the Always Prepared.

Even if I'd had one, however, I didn't see how I'd manage to avoid getting eaten by one zombie while I was *pax frater*-ing the other.

So the flame command it was.

I pulled myself together, focusing my power as best I could with the grunts and groans growing closer and closer, and then threw everything I had into the flame command. *"Exuro!"*

The backlash of the spell knocked my head into the tree behind me, making me see stars frolicking through the pillars of flame now lurching through the trees. Yes! I'd torched them good. I was a little wiped from the spell, but it wasn't like I had to engage in serious combat or anything. All I had to do was hurry home and call SA so they could take care of these zombies before they set the park on fire.

I started hauling ass back toward the bonfire, scanning the ground for my bike, realizing too late that there were only ten or twelve burning corpses. The rest of them had made it through the spell unscathed. And now that the area beneath the trees was illuminated by burning zombie flesh, they could see *exactly* where their prey was running.

Five pairs of glowing eyes and rotted hands lunged forward to meet me as I raced through the trees, making me scream bloody murder. But then, who really cared if some non-Settler heard and came to investigate? I had bigger things to worry about at the moment than blowing my cover.

I spun around as fast as I could, sliding on the leaves, my hand dipping down to land in the mud before I managed to reverse direction and start scrambling back toward Clint Street. If I could just get back to civilization, I knew I would feel safer. If I could make it to the gas station, I could run in and get the night clerk to lock the door. Then my family would be relocated for sure, but at least I'd be alive to see my sixteenth birthday.

"Come on, come on," I muttered under my breath as I dashed through the trees, dodging flaming zombies. I spied my bike on the ground but didn't dare stop. I was faster on foot than most Reanimated Corpses, so if I could just keep pulling hard toward the street, I—

I screamed again as two more RCs lurched from the trees in front of me. I skidded to a stop, flailing my arms to get my balance before falling on my ass on the cold, wet ground. *"Exuro!"* I flung the flame command at the two creatures in front of me as I hurried to my feet, but this time nothing happened. I tried again and again, forcing the power out through my fingers no matter how exhausted I was becoming, but the things kept shuffling toward me without so much as a hair on their chins catching flame.

Behind me, I could hear the other corpses getting closer, so I cut to the left, running fast through the trees. I made it over a small hill and was really putting some distance between me and the things behind me when I realized I'd made another big mistake. Possibly a deadly one.

"No!" I smelled the water a few seconds before I splashed into it. The duck pond! I'd totally forgotten it was here, and there wasn't time to go around. I'd just have to try to swim across and hope RCs wouldn't follow.

Indian summer or not, the night temperatures had been getting down in the forties, and the water was frigid. My toes started to numb immediately, but I pushed on as fast as I could go. I was up to my waist, shivering madly despite the adrenaline rushing through my system, when I heard the splashes of first zombies entering the water behind me.

I churned my legs even faster, certain I would make better time walking than swimming since my best stroke was my dog paddle, and that sure didn't get you anywhere very quickly. I pushed myself to move faster and faster, finally getting my arms into the act as the water reached my chest. I swiped cold lake out of my way, completely focused on reaching the beach at the other side . . . when it happened.

Preternaturally strong hands closed around my arm and I went under screaming. My mouth filled with ice-cold fluid and I began to choke, but still I fought, kicking and squirming, finally managing to tear free of the fingers locked around my elbow. I had broken the surface with a gasp, gagging and dizzy from the cold water, struggling to figure out which way I needed to go, when another zombie tackled me from the side.

Teeth tore into the hand I held up to block my face, but I didn't have time to scream this time before I fell under. The zombie, who didn't need to breathe, didn't loosen its hold for a second. It only tore into the flesh of my palm even deeper while another RC grabbed my leg, pulling it to the surface before sinking its teeth into my calf.

Under the cold black water, I cried out in pain, unable to help myself even though I knew I was wasting the last of my air.

There were scarier things than being chased by zombies, I realized—things like knowing you were going to die and that, the next morning on their way to school, all the kids would see what was left of your body floating facedown in the Perkins Park duck pond.

CHAPTER 14

When I woke up, the clock on the wall said it was four in the morning. I was in a beige room, lying on a bed too firm and narrow to be mine. The lights were dimmed, but the night-light across the room was bright enough for me to see my mom curled up in a chair in the corner and my dad stretched on the tile floor near her with his St. Louis Cardinals ball cap over his face. They were both snoring, loudly. I always take my iPod on family vacations where we'll be sharing a hotel room so I can plug my ears and tune out the 'rents because they both cause some major noise.

But at that moment, I didn't want to tune them out. I was just so inexpressibly glad to see them. My throat got tight and I could feel tears pricking at the backs of my eyes.

"Mom? Dad?" My voice was hoarse and scratchy sounding and not very loud, but I guess anxiety had suddenly turned my parents into light sleepers.

"Megan?" Mom vaulted out of the chair and was on her way to me before her eyes even opened all the way. "Honey, are you okay?"

I reached my arms toward her like I used to do when I was tiny and she bent over my bed for a hug. I buried my face in her wonderful, familiar-smelling hair and gave in to the urge to bawl.

Horrible, racking sobs shook my body, making my already achy chest hurt like nobody's business. But I didn't care. I was alive. Somehow, some way, I was *alive.*

I didn't think I'd ever take that fact for granted again.

"Megan, you scared the hell out of your mother and me. What were you doing out by yourself?" Dad was on the other side of my bed, wrapping his arms around me and Mom, sounding like he was about to start crying too.

"I was stupid, so stupid. I'm sorry," I sobbed, not wanting to tell the truth—that I'd gone to the bonfire to see Ethan. I couldn't ever remember feeling so dumb in all my life.

Mom pulled back to look me in the eye. "If Barker hadn't realized you were gone, you would be dead right now, Megan. Do you understand that? Dead." Her eyes were tearing up, and I could tell how hard she was working not to lose it completely. "By the time he got rid of the Reanimated Corpses and pulled you out of the water, you weren't breathing. If he hadn't been there . . . " She let her words trail off, but I'd already gotten the message.

Seemed I owed Barker a really, *really* big thank-you.

"I know. I'm sorry, Mom." My voice was so small, it didn't even seem like it was coming from me.

"Sorry is not going to cover it," she said, the tears starting to fall. "You are never leaving the house by yourself again. Ever. Not even when you go to college, not even when you grow up and get married and have kids of your own."

Then she started blubbering big-time, and so did I, and Dad was stuck there, trying to comfort both of us. Though he'd never been big on Settlers' Affairs as an organization or the Elders as people, he actually looked relieved to see Elder Thomas and Elder Crane at the door to my room.

I was surprised to see them together at first since Elders do their best to pretend they don't know each other in public, but then I looked behind them and saw more bland beige walls. SA headquarters. I should have known I wasn't in a typical hospital, not with zombie bites that would be way difficult to explain to your average doctor.

"She's awake, I see," Elder Thomas said. She was by far my favorite of the Elders, a sweet, grandmotherly type who also happened to be the *only* woman on the Arkansas council at the moment. Big mistake on the council's part. They could really use more members with a softer touch. "Elder Crane, would you go fetch the nurse on duty? I'd like to get Megan checked out as soon as possible."

"Of course." Elder Crane looked irritated to be the one sent away, but since Elder Thomas was seventy years old and outranked him, he had to deal with it.

I, however, was very relieved. If I was going to get reamed, I'd rather hear the consequences of my stupidity from her than anyone else.

"How are you feeling, Megan?" she asked, sitting on my bed once Dad moved out of the way.

"Pretty good, considering." I sniffed mightily and did my best to quit crying.

In addition to the aching in my chest, I had a pretty serious headache, and the bites on my hand and leg were sore, but all in all, I was doing okay. I wasn't hooked up to an IV, so I assumed I hadn't lost a lot of blood.

"You were very lucky," she said, leveling me with her pale blue eyes. "But I'm sure you know that."

"Yes, ma'am." I nodded and did my best to maintain eye contact, though it hurt to see how disappointed Elder Thomas looked. "I'm really, really sorry. I just . . . wasn't thinking."

"Well, the good news is that you're okay," she said, smoothing the beige bedspread. Why was everything at SA headquarters beige? You'd think people privy to a secret paranormal world would be a little more creative. "The better news is that Barker was able to track down the person responsible for these attacks."

So much for the "soft touch" thing. My mouth grew dry and my empty stomach cramped. They'd caught the psychopath. I could hardly believe it.

"Who was it?" I asked before I could control my mouth. Second-stage Settlers who had just caused big trouble didn't go around asking Elders direct questions, but I had to hear her say the words.

Monica Parsons, get ready to pay for your wicked deeds.

"Bethany Phillips, a little girl from right here in town."

What!

She tutted under her breath, obviously grieved by this discovery. "I never thought Carol would breed such a dark heart, especially in one so young."

Bethany Phillips. It took my muddled mind a few minutes to realize that Bethany must be *Beth's* full name. Beth Phillips had been raising the dead! Beth *had* been on my list of suspects, but still . . . the news was shocking.

Sweet Beth with her Barbie-blond hair, the girl who had been voted Best Personality both her sophomore and junior years and who had the intelligence of a sea slug had dipped her hands in the dark arts. Not only dipped them, submerged them. She had to have been practicing for years to be able to work so many complicated rituals in such a short time.

"She's in custody down at the Little Rock headquarters' containment center," Elder Thomas continued. "She'll be given a hearing, but the evidence against her is sufficiently damning. I have no doubt she'll be found guilty by any jury the High Council assembles. Her parents will no doubt be grieved to learn she's disappeared, but in a situation like this, there is little we can do."

I shivered at the reminder that Settlers aren't all sweetness and light and being there for dear, departed souls. SA had been dispensing its own brand of justice to those found guilty of practicing zombie voodoo for thousands of years. If you were using black magic and got on the wrong side of SA, you just disappeared. Forever.

"When Barker got to the graves of the corpses that had attacked you, Beth was still there, Megan. She had bites all over her body and . . . " Mom trailed off, then swallowed hard.

"And there were dolls that looked just like you all over the graveyard," Dad finished for her. "Thirty of them."

"Thirty," I whispered. I knew there had seemed like a lot of RCs in the woods, but *thirty*? That was insane.

"But how did she raise that many corpses in such a short time? Wouldn't she have to be working with someone? I mean, Monica Parsons was there too, and she's been acting really—"

"Megan!" Mom gasped, her eyes going round with shock. She exchanged a quick look with Elder Thomas, who was staring at me as if I'd sprouted a second head. A really ugly, crazy-talking second head. "You're accusing a fellow Settler of black magic. Do you understand how serious that is?"

"I know, Mom, but please hear me out. She was at the cornfield the other night when Beth wasn't, and she had this big bandage on her arm and—"

"I assure you, Monica is innocent of any wrongdoing," Elder Thomas said. "After her history, we were suspicious as well, but a thorough investigation revealed she had neither the time nor the opportunity to stage something of this magnitude."

"Her history?" I asked, even though I knew I was pushing it. Elder Thomas had been strangely tolerant of my questions so far, but my luck had to run out sometime.

She paused, taking a deep breath and folding her hands in her lap. "The business with Miss Parsons was a long time ago, when she wasn't much more than a child. She was reprimanded and learned her lesson. Now she's on her way to being one of our most promising young Settlers."

Promising young Settlers. Right. But she became promising *after* she'd been reprimanded for working black magic. I knew it! I *knew* she was the first Settler to go the way of the wicked. "But what if she hasn't learned her lesson? I know Monica could work the spell; she—"

"The matter is closed, Megan." Elder Thomas pressed her thin lips together, making it clear I had exhausted her limited patience. "Bethany Phillips is to blame and will be punished accordingly."

"But she couldn't have known I was going to be at the bonfire," I said, trying to sound reasonable instead of whiny. "And from the time she saw me at the Carlisle farm to the time I was attacked was only like . . . five minutes, maybe less. Could she have raised that many zombies that fast all by herself?"

"The location of your attack was immaterial. It was simply good luck that you wandered so close to the cemetery where Bethany was raising the corpses, thus giving Barker the opportunity to track the Reanimated Corpses back to their graves and capture her."

Good luck? *Good luck* that I almost died? Elder Thomas was so making her way onto my least-favorite-people list. "So the zombies would have come for me at home if I hadn't snuck out. But Barker would have been there to help stop them," I said, wondering how Barker had managed all those zombies by himself. "Enforcement must know some tricks we normal Settlers don't, I guess?"

Elder Thomas smiled at Mom. "Didn't I tell you she was a natural for Enforcement? A curious mind and a great talent. All she lacks is training and discipline."

And the will to be a creepy Enforcement person, I added silently. If I never ended up in another life-or-death situation, it would be too soon. Enforcement was *not* in my future if I had anything to say about it.

"Bethany has already confessed her plan to kill you, so you don't have to worry about any further attacks." Elder Thomas stood, making space for the nurse who came into the room. "She was deeply in love with a boy who was paying you attention and wished to remove you so that she and the boy could reconcile."

I wrinkled my brow at Elder Thomas but couldn't say anything, as the young, friendly-looking Settler nurse placed a thermometer under my tongue and then started checking my bandages. Josh hadn't even seemed interested in me the past week—not since I allegedly started going out with Ethan. But then, maybe he'd heard about our "breakup" and had said something that spurred Beth's attack tonight.

Maybe she'd been making dolls since the news of my split with Ethan broke at tryouts that afternoon. That would have given her time to get thirty assembled. She couldn't have known I was going to be at the bonfire, but like Elder Thomas said, it was just a case of being in the right place at the right time. Or the wrong place, if you weren't into risking your life to catch a psychopath.

I was safe, I realized as the nurse removed the thermometer and announced me in near perfect health.

It was hard to believe. My mind was still freaked out and on guard, which made me keep asking questions, even though it looked like Elder Thomas might be about to leave my room without issuing any punishment.

"Um, Elder Thomas, did Beth say if she was the one who called me Wednesday night, the one who created those clones?"

"She may have called you, but the council was right about the clones," Mom said, the look she shot me making it clear I should shut up while I was still ahead. "Your power interacted negatively with the murder victim's, that's all. It's something you'll need to work on so it won't happen again. SA is looking into a good tutor—probably someone like Barker, who has experience manifesting at a higher-than-average capacity."

"But then what about Monica's attack? Why was she being chased by an RC if she wasn't Beth's target?" I asked before Elder Thomas could leave.

"It seems Monica was also in the wrong place at the wrong time," Elder Thomas said, finally looking less than amused by my "curious mind." "She was foolish to respond to a prank call without contacting SA first."

"So did Beth call her too? I don't understand." I bit my lip as Elder Thomas sighed.

"The investigation is ongoing, Megan, but be assured you are safe. Beth is in custody, and Barker will be working with the rest of his team to make absolutely certain you aren't a danger to yourself or anyone else while you learn to control your power."

Oh no. Barker and *his team*? That meant I was still on the babysitting list. The big-time babysitting list.

"Barker reported eleven burned corpses in the woods, Megan." Elder Thomas smiled, but her smile wasn't comforting. It was actually kind of creepy and almost greedy looking, like she stood to cash in on the corpses or something totally weird. "That means your power is even greater than we assumed. This is a very exciting time for you and for Carol. We mean to take very good care of you from here on out."

"I guess that means no going anywhere without a bodyguard, huh?" I asked Mom as soon as Elder Thomas left the room.

"You can go to school and back, and that's it. And we're going to be relocated to the compound down by the river for at least a few weeks."

"What? Why?"

"Because you've shown you can't be trusted to follow the rules, Megan," Mom said, sounding irritated despite the fact that she was back on my bed, holding on to my hand like she'd never let me go. "There hasn't been a teenager with your level of power in about seventy years. This is something for the Settler history books. It could mean a lot more funding for Carol's Settlers' Affairs division and Arkansas in general."

So I hadn't been imagining the greedy look. What a jerk Elder Thomas was. She was so not my favorite Elder anymore.

"But," Mom continued, "it's not so great if you make the Elders here look like idiots by nearly getting yourself killed. So we're all going to the compound for a while, until you've proven you can handle yourself and your power. Even Daddy's going to have to go."

"I wouldn't want to be anywhere else but with you two," Dad said.

"Even if they don't let you go to work?" Mom asked. "Once we're in, there's no going in and out. It would draw too much attention. I had to fight to convince them that Megan has to go to school."

"What? That's complete—" Dad then proceeded to cuss colorfully about Settlers' Affairs, the Elders, and the undead in general, until the nurse popped her head in the door again.

"Um, Miss Berry, you've got a visitor. Since he's not family I figured I would ask first."

"Who is it?" Mom asked, obviously ready to take complete control of my life as punishment for the sin of my sneaking out.

"Ethan Daniel. He's with Protocol, I believe."

My mind flashed on an image of Ethan and Monica in front of the fire. It still hurt to think about it, even after the much greater hurt of nearly getting myself killed. "I don't want to see him."

"It could have something to do with the investigation, Megan," Mom said, not sounding as mad at me as she had a moment before.

Somehow, she knew. Knew that I had a crush on Ethan and had been sneaking out to see him and that he totally thought I was a pathetic little kid. And she pitied me for it. For the first time since waking up in a hospital bed, I didn't want to cry—I wanted to scream.

I hated Ethan. For treating me like crap and for making people feel sorry for me. I *hated* people feeling sorry for me more than almost anything.

"I don't care. He's unprofessional. If it has to do with the investigation, ask them to send another Protocol officer. If not, you can tell him I'm not seeing anyone but family." I tried to sound as haughty and disinterested as possible.

Pretty hard to pull off while horizontal and wearing a gown that flapped open in the back and no underwear. Where the hell was my underwear? I wanted it. Now. I was ready to get out of here and away from all things zombie-related. I wanted to go home.

But I couldn't go home, I realized with a sinking feeling in my gut. And neither could Mom or Dad. We were basically being held as prisoner by Settlers' Affairs and destined to be sent to "the compound"—a creepy place down by the Arkansas River that I'd never even wanted to visit, let alone reside at. And all this because I had been a gigantic idiot over a stupid, useless boy.

The person raising RCs had been caught, yet my life was still in the toilet.

But even I didn't realize the true lousiness of my lot until I was preparing to head to school a few hours later.

"Um, there are no dance clothes in here," I said to Mom, digging through the clothes Barker had brought me from home. "Tryouts are right after school."

"Megan, what part of 'to school and back and that's it' don't you understand? You won't be going to tryouts," Mom said, her nose buried in the cup of coffee she was nursing in the corner chair.

"What?" Not going to tryouts! This couldn't be happening. "But what about Jess? We've been working for ages, and our fourth routine won't look right if I'm not there to dance with her and—"

"There are consequences to every action, hon. I'm sorry." And then she stood and walked out of the room. Probably on the way to get more coffee.

If only my ragged soul could be so easily soothed.

I collapsed on the edge of my narrow bed and buried my face in my hands, but I refused to cry. My entire sophomore year was ruined. Tears wouldn't fix that any more than coffee. Nothing could fix it. I was just going to have to learn to live with the fact that one of my biggest high school dreams wasn't going to come true.

After nearly dying, missing my shot at the pom squad shouldn't have bothered me so much. But it did. It was just another thing my Settler powers had taken from me. Another sign that my life was never going to be normal or my future mine to decide. Not ever again.

CHAPTER 15

Quit pouting, Megan. I'm going to lose it if I'm stuck in the house with you for three or four more weeks of this," Mom said, letting her salad fork rattle back into her nearly empty bowl.

We'd been told our time at the compound might be extended if my training didn't progress as quickly as Barker and his team hoped.

Barker's *team* actually only consisted of one other big, scary guy named Smythe—apparently all of the lamo Enforcer dudes thought it was cool to have one-word names, like they were Sting or Bono or something—and a tiny woman with inch-thick glasses who told me to call her Kitty.

Kitty had already put me through my paces for two hours after school, making me practice setting frozen turkeys on fire out on the compound basketball court. After the first forty-five minutes I nailed the flame command and even learned how to snuff out fires once I'd started them. Leaving the RCs burning last night had been a huge drain on my power. That was why I'd lost the ability to torch more of them and been so worn out when I was trying to swim across the duck pond.

That sure would have been good to know before I was nearly killed.

Kitty also told me I probably could have used a single-process *reverto* spell to get rid of the corpses in the woods. It wasn't something they taught most Settlers, but she said that if I concentrated my power on one undead at a time—especially if I was able to lay hands on the RC, as I'd done with the first one who attacked me—I would be able to send them back to their Maker.

A better choice, however, would have been the *pax frater corpus*. Since my power was stronger than your average Settler's, I could conceivably put down a few dozen undead during the first speaking of the spell. All I had to do was start chanting and then focus the spell on one corpse after another with sharp physical contact. Like, say, a grand jeté to the face or a right hook, if I ever discovered my inner Muhammad Ali.

That was what Barker had done to the two zombies who had me trapped in the water—smashed their zombie skulls in while *pax frater*-ing. He'd said it was very therapeutic . . . not that you could tell from looking at him.

The big, scowly faced Enforcer was standing a foot away from my chair practically breathing down my neck. Apparently, losing track of me once had made him determined not to let me out of his sight. The only time I had privacy was in the bathroom. Even at school he'd been lurking in the hallways, under cover as a school security officer.

"Megan, I mean it. Stop pou—"

"I'm not pouting, I'm *chewing*," I said, making no effort to rearrange my face in a way that would be more pleasing to my mother. Tryouts were probably finishing up even as we ate and the seniors settling down to decide who would make the team.

"Fine. *Chew* away. I need some air." Mom shoved away from the table and slammed through the sliding glass door out to our condo's patio.

The four-bedroom condo was actually pretty nice. There were a workout room, a basketball court, and an indoor swimming pool on the premises, and the view of the river was gorgeous. It would have been a great little family vacation if we weren't all being held prisoner.

"She tried to talk to the Elders for you. She was in with Elder Thomas all morning after you went to school, so don't blame your mother for missing those tryouts." Dad sounded as pissed as Mom, making me wonder if maybe they would have been happier if I'd just died in that pond last night so they wouldn't have to deal with me anymore.

Melodramatic much, Megan?

I sighed. "I'm sorry, I just . . . I just don't understand why I couldn't at least try out. It wasn't fair to me or to Jess."

Jess had been furious when I'd told her I wouldn't be at tryouts because I was under house arrest. It was the first time in our friendship that I'd ever seen her so pissed at anyone, let alone me. She'd told me I was a selfish brat who only thought about herself and stormed away, refusing to talk to me for the rest of the day even though *she* was the one who had convinced me to sneak out in the first place.

Okay, so that wasn't really true. She'd wanted me to ask my parents for a ride. It had been my bright idea to head off to the bonfire without asking.

"Megan," Dad said, "you are not like other kids. You never have been and you never will be. That may not be fair, but that's your life. It's time to grow up and get used to it and take responsibility for your own mistakes."

"I know Dad but I—"

"But nothing. Last night was the second time in five years I've almost lost you because you weren't taking your responsibilities as a Settler seriously. My heart can't take much more, and neither can your mother's."

"I'm sorry." Now I really felt bad. I'd never really thought how scary it must have been for my parents to get that call last night.

"Sometimes sorry isn't enough." He sighed and ran his hand through his hair, making me notice how much of it had started to go gray. That was probably all my fault too. "If you're finished with supper, please go to your room. I'll go talk to Mom."

"Okay." Well, at least he had said *please*, even though I could tell he was still mad.

I trudged toward "my" room—the condo's flower-print bedroom only had two twin beds and a child-size vanity for furniture, but at least it had a private bathroom—feeling even lower than I had a few minutes ago. For the first time in my life, I suspected I was on my way to being flat-out depressed. Like, clinically.

Barker tailed me all the way to the door of my room, where Smythe met up with us. Thankfully, however, they let me go inside alone, so I was by myself when my cell began to vibrate in my back pocket.

Jess! Thank. God.

I dashed into the bathroom and turned on the shower before I flipped open the phone, hoping the sound of running water would afford me a little privacy. "Hello?"

"Hey, it's me," Jess said, still sounding weird. But then, I hadn't expected to be forgiven without at least a little more groveling.

"Listen, Jess, I just want to tell you again how sorry I am. I begged my mom to let me try out with you so our fourth routine wouldn't be messed up, but she—"

"Don't worry about it, Meg. Tryouts finished up about twenty minutes ago and I'm pretty sure I made the team. I didn't mess up a single time."

"That's great! I'm so happy for you." And I was, even though I was still feeling rather sad for myself. "Hopefully some day I'll get ungrounded and I can come watch you perform."

"So you're *for sure* grounded?"

"Yeah, for like the rest of my life, probably." I sighed as I plopped down on the fuzzy toilet lid. It was bright pink, like everything else in the bathroom. I *hated* pink. This bathroom was totally adding insult to my injury.

"That really, really sucks." She paused, and I could practically hear the wheels turning. Something was bothering her, but in typical Jess fashion, she wasn't going to come straight out and say it. "But . . . you're at home, right?"

"Um . . . right?" I was such a bad liar. That wasn't supposed to come out as a question!

"Well, since when do your parents let you have people over when you're grounded?"

"What? There's no one—"

"I just saw Monica going into your house on my way home."

"You did?" Holy crap, why would she be sneaking into my house when she knew my entire family had been sent to the SA compound?

"Yes, I did." Jess's voice left no doubt she was *pissed* and thought I was a big, fat liar. "And she not only went in, but she came out and put of bunch of your clothes in her car before going back inside again. Since when are you and the Monicster BFFs? I can't believe you loaned her your stuff, especially that new sundress. You wouldn't even let *me* borrow it."

"She had my clothes?" I asked, a horrible suspicion rising at the back of my mind. There was only one reason she would want my clothes bad enough to break into my house and steal them.

She was going to use them as totems to summon the undead.

"Yes, she did. Will you stop lying to me? I can't believe—"

"I'm not lying—I mean, I don't—I mean—God!"

I'd had enough of this. I had to tell Jess the truth. The words started pouring out of me before I could even think twice, a stream of verbal diarrhea that had obviously been building inside me for a *long* time. Fifteen minutes later Jess finally got a word in edgewise. "So, you raise dead people from their graves?"

"No, I put the dead people back in their graves after they raise themselves," I said. "Well, lately I've also been sending them back to the person who raised them with black magic."

"Black magic? That's like . . . real?" she asked, sounding understandably freaked.

"Yeah, it is . . . and I think Monica is in on what's been going on." It was freaky to say the words out loud, but it was the *only* explanation for her stealing my clothes. "You've got to go spy on her, Jess. My family is being held hostage at this Settler secret hideout. So it's up to you to find out what she's doing in our house and—"

"But she's not there anymore."

"What? I thought you said you—"

"I saw her go in after she dumped the clothes, but then she left about twenty minutes later," she said, sounding bummed that she wasn't going to be going on spy duty. Who would have guessed Jess had an inner secret agent just waiting to burst free?

"Crap," I said, rising to pace around the bathroom. "Did you see which direction she went?"

"Not really. But Megan, if you have this big secret society out there, why don't you just tell someone what I saw? Won't they track Monica down?"

"I don't know." A part of me was tempted to throw open the door and tell Barker all, but I wasn't even sure he'd believe me. "I'm not really high on the trustworthy list right now. And the thing about Monica . . . well, it's complicated." I couldn't tell Jess about Monica being a Settler. Spilling my own secret was one thing, but spilling hers would be wrong.

Even if she's been behind the plot to kill you? Hello? A clue? You need to get one.

"No, I don't think anyone would believe me, Jess. The higher-ups already have someone in custody who they're sure did it. Besides, Monica is a Settler too."

"Wait a second. How many of you guys are there?"

I barreled on, knowing there was no time to play twenty questions. "She was also attacked by a black-magically raised corpse this week. So no one is going to believe she was raising zombies unless I have proof." I quickly filled Jess in on the whole history of Settlers and how there had *never* been a Settler convicted of using black magic and that that was why no one had believed me when I told them I suspected Monica in the first place.

"You're right. No one's going to believe you."

"Thanks." My stomach cramped around my pork chop and couscous.

"But don't worry—I've got an idea. I overheard Monica and London saying they were going to post the results of the tryouts tonight before they go to London's to get ready for the dance."

"What about the game? Don't they have to—"

"The game got called off because Danderville had a bomb threat today."

"Oh, that's lame," I said, for a weird—and rather nice—moment feeling like an average teen having an average conversation with her best friend. "So they're posting the tryout results early. So what?"

"Well, they said they were going to post them on the door of that church that's back in the woods across the street from the football field."

"The haunted one on the Carlisle farm? Did someone miss the memo that the old dude is nuts and shoots people?" I asked, shivering as I recalled my bike ride last night. Even being near the edge of that farm had given me the heebs, big-time.

"Yeah, well, I guess they don't care. They're going to make all the sophomores hike through the woods Saturday morning to see if they made the team. The juniors will already be hiding out inside the church and will pretend to be ghosts to scare everyone. Then they're going to jump the four who made it and steal their clothes so they have to run back to their cars naked."

"What? They are so twisted."

"Totally. But that could be good news for us. Monica should be heading out there pretty soon. I'll just get there first and find a way to get her talking."

"To the haunted church? But Jess, that's—"

"It's not *really* haunted. Ghosts aren't real." She paused. "Are they?"

"Not that I know of, but it's still creepy, and Monica could be dangerous, and—"

"I'll be careful. I'll take that little tape recorder I use for history class and—"

"No, it's too dangerous," I said, determined to talk her out of this whacked plan.

"London will be there too."

"So what? If Monica's guilty, she's crazy. She could still try to kill you."

"How? With a zombie? I thought Monica needed to use your clothes as totems to make the zombie attack you. She wouldn't have any of my clothes."

"Still, Reanimated Corpses are drawn to the smell of blood. She could scratch you or something and then—"

"I'll be careful. Don't worry, Megan—I'll get all the evidence you need to put Monica away for good. Then our lives can get back to normal."

"No, Jess, I—"

"And maybe you'll even get another chance to try out once Monica is gone!"

"No way, it's too—" Then she hung up on me. Hung. Up! "Jess? Jess?"

I called her again and again and text-messaged her telling her she should *not* go ahead with this crazy plan, but she still didn't answer. Frantic and completely freaked, I decided it was time to call Ethan. It didn't matter that he'd been avoiding me—he was the only one who might be able to help. I called him three times, but I went straight to voice mail. Finally I resorted to texting him the lowdown and sat praying for him to text me back before it was too late.

Fifteen minutes later, I knew I had no choice. I was going to have to go after her. Despite the fact that sneaking out last night had nearly killed me and sneaking out again would break my mom and dad's hearts, I had to go.

I couldn't just call SA and tell them about Monica now, not when I'd broken the biggest Settler rule there was. My family would be relocated within twenty-four hours if anyone knew I'd told Jess what I was . . . or even what Monica was.

"Crap!" I was completely backed into a corner, with only one way out.

I turned off the shower and quickly brushed my teeth and washed my face. I changed into my pajamas so I would look the part of a girl getting ready for bed as I slipped out of my room and into my parents' room to say good night. Smythe was still outside my door, but Barker seemed to have headed for bed. Good. One less babysitter to worry about.

Back in my room, I slipped into tight black spandex pants and a long-sleeved black top and pulled my hair back into a long braid to keep it from getting in the way. As I turned off my light and made my extra blankets into a Megan-shaped lump beneath the flowery comforter, I tried not to feel guilty for the stress my second disappearance would cause my parents. I had no other choice.

The window to my room opened without a sound, but I hadn't

bargained on the screen. Before I had time to doubt myself, I pushed on the screen. It made a slight popping sound as it broke free, but I managed to lean over and catch it before it fell to the ground. Carefully I pulled it into my room, concealing it behind the drapes. When I was done, I peeked out the window, amazed to see the compound fairly deserted. Earlier in the day, there had been a good number of Elders milling around, attending to whatever business old zombie Settlers attended to in their spare time, but now the gated complex was oddly peaceful.

The *gated* complex. I'd forgotten about the gates! The *electrified* gates that completely surrounded the compound. There was no way over those suckers and only one way out—through the main entrance, where a security camera monitored anyone coming or going. The guards in the control room would surely notice a kid leaving on foot. I'd be snatched up and thrown back into my room before I could say, "There's no place like jail."

I was trapped, unless . . .

My parents were already going to kill me once they realized I was gone—how much angrier could they get once they realized their car had disappeared too?

As I climbed out onto the roof and tiptoed over to the edge of the condo closest the ground, I plotted my dash across the parking lot. Only twenty feet to Mom's Corolla, which was always left unlocked and had that extra key in the glove compartment because she kept misplacing her real keys. Then I would be on my way to *really* getting myself grounded for the rest of my natural life.

Assuming I didn't get myself or Jess killed or my family relocated, I figured it would just about be worth it.

CHAPTER 16

Twenty minutes later, I was pulling down a narrow gravel road at the edge of the Carlisle farm, shaken up but thankfully still alive. The whole driving thing was *way* harder than it looked, at least once I left the deserted roads near the SA compound and entered real traffic. People in Carol drove like maniac Indy 500 qualifiers on crack!

If I made it to tomorrow morning, I was so going to write a letter to the paper urging people to slow the hell down.

Right now, however, the living-through-the-night thing wasn't feeling like a given. It was even creepier out here knowing there weren't seniors enjoying a bonfire nearby. And of course, I would actually be *on* Carlisle's land as soon as I stepped into the woods, not skirting the edge of it. The old man would have every right to shoot me as soon as I trespassed, and I knew he'd have no problem pulling the trigger. Dude was completely, should-be-in-a-room-with-no-doorknobs insane.

All because he'd once dared to spend the night in the haunted church back in the woods behind his property.

He'd been a young man then, so the urban legend went, and there hadn't been much to do in Carol. (Not that there was much to do *now* if you weren't into the burgers at Sonic, or bowling, or if the pool was closed for the winter.) So he and some buddies had decided to camp out in the old church, one of the only remaining buildings from when Carol was settled in the late 1800s.

Nathaniel Carlisle had been the only one of the five boys to make it out alive and had been a wacko ever since. He'd babbled about ghosts, about living skeletons who had eaten every last one of his—

"Stop it!" I hissed to myself. The last thing I needed to be doing was mulling over old ghost stories. There was probably a perfectly rational explanation for what had happened in that church.

Like . . . Nate Carlisle had killed all the other boys and hacked them up and buried them somewhere on his property, and the whole living-skeleton, "I'm so crazy" story was just to throw people off his track.

Great job with the self-comfort, Megan.

But there was no turning back now. Just ahead, off to the side of the road, sat Jess's little silver VW Bug convertible, the one she wasn't supposed to be driving alone for two months. Her dad was going to be excessively pissed if he found out, but Jess had risked her father's fury. I had to get my butt in gear and help her before it was too late.

I pulled Mom's Corolla in just behind the Bug and shut it off but left the key in the ignition. I'd seen enough horror movies to know I didn't want to mess with trying to fumble the key into the slot while an ax murderer was close on my heels.

No more horror movie thoughts!

It was so much easier to freak out about pretend scary stuff than to think about the very real and very whacked Settler gone bad who could be, even now, lurking somewhere in the dark woods.

I'd been too worried about avoiding a wreck to get seriously freaked out before I got here. But now I couldn't deny the *really* bad feelings skittering across my skin as I shut the car door and started down a faint trail I was hoping led to the church. My gut was telling me to turn around and run for my life, but I couldn't. So I forced my feet to move along the path instead of cutting through the woods and across the street, where the homecoming dance would just be starting.

Ahh . . . crepe paper and balloons and the cheesy fog machine they always cranked up before the announcement of the homecoming king and queen. If only that were in my future tonight.

Instead, I was up for more dark woods and potentially near death experiences. What fun.

At least the eclipse hadn't started yet. It was only a little after nine, and there was still enough moonlight that I could find my way without tripping over rocks and tree roots, but it was too dark to feel completely safe. Anything or anyone could be hiding in the shadows, and I wouldn't know they were there until it was too late.

Still, I forced myself to move a little faster. I certainly wouldn't want to be on this path at ten o'clock, when the lunar eclipse would eliminate all the natural light in Carol—not to mention turn *up* the dark power available for Monica's ritual, whatever that might be.

It still made my chest ache to think about Ethan being so into a chick who was so evil. How could it have felt so right to touch him, how could that kiss have rocked my world so completely if he was on the verge of declaring his undying love to Monica? It just didn't seem right.

Didn't seem *right*. Hmm . . .

What if Monica had done more than raise zombies with magic? What if she'd found a way to put some sort of love spell on Ethan? That would certainly explain—

I shook my head. I couldn't dwell on Ethan right now. I had to get to the church, ASAP.

My best friend could already be dead, ripped apart by RCs, her poor little body mutilated on the floor of the old church. By now, the rats that called the place their home could be descending on her corpse, ready to—

I started to run, concentrating on dodging obstacles in the path instead of on visions of Jess's dead body, pushing myself to move as fast as I could without making too much noise.

If Monica was waiting for me somewhere in the dark, I didn't want to give her advance notice that I was on my way to kick her ass. And kick her ass I would, even though my fighting skills were probably on par with those of the grandmas who took Tae Bo down at the senior center.

But if Monica had dared to hurt Jess, she was going to pay for it. Big-time.

"Megan? Is that you?" It was barely more than a whisper, but I recognized the voice immediately.

"Jess? Where are you?" Seconds later Jess emerged from the shadows a few feet behind me. I turned to see her standing in the middle of the path, her hair a mess and mud on her T-shirt but otherwise in one piece. "Are you okay? What happened? I made it here as fast as I—"

"I'm so glad you came!" She flung herself into my arms and

hugged me like she would never let go. "Monica tried to kill me! Like, for real kill me! She had a knife, and I had to fight her. London ran away. I screamed for her to come back, but I guess she didn't hear me or maybe she's in on it too. I don't know; I—"

"Okay, just take a deep breath," I said, holding her by the shoulders. "Where is Monica? You fought her and then what happened?"

"I won, I guess," she said, looking confused. "I punched her and she hit her head pretty hard on this old stove in the corner of the church. While she was dizzy, I took off my sweatshirt and used it to tie her up."

"So . . . she's tied up?"

"Yeah. On the floor, even though I felt bad because it's super dirty." Only Jess could feel bad for leaving someone who tried to kill her on a dirty floor. "My cell isn't getting reception, so I was on my way to the pay phone near the football field to call you when I heard something on the path and decided to hide."

"So Monica's tied up because you totally kicked her ass," I said, unable to keep the smile off my face. "That's awesome, Jess! I didn't know you were secretly channeling Sydney Bristow."

"Neither did I," she said, and I heard the giggle in her voice, though she still looked pretty freaked. "Monica was so pissed. I could tell she thought she wasn't even going to break a sweat killing me."

I shivered, the *k*-word wiping away my grin. "I'm *so* glad you're okay."

"And I'm glad you're here. Now we can carry her out of there." She grabbed my hand and pulled me down the path. "Hurry, let's go get her before anyone else shows up."

I followed her a few paces while I chewed over the details of our situation. "You know what? We should probably get our cars and head back to the school."

"You have a car here?"

"Yeah, I sort of borrowed my mom's car. The place where they were holding us isn't near a bus stop."

"Wow, Megan. You stole your mom's car. That's pretty—"

"Yeah, I know, she's going to kill me. Listen, let's get the cars. I'll head over to the pay phone near the football field. I'll be in clear sight of the people headed into the gym, so I'll be safe while I call SA to come get Monica. Meanwhile, you can go home and get ready for the dance and actually enjoy your night."

"Kyle isn't picking me up until nine thirty; I'll make it home in time," she said, sounding positively chipper. "Besides, this is more important than any dance. We have to make sure Monica doesn't have the chance to hurt anyone else again. This is your future we're talking about."

"But my future won't be in Carol, Arkansas, if anyone finds out I told you I was a Settler." I stopped in the middle of the trail, tugging on the hand Jess still held, wanting to make sure she understood how serious I was. "I'll be relocated, and I wouldn't put it past Settlers' Affairs to try to do some sort of freaky mind wipe on you or something. They're *really* psychotic about our world staying secret."

"Okay, I understand. I won't say a word, but please, let's just go get Monica," Jess said, pulling me into motion once more. "I don't know how tightly I tied those knots, and I don't want her to get away. I won't be able to leave my house again if she escapes."

"All right," I said, speeding my pace despite my reservations.

"Faster, Meg. We have to hurry." Jess ran faster but still didn't let go of my hand. It was almost like she was afraid to keep going without holding on to me, which was completely understandable considering what she'd just been through.

But for some reason, I got the urge to pull my hand away, an urge that kept getting stronger as we neared the black shadow of the old church and its eerily crooked steeple. There was something wrong, something more wrong than me getting ready to take a fellow Settler into custody and potentially risking my life if she'd already set her zombies in motion.

"Come on," Jess whispered, motioning for me to lead the way around the building. "Let's go in the side door in case she's managed to get free and is waiting for us at the front."

"Okay," I whispered back, running my hand lightly along the rotted wood as we waded through the grass, the smell of decay filling my nostrils.

Visions of rats and snakes and all the other things that liked to live in old, deserted buildings were making my heart race as fast as fear of what might be waiting for us inside. Jess's concern that Monica might have somehow freed herself was totally catching. I could just imagine Monica huddled in the dark behind the old stove or whatever else was in there, waiting to pounce on me with her knife. The knife she would be entirely capable of gutting me with.

I was not secretly channeling any kick-ass crime fighter, real or imaginary. If I was channeling anyone, it was probably the pig from *Chicken Little*, the one who wanted to be left behind with some chips and ammo while everyone else kicked alien ass.

"Ohmygod!" I squeaked before slamming my hand over my mouth and stopping dead in my tracks. Oh. God. Something had just run over my foot, something too heavy to be a cute little mouse.

"What's wrong?" Jess hissed from behind me, clearly annoyed at my inability to be stealthy and quiet.

She was so much better at this. *She* should have been the one born with weird paranormal power. She probably would have loved getting on the fast track to an Enforcement career. Weird to think about since I'd never thought of Jess as the ass-kicking type, until tonight.

"Megan? What's wrong?" Jess asked again, poking me softly between the shoulder blades.

"Something just ran over my foot. I think it was probably a rat." I was shaking for real now, certain I wouldn't be able to force myself to take another step.

I shouldn't be doing this. I had to turn around and get out of here before it was too late. But Jess was so set on us going, and she'd already risked her life and nearly been knifed by a psychopath. How could I tell her I was too chicken to walk around a dark building?

I couldn't. I had to keep moving, just putting one foot in front of the other until—

"Ack!" My cell was vibrating like crazy in my back pocket. At least I hadn't turned the ringer back on, but it still nearly scared me to death. My spandex pants were really tight, so the phone was making my entire backside buzz.

"Megan! Turn it off, quick!"

"Right." I ripped the phone from my pants and pressed the mute button, but not before I saw whose call I had missed.

It was Ethan! "Jess, we have to turn around. That was Ethan. I'll call him on the way back to the car and he can come help us—"

"You really think he'd help us? Monica's his girlfriend. He'll never believe she's the one who did all those bad things to you."

I winced. The words hurt, and worse, they held a ring of truth. "If I tell him everything that's happened, I'm sure he'll at least—"

"He'll just think you're jealous because he dumped you for Monica," she said, then continued on in a softer voice. "Besides, we don't have the time to waste. She could already be loose in there. I'm not sure how good my knots are. I was never even a Girl Scout or anything, you know."

"I'd just feel better if we had someone bigger and stronger here. That's all." And Ethan was a Protocol officer and would surely know more about taking a Rogue Settler into custody than I would.

But I couldn't tell Jess that.

I'd already spilled the goods on Monica. I couldn't expose Ethan too. I was just going to have to do this and wait to call Ethan back until I had Monica bundled into the trunk of the Corolla. Besides, Jess was right—I wasn't completely sure I could trust Ethan. What if he really was under some kind of spell that made him loyal to Monica? He might untie her and take me into custody for being a crazy lady for all I knew.

"Okay, let's go. Let's just get it done," I said, my voice tight with anxiety.

"Megan, I know you're scared, but I believe we can do this." Jess's voice was soft, soothing, like she was talking to a total basket case. I had to pull it together. I was supposed to be the one experienced with creepy situations.

"Yeah, okay. We can do this." I just wished I felt more certain of the words.

"We're almost there, and if we take the path that goes straight to the football field, we won't even have to go bring Monica to the cars. We can take her with us to the pay phone and then come back and get them later, when it's safe."

"There's another path to the football field?" I asked, slowly resuming movement around the building, wondering how Jess knew so much about Nate Carlisle's property.

"Megan, I thought you turned that off," Jess whispered when my cell suddenly chimed, notifying me I'd received a text message.

"I must have pressed the wrong button," I hissed back, flipping open the phone and punching the power button without retrieving the text from Ethan. There wasn't time to worry about him right now. We had to get Monica and get the hell out of here.

I shoved my cell back in my pocket, thinking how strange it was that I was getting such great reception when Jess said she hadn't been getting any. Our phones were the exact same brand and we used the same company. We'd signed up for them at the mall together a year ago so that we'd get unlimited calls to . . . talk to . . . each other . . . all . . . the . . .

Oh . . . God. No. It couldn't be . . . It couldn't. . .

At that moment, I realized what had been bothering me since the second I got out of my mom's car. I'd never told Jess you had to use a totem to focus a Reanimated Zombie on its target. She'd supplied that information about using my clothes to make the undead attack me on her own. Just like she'd gotten out of the house and attacked me with zombies in Perkins Park.

She'd known exactly when Ethan had asked me to homecoming, and she'd known exactly where Josh and I would be going on our first date. Hell, she knew everything about me because I *told her* everything. Because I was the stupidest, lousiest detective in the world and couldn't see the truth until it was shoved right up in my face.

But it wasn't too late. It couldn't be. For some reason, she wanted me inside the church, and if I didn't let her get me there, maybe I'd be okay.

I slowed my pace and gradually worked in a tiny limp. When I spoke, I did my best to sound normal, even though I felt like I'd swallowed hummingbirds. "Hey, Jess? I think I did something to my ankle."

"Really? When? Are you okay?" She sounded so normal, so concerned for me.

Surely she couldn't sound so relaxed if she was getting ready to kill me. But I couldn't get the totem thing out of my mind. I *knew* I hadn't told her that part, knew it with the same gut instinct that was wailing for me to run like mad from the psycho behind me, to haul ass first and fake sprained ankles later.

"No, I don't think I am. I don't think I'm going to be able to carry Monica. Let's go back to the car. We can just call—"

"You're not going to be calling anyone, Megan. Give me your phone." Her voice was still calm but with an underlying coldness that banished the last of my doubt. Jess, my best friend, was the one who had tried to kill me. "And don't think about running. I have a knife and I *will* gut you."

I felt the tip of said knife poke against my ribs as I handed over my phone. "Jess, please," I said, sounding as freaked as I felt. "Why are you—"

"Get inside, Megan. Then I'll be happy to tell you why." She shoved me forward and I almost fell before regaining my footing. Jess was way stronger than I'd ever anticipated. Even without the knife she would probably have been able to take me. "I'll answer every question your tiny little brain can come up with. Then, when we're all done with our little chat, you will die. The way you should have died a long, long time ago."

She kicked me square in the back, and I fell into the open door and onto the cold, rotting floorboards. I barely managed to get back to my feet when the door slammed behind me and a light came on at the opposite corner of what had probably once been a quaint little country church back at the turn of the century, before it was sprayed with graffiti and covered in mouse turds.

"Took you long enough. Jesus, I was starting to get bored." Beth Phillips had a knife in her lap and a length of rope in her hand. A rope that was attached to the wrists and ankles of a bound and gagged and very pissed-looking Monica Parsons.

Oh. Smack. The plot had just thickened.

CHAPTER 17

*H*ow did you—I thought you—" I stammered, not sure what I could or couldn't say anymore. "But I—"

"Is she always this stupid, Jess?" Beth asked as she came toward me with more rope. "I mean, seriously, how did you fake being her friend for five years? I would have killed her year one and gotten it over with."

"Hold out your hands, Megan," Jess said.

For a second I thought about making a run for it, but then her knife was pressed against my back again. She *would* kill me. I had no doubt about that. So I held out my arms to Beth, silently vowing to wait for another opportunity to haul ass. I was going to have to find a way to escape. Otherwise, it was over. Jess wasn't going to let me out of here alive.

"She just got a text from Ethan. Looks like he was trying to warn her that you had busted out of Settler prison."

"Honestly, it was easier than sneaking out of my bedroom," Beth said. Jess laughed as Beth tied my wrists together and then shoved me down to sit on a rickety bench beside Monica before going to work tying my ankles.

"Oh, and get this," Jess said, scrolling further down the message on my phone. "They think you 'may have an accomplice.' It took them this long to figure out one artist couldn't raise all those corpses on their own?"

Beth rolled her eyes in agreement. "Yeah, you can't even work the clone spell without a partner. Stupid zombie freaks."

I'd *known* those clones weren't my fault. In your face, Settlers' Affairs! Not that the information was going to do me a lot of good now.

"They shouldn't be allowed to live in the same world as normal people," Jess said, her eyes shining in the dim light with a rage too scary to be for me and me alone. She must have been one of those fundamentalist terrorist-type people who wanted to annihilate things that violated their beliefs. It was totally weird to think about Jess that way, but at least it gave me something to work with.

"Please, Jess, I can understand that what Monica and I are might seem weird or wrong," I said in my most reasonable voice. "But I swear to you, we don't hurt people. We're not—"

"Liar! You're such a freaking liar, Megan!" She screamed the words loudly enough to make me flinch. "You're a murderer. You have been since you were a kid."

She was *totally* nuts. Still, I had to keep trying. "No, I swear, Jess, I—"

"I was there—I *saw* you do it. You and Monica," Jess said, looking like she was about to cry. "You turned the zombies on her, and they chased her into the woods. She didn't know the spell to make them stop after just a taste of her blood." She sucked in a breath and the tears standing in her eyes rolled silently down her cheeks. "So they ate her alive before they went back to their graves."

Whatever she was talking about, she had the last part dead wrong. "But Jess, you don't need a spell. Once a Reanimated Corpse gets a taste of the blood of the one who raised them, they go back to their graves. I swear, that's—"

"Bullshit! By the time I found her, the only things left were bones and . . . her hair."

Jess reached into her front pocket and pulled out a tiny braid of blond hair. "I kept it all these years, waiting until I was strong enough to work the spell I wanted to use for you and Monica. That way, it wouldn't just be my revenge—it would be Mom's too."

Mom. Her mom. Oh my God. It couldn't be. . .

I suddenly felt as if my entire world had been turned inside out, like I'd stepped through the looking glass and was living in an alternate reality. Jess's *mom* was the woman who'd run away when we were ten years old after I was attacked in the cemetery. Right after Monica and I had joined power to work the *reverto* spell. That had to be the answer. It was the only time Monica and I had ever combined forces to do anything.

"Your mom was the one who raised the corpses the night I almost died," I said, my lips feeling weirdly numb as I forced the words out. I sort of suspected I might be going into shock or something but didn't have time to worry about it since Jess was stalking slowly toward me with her knife.

"See, Beth, she's not stupid. Slow on the uptake, but not stupid."

"Please, Jess, we didn't mean to hurt your mom. I've never heard of someone who raised zombies being eaten alive. But even if we'd known that would happen, she was the one raising the dead when she shouldn't have been," I said, thinking fast. "And she was using your blood to do it, right? The blood of the innocent needed for the spell? I mean, that's not something she should have been doing. You were her kid; she should have—"

"Shut up! Mom was doing what she had to do to get rid of Clara. My dad was cheating on her, getting ready to ruin our lives. She was acting out of love for our family. We all would have been fine if you hadn't *killed* my mother!"

"No, please, I—" My words ended in a gurgle as Jess fisted her hand in my hair and wrenched my head back. I sucked in a breath and closed my eyes, waiting for her to slit my throat.

I was going to die. I was really going to die, right here, right—

"I'm not going to kill you yet," Jess whispered in my ear as she ran the knife across my jawline with enough force to pierce the skin. It stung like nobody's business but wasn't nearly as bad as a zombie bite and not deep enough to scar, let alone kill. "I just need a bit of your blood, Meggy. Monica's won't do. Everyone knows she hasn't been innocent since eighth grade."

The blood of the innocent. She was going to use my blood for the spell.

"Now, you're sure she and Josh didn't do anything?" Beth asked as Jess released my hair and carried the knife with my blood on it to a big black pot sitting where the pulpit would have been. "He told me the other night that they . . . *you know.*"

What! Josh was such a freaking pig! I couldn't believe he was spreading lies like that. Maybe *that* was why all the girls had been giving me the cold shoulder last week. They thought I had . . . that I'd— ugh, I didn't even want to think about it. And on the *first date*, no less. I was so going to kill Josh Pickle. If I didn't get killed first.

"She's never even let a guy get to second base. Trust me. Josh is a liar," Jess said.

"Josh is a liar, but Ethan's not," I said, going with my first instinct. If Beth and Jess thought they didn't have the blood of an innocent, they'd have to go looking for one. It might buy Monica and me just enough time to escape. "He was my first time, Jess. That's why I was so upset when he went after Monica."

"Oh yeah? When was this?"

"The other night, after he kidnapped me from the corn maze." The lie came quickly and easily. I was apparently much better with falsehoods when in life-or-death situations.

"You're lying," Jess said, though she hesitated before putting the knife in the pot. "You would have told me."

"I'm not lying. Ethan and I did it. And I can prove it," I said, a brilliant plan forming. "Let me text him about it, and—"

"How stupid do you think I am?" Jess laughed and dipped the knife into the pot. Whatever was inside glowed faintly green for a second, which apparently satisfied Jess that she had been right to call my bluff.

"Jess, you could have ruined the entire spell!" Beth sounded pissed. "For the summoning of the corpses to work, the ingredients have to be perfect. Right?"

"I knew she was lying. She always looks to the left when she's lying."

Argh! Having an enemy who used to be your best friend sucked!

She knew me entirely too well. But then . . . I knew her pretty well too.

"So you've planned to kill me for five years," I said in my most disdainful voice. "Seems like you would have gotten it right the first time in the corn maze instead of screwing up so badly Beth ended up in SA custody."

Jess spun away from the pot, which I guessed was their makeshift cauldron for the ritual they were getting ready to perform. "We *did* get it right. We weren't trying to kill you. I just wanted to play with you for a while, scare you a little before we got down to business."

"Right," I said, rolling my eyes like I didn't believe her, even though I knew Josh and Ethan had been the targets of the first attacks. Jess was a total freak about being right and doing things perfectly. If I could get her talking, trying to justify her mistakes, I might be able to find out what she had planned for tonight in time to do something to stop it.

"We just wanted to make sure neither of you had a date to the dance so there would be no obstacle to getting you out here for the eclipse. No boyfriends wondering where their dates had gone and getting a bunch of parents on the warpath. This was the plan all along."

So the eclipse *definitely* had something to do with this. That meant they weren't going to kill us until nearly ten! That gave me at least forty-five minutes to figure a way out of here. "Okay, so the clones and the attack in Perkins Park weren't meant to kill me. Whatever."

"No, they were. And they *would* have killed you if you hadn't gotten lucky," Jess said, practically spitting the words. "Ethan kept hanging around, asking one of you to the dance and then the other. It looked like we were going to have to kill him too, so we knew we had to get rid of either you or Monica beforehand just to even the odds."

"Two of us versus two of you; anything else wouldn't really have been fair," Beth said.

Jess nodded as if we were picking teams for beach volleyball, not some weird life-or-death game she and Beth were playing by their own rules. "We decided to go for you since you were the younger and most likely weaker one and we didn't have the power of the eclipse until tonight."

"Jess wanted to change the plans and try to get Monica that night at the bonfire," Beth added. "But I told her it was too late. I already had all the graves prepped and there wasn't time to switch out the totems."

"Yeah, I really wanted to save you for tonight," Jess said.

"She's been looking forward to watching you die up close and personal," Beth added from where she sat on the floor, stretching out like we were getting ready for dance practice, not discussing killer zombies.

Up close and personal. Whatever they were planning, it was probably going to go down here, in this church, where they would be guaranteed a good view. "So it was you on the phone the night the clones attacked," I said to Jess.

"It was, and I meant every word. I really didn't want to take you out before tonight. I'm glad that you survived the other attacks and that Ethan broke it off with Monica this afternoon."

Ethan broke up with Monica! I *knew* he would come to his senses.

Too bad he had to do it right before the dance, thus ensuring that Monica and I were both free for Jess and Beth's little party.

"Everything is working out perfectly." Jess smiled and turned back to the pot, giving it a peaceful little stir. "It just goes to show that my mom is out there looking out for me, making sure you two get what you deserve."

"You think your mom is helping you from beyond the grave?" I asked, unable to hold back my outrage. "She was a black artist, Jess; her soul is dead and gone. Forever. And that's exactly what will happen to you if—"

"Oh, shut up, I'm tired of hearing you whine. Can I gag her now, Jess?" Beth asked, already on her feet and headed toward me.

"Might as well—we don't want either of them to be able to talk when the zombies get here. Just in case they can cast spells without using their hands."

"Why not? You said two against three wouldn't be fair; how is it fair to make sure Monica and I can't command the dead if you and Beth—"

"Oh, shut up, Megan." Beth tried to stuff the sock in her hand in my mouth. I dodged it by flipping my braid around to hit her hand and kept talking.

"Screw you, Beth. Why are you even here? Jess at least has a good reason for being a nutcase. What's your excuse?"

"I am not a nutcase!" Jess screamed.

Oh yeah. I was getting them riled up now. I should have started calling names sooner. The more upset they got, the more likely one of them was to make a mistake.

"Mmmph yrrr rrre!" Monica grunted the words around the gag in her mouth, but even I could understand what she was saying. She was totally on the Megan bandwagon for once.

"You're the one who's nuts if you think running your mouth is going to change what's going to happen tonight," Beth said, not at all miffed by being called a psychopath. "You and Monica are going to be eaten alive. Then I'm going to lure our friends down to snack on the people at the homecoming dance with a little pig blood."

"Pig blood?"

"We've been prepping the ground for weeks to form a trail straight to the gym," Jess said.

The path by the track! It had to be part of their plan. Hopefully, Settlers' Affairs had disabled it so the zombies wouldn't be able to find their way to the gym, but I couldn't be sure. I *had* to get out of here!

"I'm going to dump the blood and let the undead swarm all over the homecoming court. It's going to be fabulous."

"You're kidding me. You're helping Jess work black magic because you didn't get voted onto the court?" I couldn't believe it. In a way, I'd been right all along. Jess had her own motives, but for Beth this was all about some stupid high school stuff.

I suddenly realized exactly why Ethan and the Elders had been so reluctant to believe me when I'd first posed that theory. After being faced with the possibility of dying so many times the past week, I thought Beth's motives were completely ridiculous. She'd lost a high school popularity contest. So. What.

Beth was willing to kill two people—well, more than two if you counted the attacks on Josh and Ethan and the plan to destroy the homecoming court—because she wasn't a homecoming princess? WTF?!

My thoughts must have shown on my face, because Jess leapt to her psycho friend's defense.

"It's not just the court," Jess said, coming to stand beside Beth, looping an arm around her waist. Standing there together, both of them so blond and delicate looking, it was hard to believe how completely evil they were. Just went to show that not every bad guy was ugly on the outside. "We're going to douse the entire gym. We've got to make sure a lot of people die."

"Why? Because the football team deserves to get theirs for using their votes for a prank?"

"Because we've got to make sure everyone believes we're dead too," Beth said. "Otherwise we'll never be free."

"Our parents will never accept us. We have to do this." Jess turned her eyes to me, as though she expected me to understand what she was talking about. "We have to run away."

"Run away? All this time, you've been planning to run away?" She nodded at me like *I* was the crazy one. "Then why were you so worked up about tryouts? You're not even going to be here to—"

"Anything worth doing is worth doing right, Megan. How many times have I told you that?" Jess rolled her eyes and sighed. "I mean, I feel bad about killing all those people, but it's the only way to do this right."

"It's okay, Jess. Most of those people are nothing but sheep anyway. Who cares if they're dead?" Beth smiled before she gave Jess a kiss on the cheek. Jess sighed and turned to Beth, and suddenly their kiss became a lot more than friendly.

God! My best friend was not only secretly evil, she was also secretly a lesbian! Why had she never told me? I could have been cool with it. Well, with the lesbian part, not the evil part. Obviously.

"Mmph frkgg gwds," Monica grumbled around her gag.

I was pretty sure Monica had called them gaywads, but I couldn't get up to defending Jess and Beth at the moment. Sure, I felt awful for Jess. Her mother dabbling in black magic and then getting herself killed had obviously messed her up big-time. I also felt bad for the two of them. I could almost understand why they felt they had to stage their own deaths and run away.

Their families were two of the richest and oldest in Arkansas. If either the Thompsons or the Phillipses found out their little girls liked other little girls, they would flip out. They'd probably have Jess and Beth committed to the psych ward for electroshock therapy to cure their gayness and would be damned sure never to let the two girls see each other ever again.

But at the same time, *I* hadn't done anything wrong. And neither had any of the people at the homecoming dance.

Jess's mom was going to use those zombies as a murder weapon, to kill Clara. Any way you sliced it, that was just wrong. Monica and I had only been defending ourselves. I was just a kid in the wrong place at the wrong time. But luckily, with the help of a friend—or sort of friend, anyway—I'd used my power to save my life.

I wasn't going to feel bad about that or about using that same power to take down the girls in front of me, no matter what. They'd made that decision easy. I'd never been anything but a good friend to Jess, a loyal and loving friend whom she had betrayed as surely as her mother had betrayed her by dragging her to the graveyard that night five years ago.

So it was with very little regret that I invoked the *exuro* command, aiming it toward the black pot, knowing I would have to thank Kitty for the lesson in roasting turkeys.

CHAPTER 18

I'd done enough research on Reanimated Corpse spells to know there had to be something dead in that pot. Something dead that—thanks to Kitty—I knew how to make burn like a thousand white-hot suns.

Okay, maybe not *that* hot, but I could feel the flames scorching my face. Both Jess and Beth—who had been closer to the cauldron—were screaming bloody murder. Beth fell to the ground and Jess flung herself on top of her girlfriend, acting as a human shield, but I didn't let myself feel sorry for them. Instead, I poured even more power into the spell, until the flames rose at least six feet in the air. My bones buzzed with the force of the magic I was working, but I didn't tire out nearly as quickly as usual.

Guess fear of certain death had ramped up my personal mojo. Thank. God.

I turned to Monica, knowing this was our only chance. "Come on, follow me!" I stood up and began hopping toward the front door.

Just a few more hops and—

"Ahhh!" My screams replaced Monica and Beth's as I fell through a rotten place in the floor and my fire abruptly went out.

Thankfully, I'd only fallen a few feet. I could still find a way to free myself if I could just—

"That's it! Stuff the sock in her mouth," Jess yelled.

Seconds later Beth had ahold of my nose and was cramming the sweat sock into my mouth, shoving it so deep I started to gag. It was only with a great degree of effort that I managed to stop myself from puking. Call me crazy, but I had a feeling Jess and Beth would let me choke on my own vomit before they gave me another chance to talk.

"I thought they couldn't work spells on living people," Beth said, turning back to Jess with an accusing glare, showing me the left side of her face, which looked painfully red. At least I'd left my mark. "It was the dead cat in the pot." Jess cursed and stamped her foot on the ground, looking like a five-year-old throwing a tantrum. "Now I have no idea how many of them we'll get out of their graves. The ingredients weren't supposed to be set on fire until the moon was dark."

"What if it's not enough, Jess? This is the only lunar eclipse this year. I can't wait until next year," Beth said, her face scrunching as she prepared to have a come-apart. Man, these two were the whiniest couple ever. "We'll never be able to stage something big enough, we'll never get out of this town, we'll never be together, and—"

"Don't worry." Jess pulled it together a little bit, pasting a smile on her face. "If worse comes to worst, we can book it over to Mount Hope and raise a few more."

"No way, I don't want any zombie bite marks on my skin. That could scar. And scars are like . . . forever." Ah, Beth, vain as ever, her mind on the future of her flawless skin even in the midst of murder. "The Settlers could turn those zombies back on us since they're not as old as the Indians."

"The Indians can still be turned on us, but they won't be," Jess said, calmly explaining the situation to her partner of very little brain. "They're corpses, after all, the same as any other zombie."

"Jess! There are more than three hundred bodies under here. If the spell still raises them all, we'll be—"

"We'll be fine."

"But the blood we stole from the blood drive is almost gone." Beth wrung her hands.

Aha, so *that* was how they'd been getting their RCs back in the ground without a bunch of bite marks. They'd donated blood and then shoplifted it for their own nefarious purposes, letting the zombies take a sip whenever they came running back to their Makers. One small needle puncture versus a bunch of festering zombie bites—it made sense.

"We're not going to need it. We don't have to worry about Settlers anymore. These two are going to be dead, and there's no way Ethan will be able to handle all those zombies by himself."

So Jess didn't know there were other Settlers in town besides me, Ethan, and Monica. Maybe there was still a chance to stop this craziness before anyone got hurt. Well, anyone except me and Monica. At this point, it looked like we were pretty much done for.

"We'll be halfway to Louisiana by the time they figure out how to get rid of the corpses. We'll be totally safe," Jess said. "Their spell doesn't work at that kind of distance."

How did she know so much about Settlers? Someone other than me had been telling tales out of class. But who? Monica wouldn't have told Jess or Beth anything. She wasn't weak enough to need support from her non-supernatural friends in order to continue on her Settler path.

"So don't worry. Okay?"

"Okay." Beth sniffed and then grabbed Monica—who had hopped in the opposite direction from the one I'd indicated, *of course*—and pulled her back to where I was now sitting and heaving my legs back above the floor.

I tried to wiggle away, but Beth still managed to get Monica and me tied together in a less than a minute. Now we were bound together, back to back on the mouse turd–littered church floor, stuck here to wait for the zombies I'd unintentionally caused to rise a good thirty minutes early. Way to go, Megan.

"There, all ready to go." Beth crossed back to give Jess a hug. "Speaking of going, I'd better jet down to the gym and get ready to spill some blood."

"Awesome. I'll call you to give you the cue when the zombies are done with these two," Jess said, a smile on her face once more. "I'd better hurry and get in position too. I want to make sure I have time to turn the video camera on."

"Take care of you," Beth said.

"Take care of you." Jess leaned up to give her a quick kiss before Beth ran for the other door—the one they'd been using because the floorboards near the front of the church were rotten, duh, Megan— and Jess made for a rope hanging near the cauldron.

In seconds, she had scrambled up to the ceiling and crawled out onto one of the rafters, where she began to arrange a tiny video camera. Not only was she going to watch us being eaten alive, she was going to *record* it so she could relive the magic again and again.

In that second, I realized I hated Jess. I couldn't think of anyone

225

I had loathed more in my entire life—even the evil minion presently shoving her back into mine.

"Whhmm?" I asked, hoping she understood gagged Megan as well as I understood gagged Monica.

"Pmm yrr fmm imnu frrr."

"Whhm?"

"Yr fmm imnu m frr!" Her butt lifted an inch or two off the ground before dropping back to the floor.

Floor! Push my feet into the floor.

If we both pushed our feet into the floor and pressed our backs together, we might be able to stand up. Whether we'd be able to get out of here in time with both of our ankles tied together and our upper bodies connected by Beth's rope was another question, but we had to try. Anything was better than sitting here waiting to be eaten.

"Yr rree?" Monica asked.

Hell, yes, I was ready.

"Un-hnn." I bent my knees.

"Un, mmu, free," Monica grunted, and on three we both dug our heels into the church floor. Slowly, inch by torturous inch, we made it to a squatting position before falling back to the ground.

"You two might as well give it up. The zombies are already on their way. The burial ground is right beneath us. A few hundred skeletons should be clawing their way to the surface as we speak," Jess said, her voice echoing eerily through the rafters. "They're nearly three hundred years old, so they're going to be really hungry."

God, no. We were too close; we didn't have a chance.

"Whh rr uu rrng rs?" I screamed around my gag, tears of frustration in my eyes.

"I think we covered the 'why' pretty well, Megan." Jess obviously understood gagged Megan too. "I actually figured you'd prefer this. I thought about killing your mom to really make the punishment fit the crime but then decided it would be more fair to take you out."

Just when I thought I couldn't hate her any more.

She'd thought about killing my mom? My mom! My mom, who had treated her like another daughter? Who had been there the day she started her period to give her hugs and take her to buy pads so Jess wouldn't have to tell Clara? Who had brought us snacks and driven us to the mall and summer camp and a zillion other places over the years and even taken us for a spa day for Jess's fifteenth birthday?

How *dare* Jess even *think* about hurting someone who had gone above and beyond to care about her, even love her?

Monica continued to shove against my back, frantically trying to stand up, but all I could think about was what an ungrateful, horrible, evil person I had once called my best friend. Talk about killing me all you want, but apparently, bringing my family into the picture was enough to make me completely lose it. Big-time.

"Mmmph!" Monica screamed as I leaned to the right, tipping us both over onto the ground.

I ignored her, staying totally concentrated on slamming my cheek into the floor. If I could just get the freaking sock out of my mouth, I'd torch whatever was left of that cat, make it burn so high Jess's bleached blond hair would light up like straw drenched in gasoline. I had the power, and I was no longer afraid to use it.

"Give it up, Megan," Jess said. "If you get the gag out of your mouth, I'll work a spell to call more blood from the cut on your neck. Not enough to kill you, of course, just enough to make the zombies go crazy."

Go ahead and try it, witch. We'll see how strong your magic really is.

I moved faster, scraping my cheek along the floor until it stung even as I shoved my tongue against the sock from the inside. I wasn't scared of Jess anymore.

The rage burning through my veins made me positive I could take out Jess and however many zombies she invited to the party if I could just—*slam, scrape*—get—*shove, shove*—the—freaking gag— *slam*—out—of—*scrape*—my—*shove, shove, shove*—mouth.

Yes! *"Exuro!"* I screamed the command at the same instant Jess screamed the words to a spell. I had just enough time to realize she'd been bluffing about her ability to summon blood before all hell broke loose.

Monica started thrashing, spinning us in a circle on the ground, while up in the rafters Jess screamed like her eyes were being gouged out. Not about to show my ex–best friend mercy, I poured even more power into the flame I could feel burning behind me, willing it to climb higher and higher, to rise and feed and destroy.

I was so concentrated on the *exuro* spell that I didn't notice the crashing sounds at first. It was only when the floor started to vibrate and first one skeletal fist and then another burst through the rotted boards that I realized we had company. I heard them before I could see them. The unmistakable grunts and groans of the undead filled the room, making Monica scream around her gag as they closed in on where we lay.

"*Exuro!*" I invoked the flame command on the first red-eyed zombies that crawled through the hole I'd made when I fell through the floor.

"*Reverto!*" I screamed the command into the face of the first zombie to fall on top of me with teeth bared. No matter that it had no internal organs and therefore no stomach to put my tasty human flesh inside; it was still going in for the kill.

The zombie spun away, searching for either Jess or Beth—I had no clue which it'd hunt down since they'd concocted the spell together—as I thanked God for Kitty. Without Kitty's afternoon of coaching, I wouldn't have lived this long.

Summers at Camp Junior Enforcer were looking like a better idea all the time. Like Dad said, I'd never be normal, but I *could* be properly prepared to fight for as much normalcy as possible. And to defend innocent people who deserved my protection.

"*Reverto!*" I lashed out with my legs, kicking at the zombie headed for Monica, bringing it down to our level before invoking the command again. Soon both it and the two RCs behind it were reeling around and shuffling away. We were safe.

But not for long, I realized, as I got my first clear look across the room.

Looked like Jess shouldn't have worried about lighting the ingredients on fire too early. There were at least sixty zombies already in the church, and more were still bursting through the floor and trudging in the door, relentlessly shambling toward me and Monica.

There was no way I'd be able to get rid of them all, not without Monica's help or my arms free at the very freaking least.

God! If I could just find a way out of the—

"Monica, I can't believe—" As if summoned by my deep, persistent need, strong hands started tearing at the ropes binding me and Monica together. "Megan? What the hell are you doing here?"

Ethan! I'd never been so happy to see anyone in my entire life. Especially considering how horrified he sounded to see me here. Maybe he did feel the same way I felt about him after all! Maybe the thing with Monica had all been a horrible mistake, maybe—

"Untie us first, ask questions later," Monica, whose mouth was apparently now sock free, snapped. "We're all about to die, in case you hadn't noticed."

Maybe Monica was right and I needed to maintain my focus on the undead.

"Exuro! Exuro!" As Ethan finished untying us, he and I both cast, and more zombies burst into flames—which was the good news. The bad news was that I was forced to put out the flame burning in the cauldron to conserve energy, which gave Jess the psychotic another chance to cast her spell.

"Ohmygod!" Monica screamed as blood gushed from the wound at my jaw.

So much for bluffing. Looked like Jess had more power than I'd anticipated.

"Megan? What's happening?" Ethan asked, pressing the sleeve of his sweatshirt against my face, applying pressure to the cut.

"Up there in the rafters. It's Jess; she and Beth are witches—" Jess shouted again. Ethan pulled me close and spun us toward the corner of the room, dodging the spell. We got out of the way just in time. Unfortunately, Monica wasn't so lucky.

"Ahh!" Monica screamed and clenched one hand around her shoulder. From the blood seeping through her fingers, it was obvious she'd been hit.

Though probably not too badly since she was running for the door seconds later.

"Parsons, don't you dare—" Ethan cursed as Monica disappeared.

Of course the floor held for that skinny little turd while I had fallen through. As if I needed further evidence that life wasn't fair.

"Go, Megan. Run," Ethan said, pulling me across the room, dodging zombies as we went. "I'll stay and make sure Jess doesn't—"

"No way, I'm not leaving you here."

"Settlers' Affairs are on the way," he said. "I'll use the *exuro* command until I run out of power. I only have to hold them off for ten, fifteen minutes until—"

"*Reverto!*" I grand jeté kicked the first zombie to make it through the flaming corpses. It stumbled backward before turning around. "You only need ten minutes to get killed."

"How did you do that? The *reverto* spell shouldn't work unless—"

"I've been training with some Enforcement people," I said, feeling pretty proud even though I did my best to make it sound like no big deal.

"When was this?"

"While you were busy making out with Monica." Why did my mouth have to go there? This was *so* not the time or place. "*Reverto! Reverto!*"

231

The zombie skeletons were getting creative, swarming across the floor on all fours, leaping over each other in their haste to get to our yummy flesh. *"Reverto!"* The command was still working, but I was feeling the drain on my power from working the *reverto* and *exuro* commands at the same time. The buzzing in my bones had turned into a full-body tremble. I couldn't maintain this level of power much longer. If Settlers' Affairs didn't get here soon, Ethan and I might still end up zombie food.

Unless we risked getting zapped with some wicked magic and made a run for the door . . .

"Reverto! Reverto!" Two more down and there was a little break in the RC action. "Maybe we should both make a run for it."

"But Monica could be waiting outside."

"Monica? But Monica isn't in on this."

"She definitely raised the corpse that attacked her at the cemetery that night," he said, looking pissed. "It took a few days of searching, but I finally found the evidence in her room. She had the spell to raise the dead written in a journal and some extra dolls with long brown hair. I was on my way to headquarters to turn in the evidence when I got your text."

Searching? Evidence? Suddenly, the pieces all fell into place. Ethan had been pretending to date Monica to get close enough to her to find out if she was the one who had it in for me! He must have thought her "attack" as suspicious as I did; hence the sudden shift in his behavior since that night. It wasn't a confession of undying love, but it certainly meant he cared.

Too bad there wasn't more time to celebrate.

"Exuro!" Gathering my strength, I set a few new zombies aflame

while relaxing the amount of power I was funneling toward the corpses already burning out on the floor. My breath was coming heavier by the time I turned back to Ethan, but I already felt a little better without so many zombies burning at the same time. "She might have raised that corpse, but I'm pretty sure she had nothing to do with the rest of this." I quickly gave Ethan the lowdown on Jess and Beth and their motives and plans for the rest of the evening.

"And you've been using the *reverto* spell?" he asked, disbelief in his tone. "When you knew Beth was already headed down to the dance?"

"Well, yeah," I said, stomach sinking. "I didn't really have much of a choice, and I wasn't sure which of them the RCs would go for. I was just trying—"

"Now we've *got* to get out of here. If we don't get to those zombies in time, we're going to have a Class Three Containment crisis—not to mention a bunch of dead high school kids." He darted to the left, setting another zombie on fire as he moved, then stopped to scan the rafters. "Looks like your friend made a run for it."

"Okay, but what—"

"Come on." Ethan grabbed my hand and pulled me toward the door before I could finish my sentence. "Borrow my power and torch as many of them as you can. The fewer following us down to the school the better."

We charged into the center of the swarming undead, groaning, hungry skeletons closing in all around us.

I let down the last of my shields and pulled Ethan's power into my body, waiting until I felt like I was about to burst before I spoke the command. *"Exuro!"*

Ethan caught me when the force of the backlash threatened to knock me off my feet, then pushed me down to the ground as everything around us exploded into flame. Soon I was facedown on floor, tucked under Ethan's body while unearthly shrieks filled the air. Even with another person between me and the heat, I still felt like a lobster thrown into a pot of boiling water. I tried to will the flames to die down a bit without much effect. Somewhere along the line, I'd lost control of the blazes I'd started.

I'd obviously underestimated what I could do with a little extra power.

"We have to go now!" Ethan said, shouting to be heard. The fire had taken on that sort of ocean waves quality I had always associated with wood burning, so I suspected the blaze had spread to the building itself.

A loud pop sounded above the roar of the flames and the wailing zombies, and seconds later a huge chunk of the rafters crashed to the floor beside us. The roof was on fire. We had to run for it or risk burning up right along with the corpses stumbling around us.

Ethan grabbed me beneath the arms and hauled me to my feet, kicking zombies out of our way as we dashed toward the door I'd come in with Jess. That felt like ages ago. Time really tended to drag when you were waiting to die by zombie attack. Judging from the black circle slowly easing across the full moon hanging low on the horizon, I'd only been inside for forty-five minutes.

It was nearly ten. The eclipse was getting ready to happen and there were already zombies shambling through the forest toward the homecoming dance.

We were going to have to haul some serious ass.

Ethan must have been on my wavelength because he grabbed my hand and was booking it through the woods before I could say a word. Despite the adrenaline dumping into my system, I was grateful for the help getting my move on. The last *exuro* spell had drained my energy big-time. But Ethan didn't even slow down as he grabbed his phone from his pocket and contacted Settlers' Affairs to give them the update on the situation at CHS. Unfortunately, from what I heard of his side of the call, our reinforcements were still at least ten minutes away.

That meant it was up to us to stop Beth and Jess. Jess was never going to let me live, not as long as there was breath in her body. I knew that for a fact.

So I guess I shouldn't have been surprised when one of the shadows lurking in the trees suddenly came to life and tackled me to the ground. But I was. Surprised, that is. So surprised I didn't even struggle at first, giving my ex–best friend plenty of time to slide the sharp blade of her knife under my chin.

CHAPTER 19

Don't even think about it, Ethan. Stay right where you are. I'll kill her right now if you take another step," Jess said, pressing the blade into the soft skin beneath my chin until I had to fight the urge to gag.

After all the zombies and magical madness, *this* was how I was going out. The irony was not lost on me, no matter how terrified I felt.

"Listen, Jessica, relax. Let's talk about your options." Ethan's voice was calm and collected, like we were all discussing which diner to go to for burgers after the dance.

Bonus points to him for the cool head in the midst of a crisis, but I doubted anything he said was going to make a difference. I could feel Jess trembling all over, feel the tension in her hand that revealed she was only a breath away from slicing open my throat. She was too close to the edge to be talked back now.

The realization made *me* start shaking.

I'd thought all I had to worry about was helping contain a few hundred zombies—like that wasn't enough. But here I was, getting ready to die for the third or fourth time tonight.

I suddenly wished I'd told Ethan how I felt about him. In the midst of fighting zombies certainly wasn't the time or place to tell the first boy you'd ever loved how you felt, but it sure beat dying before you had the chance to spill your guts.

In that moment, the true importance of my job became blindingly clear. *That* was what was so amazing about being a Settler, what Mom had been trying to tell me for years. We gave people the chance to finish up their earthly business, to say or do those things their souls had been craving so they could truly rest in peace.

It was a priceless gift, but it wasn't one I wanted to take advantage of myself. I didn't want to crawl out of my grave—I wanted to live to see my sixteenth birthday! And preferably a few dozen birthdays after that.

"We're not going to talk about anything," Jess snapped. "I'm going to take Megan to her mom's car and she's going to drive me out of here. That's how it's going—"

"And where is she going to take you?" Ethan asked, edging slightly closer in the near complete blackness. "Back to your house for a slumber party? I can swear to you Settlers' Affairs isn't going to let you get away with this even if there isn't enough evidence to convict in human court. They've been specializing in making people like you disappear for thousands of years."

What was he doing? Giving her an excuse to off herself after she finished with me?

"Beth got away from them. I'm sure I can—"

"Beth got away because SA underestimated her, thought she was just a kid. After tonight I don't think they'll be making that same mistake."

"Whatever. I'll figure out where to go. I'll figure out something." Jess's voice rose hysterically as the moon's light was snuffed out and the woods suddenly became as dark the inside of her giant walk-in closet, the one we used to hide in to tell ghost stories when we were in junior high.

Tears pricked at the back of my eyes, and it was suddenly all I could do not to cry. We'd been best friends, as close as sisters. I'd never dreamed that someday she'd be sitting on top of me with a knife at my throat.

Then I heard a muffled grunt and Jess's weight was knocked off my body. She screamed, and metal clanged against bone.

Heart racing, I scrambled to my hands and knees in the utter blackness. Even with a small sliver of moon beginning to shine through, it was still too dark too see what had happened.

"Watch out!" Ethan's shout was drowned out by Jess's scream as the Reanimated Corpse on top of her dug its teeth into her arm.

I couldn't believe it. I'd been saved by a zombie. One of the RCs I'd worked the *reverto* spell on, no doubt. Jess hissed a few words in what sounded like French—I guess whatever spell she thought she had to use to keep the zombie from eating her—but the RC had already pulled back from her skin. Soon it was stumbling away through the quickly lightening woods, headed back to its grave. Ethan was behind Jess a second later, hauling her to her feet with her hands behind her back.

"Thanks," I said, feeling strangely numb as I struggled to stand.

"Megan, are you okay?" Ethan asked.

"Yeah, I just . . . um. Yeah, I'm fine." I pushed away the dizzy feeling trying to get started in my head. I didn't have time to be dizzy. We still had zombies to take care of.

"You won't be for long," Jess screamed, her words barely

intelligible as she was now full-on bawling. "Beth will kill you. She loves me, she—"

"I think it's time you shut the hell up," Ethan said, spinning Jess around and marching her toward the dance. "Come on, Megan. We'll tie this witch up somewhere out of the way. We've got to get everyone out of the gym before—"

"It's taken care of, but hurry. We don't have much time." Monica appeared on the path just ahead, frantically motioning for us to follow her back toward the school. "I pulled the fire alarm before the RCs got there, but they've reached the gym for sure by now. And I have no idea where Beth is."

So Monica hadn't cut and run after all. She'd actually had the forethought to go clear out the gym before the student body of CHS had the chance to get up close and personal with a bunch of hungry skeletons. The chick was evil, but she was certainly not stupid.

And maybe not so evil, really, at least not when compared to the blonde sobbing her eyes out as Ethan tugged her along the trail. I still couldn't believe Jess had done all of this. I didn't know if I'd ever be able to reconcile the person she'd turned out to be with the best friend I'd counted on for so much of my life.

"Let's cut over to the gravel road and go around to the back entrance of the gym. Less likely to run into any RCs on the way," Ethan said, already on the move.

"Yeah, there were like fifty of them crossing the street a few minutes ago."

"Crap," I said, that dizzy feeling sweeping over me again. "We're going to need a miracle to keep them contained."

"Elder Freedman was undercover chaperoning the dance; he's

doing his best to keep the rest of the chaperones and students away from the gym," Monica panted as we fell in step beside her, Ethan pulling Jess along so fast her feet barely touched the ground.

"I guess that means we're on our own until SA arrives," Ethan said, moving even faster.

"So what? We've got super-Settler Megan Berry. What do we need a bunch of old Elder farts for?" Monica asked. And, wonder of wonders, there was only the slightest trace of sarcasm in her tone.

"And I think I've got a spell that will take care of the rest of these things. I'll tell you on the way," I said, a plan forming in my dizzy brain.

"Cool," Monica said.

Wow. Who would have thought? This might actually be the beginning of a friendship. . .

Okay, maybe not. But a truce was definitely looking good.

• • •

By the time we tied Jess to a tree behind the gym and hustled down to the back entrance, there was no doubt the zombies were running amok inside. Even from ten feet outside the shut doors we could hear horrible crashing sounds, underscored by the hungry groans of the undead.

Thankfully, Elder Freedman had managed to get the rest of the student body pulled back to the lawn in front of the main school building. But RCs wouldn't stay contained in the gym for long, not when there wasn't anything flesh possessing running around inside to feed upon.

"You're sure about this, Megan?" Ethan asked.

"Positive. I know the spell, and I'm the only one who can work this version of it. Just cover cleanup duty and I'll handle the rest," I said, forcing away my last shreds of doubt.

I'd never actually worked the version of the *pax frater corpus* spell Kitty had taught me—or *any* version of the *pax frater corpus* spell— but at least I had it memorized. Besides, it was the only thing I could think of that could get this situation under control.

There were already at least twenty corpses out there that I'd worked the *reverto* spell on and who would be looking for a bite of Beth or Jess. We couldn't risk any more.

The *pax frater* was our only hope. I had to put those zombies down, and we had to get the gym cleaned up before the human firefighters responded to the alarm. SA had an operative undercover at the fire department, but she would only be able to buy us so much time. We were down to the wire, and every second counted.

"Be careful," Ethan said, looking like he wanted to say more.

But there wasn't time to find out what. Together, Ethan and I flung open the door, and the three of us exploded into the gym.

"This way!" I heard Monica scream as she pulled Ethan toward the equipment storage room, but then my awareness of everything else faded.

The world narrowed to the blood-smeared gym floor before me. Hundreds of zombies swarmed over what remained of the homecoming dance decorations, like flies on a ruined birthday cake. Beth must have made it here and dumped the pig blood, even though there were no longer any students left to baptize. It was the only explanation for the red-stained crepe paper and the mounds of soaked cotton that had once been puffy clouds artfully scattered throughout the room.

A walk in the clouds. That had been the theme for the dance, but now it looked more like a walk through hell.

Blood dripped off the edges of the refreshment table and the stage where the homecoming court would have sat, and the zombies had been whipped into a crazed frenzy by the pure abundance of the red stuff. They were down on the floor, smearing their bony fingers and faces in the blood puddles, frantic to consume something that had once belonged to the living.

And in the areas where they were running out of pig blood, the zombies had turned on each other, howling in desperate fury as they lunged at the red fingers and faces of their undead comrades. It was the most horrible thing I'd ever seen: a horror movie brought to life for my own personal viewing displeasure.

Then suddenly a calming breeze seemed to sweep over the RCs as first one and then another sensed a living, breathing human in the room. A human with blood even fresher than the stuff splattered across the basketball court.

Dozens and then hundreds of glowing red eyes turned toward where I stood, but, strangely, I wasn't afraid—at least not as afraid as I'd thought I'd be. I was Megan Berry, Settler of the Dead, and in that moment I knew I'd been given crazy amounts of power for a reason.

I was ready to get this situation *Settled*. Permanently.

"Pax frater corpus, potestatum spirituum," I began chanting as I rushed forward to meet the first wave of zombies.

The first two I kicked square in the ribs with as much force as I could muster, beyond grateful to see them crumple to the ground and lie still as soon as my tennis shoe connected with bone. With a shout of celebration I spun around, landing another kick to an RC closing in behind me before turning back to the corpses stumbling over the bones of their fallen comrades.

"Inmundorum ut eicerent eos et—" A round-the-world jazz kick knocked out another three zombies, but the corpses pushing in behind got up close and personal before I regained my footing.

On instinct, I lashed out with rapid punches, using sharp upper thrusts with the heel of my hand to fell half a dozen of the RCs. My dad had assured me the move could break an attacker's nose and would certainly make any normal bad guy think twice about coming for me again. Thankfully, it worked on the nonliving as well.

Another dozen zombies fell to the ground as I continued to chant and punch, pushing my way deeper into the gym, leaving a trail of bones behind me that I leapt over with a dancer's grace. Thankfully, my balance didn't falter for a moment and my concentration was complete. My entire body was finally vibrating on the right frequency, flowing with the power instead of fighting it.

It was almost like dancing. Which meant the usually klutzy Megan was replaced with the one who could seamlessly blend one move into another, who could make a choreographed dance look like an organic improvisation.

Or in this case, make improvisation work as smoothly as any rehearsed performance.

"Curarent omnem languorem," I chanted, actually feeling a smile stretch across my face as I dipped and swung and kicked, finding I needed less and less force to deactivate the undead.

A part of me realized Ethan and Monica were fighting a few feet behind me, working the *pax frater corpus* the old-fashioned way, with javelins they'd lifted from the equipment room, but the rest of me was riding the wave of energy flowing through my cells like a whirlwind.

More Settler power than I'd ever felt before rushed across my skin, burst from my hands and feet as I lashed out at the zombies. The dizziness I'd been feeling since leaving the church in the woods was still there, making my lips buzz and my teeth tingle, but it couldn't compete with the force of the raw energy surging inside.

It felt like I was pulling power from everywhere, from the undead I was Settling, from the blood on the floor, even from the stale air filling the gym. I was practically floating off the ground as I leapt over another pile of bones, the movement nearly effortless.

Until I forgot to turn around quite fast enough.

"Et omnem infirmitat—" Skeletal arms grabbed me from behind. I slammed my knuckles back, aiming for where I assumed its face would be and thankfully connected, but two more RCs tackled me before I could shrug off the bones encircling my chest. I caught a glimpse of Ethan and Monica being overwhelmed by their own mess of zombies before I fell to the ground.

I kept chanting the *pax frater corpus* for all I was worth as I thrashed beneath a mounting pile of skeleton zombies, but I could feel my power rush fading fast. I'd taken out nearly a hundred of the undead, but there were still so many, too many for one Settler to take out on her own.

For what felt like the millionth time, I was sure I was going to die. A scream of frustration and rage erupted from my chest as I fought even harder. It was a hopeless situation, but I could at least—

"Pax frater corpus, potestatum spirituum." A woman's chants

suddenly broke through the wailing of the remaining undead. Seconds later the zombies on top of me stopped moving and a tiny hand appeared through the skeletons.

Kitty! I never thought I'd be so glad to see a member of Enforcement in my life.

She tugged me free of the zombie pig pile and then turned back to the gym floor. I fell in behind her, wobbling with exhaustion. I managed to take out a few more RCs as we worked our way across the room to where Smythe and Barker were *pax frater corpus*-ing the last of the remaining undead, but that energy wave I'd been riding before didn't return.

Instead, I felt like I was moving through Jell-O, each kick and punch more difficult than the last. By that time the final zombies were on the ground, hastily being gathered into volleyball carts by the half dozen Protocol officers from Settlers' Affairs who had appeared on the scene, I was completely wasted.

It was all I could do to stay on my feet. I was dizzy. Everything was spinning. . . . I stumbled and would have fallen if Ethan hadn't grabbed my arm.

"Megan, are you okay?" he asked.

"Yeah, I just . . . um. I'm just not really feeling that well." That was the understatement of the year. I actually felt like my head was about to float off my body and my stomach was going to sink down to the bottom of my feet. Weird sensations alone, but together they were especially awful.

"Let me help you out of here. The fire trucks are headed down Main right now; we've only got a few minutes—"

"Scratch that, a few seconds," Monica said, jumping over a pile of zombies to reach us. "Enforcement said they're going to torch the rest of the skeletons. There's no more time."

"Come on, let's go," Ethan said, looping an arm around my waist.

"Okay, yeah . . . but I think I'm—" My knees buckled and I fell to the ground despite Ethan's attempt to catch me one-handed.

"What's wrong with—" Monica's face swam into focus above me as I struggled to keep my eyes open.

"Are you still feeding that *exuro* spell?" Ethan asked, sounding freaked. "You've got to stop, Megan. You can die from—"

"She's burning up," Monica said, laying a cool hand on my forehead. "You've got to shut off the heat, Berry."

"I can't. I tried . . . when we were still . . . in the . . ." The world was spinning; I was getting sucked under, pulled into the black center of the lights swirling around me like trippy peppermint candy.

The last thing I heard was Monica muttering something about little Settlers biting off more than they could chew. I felt her take my hands in both of hers and then I was out, sinking into fuzzy blackness.

CHAPTER 20

When I woke up, I was lying on something soft and was covered with a blanket. It was a beige blanket and I was in the back of a primarily beige ambulance of some kind. Settlers' Affairs' work. It had to be, since beige was their signature color.

"Are you finally awake?" I turned to see Monica seated just behind me, her wounded shoulder wrapped in white gauze.

"Um . . . yeah." I smacked my lips, trying to get enough saliva together to actually swallow. Man, I was thirsty. *Pax frater corpus*-ing my way through a gym full of zombies and then nearly burning myself up with an *exuro* spell had left me with major cotton mouth.

"Here, drink this." Monica handed me a bottle of water. "Now listen up, because we don't have much time." She slid down the padded bench she was sitting on until she was even with my elbow. "Settlers' Affairs called their contact in the Little Rock Police Department, and he came to get Jess and Beth."

"Where was Beth?" I asked, grateful she hadn't escaped.

"Some of the RCs you worked the *reverto* spell on followed her to the gym. She dumped the blood to distract them, then locked herself in the girls' toilet. The Settler from the police department took her into custody before the fire trucks got here," Monica said, words coming out in a breathless rush, making me wonder what she was so freaked about.

"Okay, that's good, so why are—"

"Shh! Just listen." Wow, spaz much, Monica? "We're going to have to testify in court that they were trying to kill us because they were jealous or something. SA will have the cover story ready tomorrow and debrief us before we go to give our statements, but I wanted to talk to you about something else first."

"Okay," I said, sounding semi-normal when I spoke. "So why are you freaking out?"

"So . . . Ethan told me he told you about what I did, raising the zombie the other night to make it attack me. I just wanted you to know I only did it because I was jealous, because I've always liked him and suddenly he was all over a sophomore loser nobody." Her eyes shifted to the floor, and I could tell how embarrassed she was to be having this conversation, especially with said loser nobody. "But I swear I didn't have anything to do with the rest of it. I never planned to hurt you."

"So you just happened to be at the same cemetery where Shane was buried? Come on, Monica." My mind was fairly sharp, considering I'd almost been killed several times tonight.

"I followed Ethan. I thought he was just going to meet you. I didn't know you two were Settling a corpse."

"Hmm . . . convenient explanation."

"Listen," Monica said, obviously getting frustrated, "Ethan believes me and said he wouldn't out me to SA if you wouldn't." She actually seemed like she was telling the truth, but I wasn't feeling in a very charitable mood.

"You want me to lie for you. Why should I?"

"How about because I saved your life about twenty minutes ago? If I hadn't helped you turn off that *exuro* spell, you would be dead right now."

"How did you know how to do that? You're not third stage yet."

"You're not the only one to think of looking ahead, Megan. I've been studying third-stage stuff for over a year. I may not be as powerful as you are, but I'm stronger than most, and I want to be ready for the Enforcement training program if they accept me after graduation."

Monica wanted to be an Enforcer. Not surprising. She was all about getting off on being more powerful than other people.

"Kitty or one of the other Enforcers could have helped me turn off the *exuro* spell," I said, so not willing to give Monica props for saving my life. "So thanks, but—"

"They could have. But they didn't. *I* did," she said, a note of real desperation in her tone. "Please, Megan, I'll never get the chance to apply for Enforcement if I get another black-magic mark on my record."

Ahh . . . groveling, sweet groveling. If only there were more time to draw out the Monicster's torment.

"So what did you do to get the first black-magic mark anyway?" I asked.

"None of your business."

"Let's make it my business, shall we?" I smiled, relishing this moment of power over my nemesis. "I want to know what you've dipped your hands in before I agree to lie for you."

"I tried to raise Dexter," she whispered.

"Dexter?"

"My pet rat, the one that died when my mom accidentally stuck it in the washing machine." Before I could marvel that Monica actually had enough of a heart to get *that* attached to a pet rat or ask how someone could *accidentally* stick a rat in the washing machine, muffled voices sounded outside the ambulance.

"Please, Megan. It was just a stupid kid thing. Keep this our secret and I'll do anything you want."

Anything? Hmm . . . now that Beth was in police custody, Monica would be captain of the pom squad, not cocaptain, which might give her something to bargain with. Call me crazy, but even after all the horribleness of the past week I *still* wanted one of those places on the pom team. And I wanted it badly enough to make a deal with the devil.

Well, maybe not the devil, but the Monicster anyway.

"First, you've got to swear never to work black magic again," I said, knowing I had to think of the greater good as well as my own selfish desires.

"I swear." She held up one hand and placed the other across her heart.

"And second, you've got to vote me into one of the empty places on the pom squad."

"You're kidding," she said, her sweet facade cracking a bit as she wrinkled her nose in obvious contempt. "You didn't even try out."

"So what? Give me another chance to dance for the seniors after school on Monday. You'll have two extra spots on the team now that

Beth and Jess are both gone," I said, knowing my argument was perfectly rational. "No one would think it was strange if you gave the girls who didn't make it another chance to show you what they've got."

The voice outside the ambulance grew louder. Monica's eyes widened before she leaned down to my ear. "Fine, it's a deal. As long as you keep your trap shut," she hissed.

"I'll keep it shut as long as you keep your hands clean."

"Whatever, Berry."

Before I could think of a comeback, Mom and Dad were climbing inside the ambulance.

All worries about black magic and Monica faded as I was enfolded in a two-parent hug. Thankfully, it seemed they'd gotten the lowdown on what happened from Ethan and the other Elders on-site. Though in the version of the story they'd heard, I'd snuck out because Jess threatened to kill Monica if I didn't come meet her on the Carlisle property without telling anyone. I suspected I had Ethan to thank for that little falsehood and knew I had him to thank for freeing me and Monica before we became zombie kibble back at the old church.

Evidently he'd put a tracking device in her phone once he'd started suspecting her of being the one out to get me, and that was how he'd been able to find us and tell SA exactly where we were. He might have had the wrong suspect, but Ethan still got some of the glory for saving the day—the portion not doled out to yours truly for *pax frater corpus*-ing the zombie skeletons or to Monica for emptying out the gym before SA had a Class Three Containment crisis on their hands.

Amazingly, between the three of us and the Enforcement officers, we'd managed to get the whole crazy situation under control without any of my classmates coming in contact with the undead.

Mom said there was even talk of letting Ethan and Monica start training with Kitty and the other Enforcement officers—who would be moving to Carol full-time to help train me instead of holing up at the compound for three or four weeks. I wasn't sure about the Monica angle, but training with Ethan certainly sounded nice—almost as nice as hearing that the Elders were totally backtracking with regard to their opinions of my power and how well I could control it.

They knew they'd been wrong about the clones, and Monica hadn't told anyone about turning my *exuro* command off for me, so I guess everyone thought I'd just fainted from stress or something. Whatever they thought, I was willing to go along with it as long as it meant I was out of trouble and my family got to be released from SA compound prison.

"They said we can go home tonight," Mom said, smiling at me. "I think you showed them the compound wasn't so secure anyway."

"You're grounded for stealing your mother's car, by the way," Dad added, also smiling. I guess they were just so glad everything was over they couldn't muster the energy to put up the full-throttle parental disciplinary front. "And for not telling us about the call from Jess right away." Mom put in. "You should have trusted us to help you, even if we were fighting earlier."

"I know, and I'm sorry," I said, not feeling as bad as I probably should have felt for going along with Ethan's false cover story. "So . . . how much grounding are we talking about?"

"A month with no weeknight activity, and you have to be in by five on weekends," Mom said.

I tried to look sad about that news, even though it was *way* better than I'd thought it would be.

"But we'll wait and start that tomorrow," Dad said. "We figured you deserve a reward for single-handedly saving hundreds of lives." He leaned in and said the next words in a whisper. "We're really proud of you, Meg."

Sniff! God, I loved my dad. Even if he did make me get all teary sometimes.

"So if you feel well enough, you can go down to the dance. Since the gym was wrecked, they've moved the DJ outside and are having the dance in the parking lot," Mom said, continuing on before I could protest that the last thing I wanted to do was go to homecoming. "Ethan said he'd have you home before midnight."

Ethan?

The boy in question suddenly appeared at the entrance to the ambulance with a nervous smile on his face.

My heart started racing like I was still back in the gym fighting zombies. I still had no idea whether Ethan considered me a little-sister type, a friend he'd randomly kissed one time after a stressful situation, or whether there might be something more in our future. And the uncertainty was driving me insane!

Mom laughed, evidently amused by whatever expression I had on my face. "See you in a few hours, honey." Then she and Dad both leaned over and kissed me on the cheek and climbed out of the ambulance.

I followed a second later, even though nerves were making my stomach turn backflips. No matter how nervous I was, I didn't want to waste another second sitting in an ambulance with Monica when I could be with the only guy who'd ever made my whole body light up with just a smile.

CHAPTER 21

So that's why the Elders didn't believe us in the first place," Ethan said. "Jess and Beth weren't the only ones raising zombies. Apparently some sicko in Little Rock was starting a zombie harem and using his 'girls' to attack old girlfriends who'd dumped him."

"Ew. That's deeply disturbing. Have they caught him yet?"

"They were taking him into custody tonight. That's why it took some time for them to get back to Carol when I called for backup." Ethan stuffed his hands in his pockets as we walked. An awkward silence fell between us that I tried my best to fill.

"Thanks for the cover story about why I was here," I said as we continued down the hill toward the gym. "I'm sure it made SA and Mom and Dad go a lot easier on me than if they'd known the truth."

"That's cool. I figured I could help you out a little since you weren't awake to help yourself," he said, shrugging. "What *was* the truth anyway? How did she get you out here?"

"Jess didn't tell you?" He shook his head.

I filled him in as briefly as possible, then hurried to make my apologies for misjudging him. "I'm sorry I believed you were so gone on Monica. I should have known you would have called after you were reassigned if there hadn't been something big going down."

"Once I had the evidence and got to 'break up' with Monica I was going to call, right after I dropped the stuff off at SA headquarters. I felt awful knowing people thought I was into her. Especially you."

Especially me? What did that mean? Gah! I was going to lose it if he didn't stop saying things my poor deluded heart could latch onto in a pathetic attempt to believe he liked me as more than a friend.

"Right. I mean, I understand. Even when I saw you two kissing by the bonfire, I should have known that—"

"It was only to make her drop her guard. I swear." He stopped and turned to me, his eyes all nervous looking again for some reason. "I should have told you everything. And while we're on the subject of what a jerk I am, I have a confession to make. I sort of lied to you and Settlers' Affairs."

"You did?"

"Yeah, that time I summoned the daytime zombie? My fault. I let my shields slip. It didn't have anything to do with your power transferring to me or anything like that," he said, hurrying on before I could think of how to respond to that. "But I've already told Settlers' Affairs the truth and told them why I lied at the review."

"Because you thought Monica was to blame for everything but didn't think they'd believe you," I supplied, wondering why Ethan had lied to me in the first place. A part of me prayed it was because he was as affected by the attraction between us as I was.

"Yeah. I knew they wouldn't. But you would have, and I should have told you I suspected Monica instead of just cutting you out of the picture like that. I guess I thought you'd be safer if you didn't know, but now I just—I can't believe—"

He sucked in a breath and shoved his hands deep into the pockets of his jeans. He looked so unbelievably gorgeous in just jeans and a black sweater. Even smelling vaguely of burnt zombie, he was going to be the yummiest guy at homecoming. I, with my black spandex and braid and scratched-up cheek, was entirely scruffy in comparison.

"What I mean is, I'm the one who should be sorry. You were almost killed, several times, because I made the wrong call. I wanted to kick myself when I heard you were in the hospital the other day. I can't ever remember being that scared. And when you wouldn't even see me . . ."

My heart did another flip and I had to fight to keep a smile from my face.

I stepped a little closer, trying to contain my excitement. "It's not your fault, Ethan. Really, I—"

"No, it is, at least part of it is, and I know that." He reached out and took my hand, but even that small touch made my entire body shoot into tingle overtime. "Do you think you'll ever be able to forgive me? That we can be friends again like we were?"

Friends. He wanted to be friends and was nervous because he thought I'd hold a grudge. And here I'd been about to throw myself at him like the completely pathetic sophomore nobody Monica had said I was.

I suddenly didn't want to stay out with Ethan until twelve, not when thirty seconds of knowing he just wanted to be friends was cutting my chest apart.

"Yeah, sure. We can be friends." I pulled my hand away from his, keeping my eyes on the ground. "You messed up some, I messed up a lot, but everybody's alive, so it's cool."

"Good. It would have been really weird starting to train with you and Kitty if you hated me," he said, sounding relieved. "I talked to her after you passed out. She seems really great and was psyched about having another potential Enforcer to train."

Ouch. So he didn't even *really* care about being friends; he just didn't want any awkwardness interfering with his new job opportunity.

I had to get out of here. Maybe if I booked it back behind the gym, I could still get a ride home with my parents.

"Yeah, training together will be great. But, you know, I'm not really feeling as well as I thought." I started backing away, still doing my best to look anywhere but at his face. "I'll just go catch my parents and see you around, okay?"

"Oh . . . okay." He *did* sound disappointed, but he was probably just faking it. I doubted the big, important, gorgeous college guy was bummed to miss a high school dance.

"Yeah, so . . . have a nice night." I spun around before the tears could make it to my eyes and started walking away.

After everything I'd been through, after being betrayed by my best friend and nearly killed more than once and facing down a few hundred undead, it was a boy who finally made me cry. It just went to show how stupid I was. How stupid and deluded and pathetic and—

"Megan, wait!" I heard Ethan's footsteps behind me but only sped up, not wanting him to see my face.

"I'll see you later, Ethan." I sucked in a breath, trying not to cry any more as I waved a hand back in his direction. "Really, I just—"

"I can't wait until later," he said before he grabbed my elbow and spun me back around. "And I'm not going to have a nice night if you walk away from me."

And then, before I quite realized what was happening, he was kissing me. Pulling me into his arms, hugging me so tight my feet came off the ground kissing me. Humming against my lips like they were the best-tasting thing in the world kissing me. Mouths open, tongues doing things way too exciting to be merely French kissing kissing me. Kissing me until I was dizzier than I'd been after the extended *exuro* spell and the *pax frater corpus*–ing, until I felt like my heart was going to explode because I'd never even dreamed about being kissed like this.

Okay, I'd dreamed about it but never really thought it would happen. This kiss was even better than the one in the cemetery. It was hotter, heavier, yet somehow sweeter, too. And this time I knew Ethan wasn't kissing me because I was upset or—

"Wait a second," I mumbled against his lips, a part of me still freaking out that Ethan and I were this close. Like, attached-at-the-lips close.

"Yeah?" he mumbled back, still holding me so tight I couldn't get my brain to function.

"Um . . . could you put me down for a second?"

"Oh, sure," he said, sort of breathless and looking a little nervous again as he set me back down on my feet.

God, he was so beautiful. Even more beautiful than when I first re-met him. Was he getting cuter every day or was this just a side effect of how progressively hung up on him I was becoming?

"Megan?"

"Yeah?"

"You . . . were going to say something?"

"Oh yeah." Could I be more of a loser? Getting sucked into Ethan's gorgeosity to the point of zonage? "So, I was just wondering— I mean, you know that was . . . yeah . . . but— well, the other time that we kissed, you know I was sort of upset and—"

"Megan! Ethan! Heads up!" Seconds later something wet exploded on my butt. I spun around to see London and Alana a few yards away, giggling like crazy.

"Come on! They moved the dance outside because some freak sprayed the gym with blood and it's like a biohazard or something, but it's totally turned into a big water-balloon fight! Andy brought like four hundred in the back of his pickup truck." London started giggling again after this announcement, and she and Alana ran back around the other side of the gym, stumbling over each other in a way that left no doubt they'd been drinking something other than cola before the dance.

Well, at least they didn't seem mad at me for hanging out with Ethan anymore. And they hadn't noticed that Ethan and I were hardly dressed in semi formal attire.

Maybe we *should* go join in and just put off talking about whatever was going on until a later date. As badly as I wanted to know how Ethan really felt, a part of me *didn't* want to know just as strongly. Especially if he was going to confess that he always made out with girls whenever they cried, like it was some sort of weird compulsive thing he needed to seek therapy for or something.

"Your butt's wet, isn't it?" Ethan asked as I turned back around.

"Yeah, it is," I said, blushing a little to hear Ethan talking about my butt. Slowly, I started edging down the path. "So, since I'm already wet, we might as well go join the rest of the freaks out there on—"

"You know, you've got the cutest butt I've ever seen. Like, in my entire life," Ethan said, grabbing my hand and pulling me back to him as I struggled to breathe properly. "And your eyes make me crazy and the way you smell just—"

"I smell?"

"Good! You smell good. Great, actually, and—" He broke off with a little laugh. "You're just completely gorgeous, Megan. Every single part of you."

"I am?" I asked, my voice not much more than a squeak.

"Yes, you are," he said, sounding annoyed. "That's why losers like Josh Pickle are after you, because you're hot and only going to get hotter. But that's not why I kissed you tonight."

"It's not?"

"No, well . . . not the only reason." He actually blushed a little then, which almost made me want to believe he meant everything he was saying. "Yes, you're hot, and yes, I can't think straight half the time around you because all I can think about is how much I want to touch you, but the reason I kissed you tonight is . . . I care about you. A lot." His breath rushed out really fast and he rolled his eyes, but I could tell it wasn't at me. "Just say it, idiot . . ."

"Say what?"

"I . . . love you," he said, though it looked like the words caused him indigestion.

I was going to have a heart attack. There was no doubt about it now—I was going to set a record for world's youngest coronary victim.

"I know that sounds stupid," he said, obviously misunderstanding my stunned silence. "We've only known each other again for a couple of weeks, but I've always trusted my gut. And my gut is totally gone on you. Every time I heard you were in danger or hurt, I just . . . I couldn't breathe. It scared me more than being surrounded by those zombies tonight. I don't want to see you with any other guy, and I don't ever want you to get hurt because I wasn't there with you."

"Ethan, you can't go out with me just because you don't want me to get hurt. And I think I handled myself pretty well in the gym," I said, because apparently some perverse part of me was intent on talking Ethan out of loving me. Couldn't I just shut up already?

"That's not why I—hell, at first I was afraid to *start* anything because I thought hanging around someone in Protocol would put you in danger." He laughed and pulled me closer, until I was once again surrounded by Ethan arms. This *had* to be the best feeling in the world. "Now I realize you totally outclass me in the ability to get yourself into major amounts of trouble. I really should stay away from you if I value my life, but I think I'm too far gone."

"Too in love with me?" I asked, needing to hear the words again.

"Yeah, too in love with you." He smiled and kissed me, really softly, on the tip of my nose and I felt the truth of his words in every shiver sweeping over my skin. Ethan loved me! "And it's okay if you don't feel that way about me yet. I think I can convince you I'm worth the trouble if you give me the chance."

"I think that can be arranged." And then I was kissing him.

Pulling his mouth down to mine and showing him how completely gone I was on him kissing him. Smiling against his lips when another water balloon exploded on his back and still another one caught me on the leg and kissing him some more. Kissing him until we were both soaking wet and were finally forced to turn on our attackers and retaliate.

And once we'd found the stash of water balloons and pelted London and Alana until their mascara was dripping black down their cheeks, we kissed some more. Right in the middle of the CHS parking lot, where anyone could see, and I didn't care. An hour ago I might have been Megan Berry, zombie queen, but right now I was just Megan, average teen, a girl learning that even nights like this one could have a happy ending. . .

ACKNOWLEDGMENTS

So many people to thank, so I'll just dive right in. First off, thanks to my amazing agent Caren Johnson. You rock in so many ways I cannot count them all. Thanks so much for your unfailing support. Thanks also to the entire Razorbill team, and especially to Laura Schechter and Ben Schrank who were vital in making this book something I am so proud of.

And more heartfelt thanks to some of the people who offered encouragement and support along the way: To Susannah Berryman, teacher, friend, and amazing lady. Thank you for being one of the first people to make me think I could do this writer thing. To Aida Iglesias, the best ex-mother-in-law in the world, for all her help when I was a new mommy and a new writer and struggling to balance the two. (Also a big shout out to Dr. Hector, Aida's partner in crime, and a man who has pulled my sickly family back from the edge of a zombie outbreak countless times. Thank you!) To my critique partner, Stacia Kane, without whom I could not have made it through some of the stickier bits of this writing life. I treasure your friendship so much, you talented woman!

And because I like to save the best for last, an enormous, slightly teary and emotional thanks to my family. To my mother, Carol, my friend and guide and one of the best people I know. To my husband, Mike. I don't know what I did to deserve such a fabulous, loving, best friend of a partner (but I'm keeping you, so don't even try to escape). To my girls, Laura and Ashton, and to my boys, Riley and Logan. I never thought I'd be helping raise four kids, but I wouldn't trade any of you for a huge sack full of money. Lots of love and thanks for understanding that "mama has to work".